SWEETS, BEGORRA

Connie Shelton

SWEETS,
BEGORRA

The Seventh Samantha Sweet Mystery

Connie Shelton

Secret Staircase Books

Sweets, Begorra
Published by Secret Staircase Books, an imprint of
Columbine Publishing Group
PO Box 416, Angel Fire, NM 87710

This book is a work of fiction. Names, characters, places and
incidents are either the product of the author's imagination or are
used fictitiously. Any resemblance to actual events or locales or
persons, living or dead, is entirely coincidental.

Book layout and design by Secret Staircase Books
Cover illustration © Thye Gn
Cover cupcake design © Basheeradesigns

Publisher's Cataloging-in-Publication Data

Shelton, Connie
Sweets, Begorra / by Connie Shelton.
p. cm.
ISBN 978-1945422225 (paperback)

1. Samantha Sweet (Fictitious character)--Fiction. 2. New
Mexico—Fiction. 3. Paranormal artifacts—Fiction. 4. Ireland—
Fiction. 5. Women sleuths—Fiction. 6. Honeymoon—Fiction. 7.
Magical items—Fiction. I. Title

Samantha Sweet Mystery Series : Book 7.
Shelton, Connie, Samantha Sweet mysteries.

BISAC : FICTION / Mystery & Detective / Cozy.

813/.54

*For Dan, who will always be my travel partner
on this journey called life.*

Begorra: Irish—used as a mild, usually jocular oath. Euphemism for 'by God.' First known use: 1715
--*the Miriam Webster Dictionary*

Chapter 1

Ladies and gentlemen, please raise your seats to their full upright position, came a too-loud voice over the 747's intercom system. Samantha Sweet gathered the soft blanket which had covered her during the overnight flight, gazing over the short divider between their seats to find that Beau was already sitting upright, looking as fresh as if he'd showered and shaved.

"Morning, Mrs. Cardwell," he said with a grin. He'd taken to using her new last name ever since their wedding two days ago. She liked the sound of it.

Sam smiled back at him then pressed a button on the console beside her. The automatic seat began doing about four different things, lowering her legs, raising her back, switching from the flat bed where she'd actually slept awhile, to an upright airline seat. She ran her fingers through her hair and wished she'd wakened a tad earlier. Freshening up would now have to wait until they were inside the terminal.

Beau handed her a small napkin-wrapped bundle. "You

missed breakfast but I saved this for you."

The savory slice of meat enclosed in soft bread tasted heavenly, although she would have loved a cup of coffee to go with it. No time. The first-class cabin attendant passed through, collecting the napkin and reminding passengers to stow their loose items.

Welcome to Shannon, Ireland, where the local time is six a.m.

They had pre-cleared customs back at JFK so the trip through the airport went quickly. Slightly past the baggage claim area Sam spotted her name on a placard. The young woman holding it brightened as soon as they headed her direction. She had blond hair that grazed her shoulders in a ragged cut, brilliant blue eyes, and a ready smile with perfect teeth.

"Good morning, Ms. Sweet. I'm Kathleen, your driver to Galway." She reached for the handle of Sam's wheeled bag and led the way, with Sam and Beau close behind. Across a parking lot she stopped in front of a large black car. "We're right here."

As Kathleen deftly stashed the bags in the roomy trunk, Sam looked around. Beyond a row of small warehouses she caught a glimpse of brilliant green. Small puddles dotted the lot and the pavement was dark with moisture. She touched her hair; it had already begun to curl with the humidity.

"Rained all night," Kathleen said. "And it'll rain again today. And every day for the foreseeable future."

"But it makes all this beautiful green."

"Yeah, you got that right. Mr. Ryan says you come from New Mexico?" She sighed. "I'd love to see that myself sometime. All that blue sky. Sunshine every single day."

She had walked around the car and opened the back doors.

"That part is nice," Sam said as she slid into the back seat. "I guess we always want to go places that are new to us."

Beau had joined Sam on the roomy bench seat, while Kathleen started the engine and pulled away, driving on what felt like the wrong side of the road. Beau asked how long it would take to get to Galway and, after telling him it would be about ninety minutes, Kathleen went into a story about how her brother had taken a wrong turn once and spent two hours getting back on track. Apparently the car service was family-owned and he'd cost their father a fair amount of cash for the mistake.

Sam found her thoughts drifting as the young woman chattered on. Less than a month ago she'd been completely occupied with her bakery, Sweet's Sweets, plus her little sideline of breaking into houses, along with planning her wedding. She had known nothing of a family connection to Ireland, much less the fact that she and Beau would be taking their honeymoon trip here. The unknown still awaited—an inheritance of some sort. When the letter and first class air tickets came from a law firm in New York, she'd first discounted it as a hoax. But Beau had used his pull as Taos County Sheriff to do a background investigation, discovering that the attorney, and the news of the inheritance, was real. Now they would meet with the lawyers in Galway, where her great-uncle Terrance O'Shaughnessy had lived. She had verified the family connection as well; the main thing she didn't know yet was what, exactly, she'd inherited.

"You'll love the Harbour Hotel," Kathleen was saying. "It's right beside the dock for the small boat harbor. Big excitement there last year when the racing yachts came in. Galway was the finish line for the race that went round the whole world. We partied for a week, begorra!"

She went on to describe fireworks and cannons, food vendors and more than a few people who overindulged as they listened to shows by rock bands. Sam found herself wondering just how noisy an area it might be.

"This time of year should be quieter, even though the hotel will be full," Kathleen told them. "The horse races start soon but that's off on the other side of the city."

Sam loved the young woman's accent with its rounded vowels and crisp consonants.

The miles rolled by and she caught herself dozing lightly, despite thinking she'd slept fairly well on the flight. Kathleen chatted on, prompted once in awhile when Beau would ask a question. Soon, they began to slow for traffic. Open fields in every shade of green gave way to neat yards surrounding two-story brick and stucco homes, many with B&B signs out front. Larger hotels appeared and, after a confusing series of turns, a railway station. A large park across the road from it seemed to be the site of an event of some sort. Kathleen negotiated the narrow streets, the many turns, and avoided throngs of pedestrians who walked with an intensity in their strides.

About the time boat masts appeared beside a long concrete dock, Kathleen made a quick turn and stopped at the entry to the Harbour Hotel. A uniformed man took their bags and Beau headed for the long teak desk. Sam took in the polished marble floors, pale walls, heavy glass doors leading to the wings, groupings of chairs upholstered in primary purple and blue, with a sleek marble fireplace against one wall and a pub entrance beyond it. While Beau dealt with checking in, Kathleen turned to Sam.

"Mr. Ryan would like to take you out to breakfast," she

said, after a glance at a text message. "Shall I tell him that's all right?"

"That would be very nice," Sam said. Although it wasn't yet nine o'clock, the small sandwich aboard the airplane might have been eaten days ago.

Kathleen began tapping keys on her phone. "How much time would you like?"

"Thirty minutes?"

"Perfect." She sent the message and received a response as Beau joined them. She looked up. "Mr. Ryan will meet you here in the lobby in a half hour."

Beau reached into his pocket for the unfamiliar cash he'd received in exchange for dollars at the airport.

"No need," Kathleen said. "Everything's been covered." She flashed a smile, turned back to the limousine, and had driven away in less than a minute.

"She's right about being covered," Beau said. "They didn't even want a credit card for incidentals when I checked in."

A bellman appeared, taking the handles of their bags and leading the way toward a group of elevators. On the third floor he opened their door, rolled the bags inside and vanished before either of them could reach for money. Sam and Beau exchanged a wide-eyed look. Seriously? No hand reaching out for a tip?

With its thick duvet and plump pillows the king-sized bed looked inviting, but Sam reminded Beau that the attorney would show up in a few minutes.

"Look at this view," he said, while she opened her suitcase and rummaged for the makeup kit that held her hairbrush.

She stepped over to the large window, which he had

opened to the fresh morning air, and saw that they were near enough to the corner to see both the street and the boat harbor. Below, at least a hundred small and mid-sized sailboats bobbed at their moorings. A few people milled about, some with mugs in hand, obviously just awakening and coming up onto their decks. Across the busy street stood a high, moss-covered rock wall. From below, there had been no clue what was behind it, but from this vantage point Sam could see neat rows of tombstones. Few of the graves had flowers and no one was in sight. Rail cars sat on a siding a few blocks beyond the cemetery, and in the distance she heard the long, low blast of a freighter's horn.

"So," she said to Beau as she brushed her hair at the bathroom mirror, "what do you think of Ireland so far?"

"Friendly, pretty, smells like the sea." He came up behind her and snaked his arms around her waist. "I'm ready for the honeymoon to begin."

"If we weren't to meet the attorney in ten minutes, I'd say yes to that."

He nuzzled her neck.

"Seriously, I don't have time for a shower but I'd better brush my teeth before I have a conversation with anyone. Do you think I should change clothes?" She'd worn stretchy slacks and a loose top on the plane.

"You look fine. He'll expect us to be slightly travel-worn." He edged away so she could finish trying to tame her hair.

When Sam came out of the bathroom she saw that Beau had been into the suitcases and had pulled out two umbrellas.

"By the look of those clouds racing across the sky, I'd say Kathleen was probably right about the rain. We better have these with us."

They donned jackets and she decided to lighten the load of her bag, the small leather backpack she always carried at home. At the last minute when she was packing for the trip, she'd reached for the wooden box that normally held her jewelry. Undecided about what to take, she'd placed the box and its contents into her carryon bag. A silly move, she told herself now, but here it was. She stuck it into the room's safe.

"Okay," Beau said. "Let's go find out about your big inheritance."

She laughed. "No one has ever used the word 'big' about this thing." It was something they'd speculated about since the day they'd verified the letter from the lawyer. Beau's guesses leaned toward castles, titles, and fat bank accounts. Sam tended to think it was going to be something like a crotchety old cat that she would be obligated to feed for life. Actually, if the entire estate consisted of their plane tickets and a stay in this wonderful hotel, she wouldn't mind a bit. But she had to admit that her pulse quickened just a little. There must be more—otherwise, why would the attorney be so eager to meet with her immediately after their arrival?

She tucked the folded umbrella under her arm and preceded Beau to the elevator. A man rose from one of the upholstered chairs near the fireplace when they stepped into the lobby.

"Ms. Sweet? I'm Daniel Ryan, with Ryan and O'Connor."

"I'm Sam." She shook hands with him, then introduced Beau, admitting that she wasn't yet accustomed to using her new married surname.

"I trust first names are fine then?" Ryan said. "How was your flight?"

"My first time to fly first class, I have to admit, and it was wonderful."

He pointed to a door at the other end of the lobby. "We can eat here if you'd like, but if you'd be up for a short walk there's a better spot, actually, just up the way. And it's the direction we're going anyway."

"Sounds perfect."

Daniel held the thick glass door open, then led the way to the left. Beyond the hotel's dove-gray walls, the sidewalk widened and they strolled past the boat harbor. Gulls swooped and called out, hoping that some boat owner would toss a few scraps their way. Rigging clanked against metal masts, ringing like chimes in the morning air.

"It's peaceful here this morning," Daniel said, pressing the button for the crosswalk light when they approached an intersection. "Weekends get pretty crazy. Always some lot on the lash."

By his expression, Sam took it to mean drinking and partying were pretty common. The light changed and they crossed, walking down a narrow street with skinny sidewalks, in the shadows of the three-story buildings on either side. Each time a car came along they had to move single-file.

"You'll find the architecture a curious mix here," Daniel said when they reached the next cross street and waited for the light to change. "Four- and five-hundred year old buildings sit next to modern ones. In old times a lot of them were built of wood, and fires were a constant danger. The stone ones survived. The wooden ones got rebuilt in newer styles. And then there's the growth. Since tourism has become popular, hotels and B&Bs are all over the place, all pretty modern by Irish standards."

As they walked, he gave a quick history that involved

the Normans and a lot of tribes and dates way more than five hundred years ago. Sam started out trying to remember details, but decided she would have to read more about it—when she wasn't quite so jetlagged.

"Here we are," he said, ushering them into a narrow café filled with people chatting and lingering over coffee. Most of the clientele seemed to be college students and women with babies in strollers.

"My wife started me coming here," he explained. "They make terrific omelets. But there's all sorts of other choices too."

They placed their orders at a long counter then edged toward the back to find a table.

"I'm sure you're quite anxious to know about your uncle's will," he finally said when they'd settled at a table, shed their jackets and taken sips from their coffee, which Sam found delicious. "There's been a charitable trust in place for a number of years, so certain items were already earmarked for that. I know you're here on your honeymoon, so you don't want to spend the whole time talking business. We'll take a quick look at the property this morning and there's a little paperwork. Won't take too long."

The cryptic explanation did nothing to answer Sam's questions, and a waitress stepped up just then, arms laden with plates. It took a few minutes to sort out the orders and settle into eating.

"You mentioned property . . . is it something here in the city?" Sam asked.

"Oh, yes, very nearby." Ryan spread jam on a piece of toast and took a huge bite.

Sam suppressed her impatience. The question had remained unanswered for weeks now, it could stay that way through the meal. Plus, she found that the eggs and vegetables in the omelet were working wonders to restore her flagging energy. By the time they pushed their plates aside and started gathering their belongings she felt ready to face the day, whatever it might bring.

Chapter 2

The rain had started again, a gentle sprinkle, when they walked out of the café. Daniel Ryan turned to Sam. "Umbrellas?"

She and Beau nodded, holding them up.

"We're off then," Ryan said. "It's only a couple of blocks."

The attorney led the way along the narrow sidewalk, as they held their umbrellas high and dodged oncoming pedestrians who came at them in single-mindedly straight paths. At the next intersection, they turned left into a wide pedestrian mall rimmed with shops and restaurants in stone buildings. A young couple stood under an awning; he strummed at a guitar and she wailed out a folk tune while passersby ignored the open guitar case that held more raindrops than coins. Across the way, a woman was carrying a wire rack of postcards back inside her tiny shop. Sam and Beau followed Daniel to the center of the open area, where he stopped and faced the small stores.

"Well, here we are in Shop Street and this is it," he said.

What's it? Sam stared through the rain at the gray buildings.

"Just there." He pointed directly in front of them. "O'Shaughnessy's Fine Books. It's yours."

Sure enough, high on the gray stone building, a carved wooden sign with burgundy background and chipped white lettering spelled out the name of the shop. A display window showed an assortment of books with covers long since faded and curled. A red wooden door, its upper half done in small glass panes, led to the dim interior.

A bookstore? Uncle Terry left me a business? She looked up at Beau, certain that her eyes must be as wide as his. What on earth would she do with this?

She turned to Daniel and opened her mouth but couldn't formulate a question. There were too many.

"Come on, then," he said. "Let's go inside and meet your crew."

"So it's open? I mean . . . well, it looks sort of—dark." *Abandoned.*

His forehead wrinkled. "Yes, I suppose, now that you mention it. Better lighting in the window, that would fix it right up."

She managed a weak smile. Maybe it was more inviting inside.

"The building is, as you can see, in the historic district— eighth century. Many of the shops date very far back." He pointed as he led the way. "The claddagh goldsmith on the corner, for instance, has been in that location since the

1700s, and Aran woolens have been carried by the shop next to yours for centuries."

Nearly as old as the mold on some of those paperbacks, she thought, cringing a little. Well, there was nothing to do but take a look. In her sideline job at home, breaking into abandoned houses and cleaning them up for sale, she'd certainly seen worse than this. She squared her shoulders and folded her umbrella as Daniel led the way inside.

A man stood behind the vintage mahogany sales desk, his gray hair curling over his ears, bushy sideburns widening his cheeks, and dark brows pulling together fiercely over the bridge of his nose.

"Ambrose," Daniel said brightly, "I'd like for you to meet Terrance's niece, Samantha Sweet-Cardwell."

Sam stepped forward, hoping that her smile didn't look as frozen as it felt. No matter—the man only grunted and didn't offer his hand.

"Ambrose Piggott is manager of the shop," Daniel was saying with as much positive spin as he could muster. "He knows every inch of it, I'm sure."

"I've worked here forty years, know every little detail of the business, too, I daresay," muttered Ambrose. "Except for the fact about this *niece*, which I never heard of."

Daniel cleared his throat. Sam noticed that Beau was staying quiet as the proverbial mouse in the corner.

"Are the ladies here, Ambrose? Samantha wants to meet them as well."

From behind a tall wooden bookcase a heart-shaped face, framed by long strawberry curls, peered toward the newcomers. When the young woman stepped forward Sam saw that she was under five feet tall, very curvy, with a ready smile and a sparkle in her green eyes.

"Bridget, this is Samantha," Daniel said.

"You can all call me Sam." She extended her hand and Bridget edged forward. Despite her shy approach, her handshake was firm.

"Bridget O'Henry. Pleased to meet ya," she said, with a slight dip that might have become a curtsy in a more formal setting.

Sam guessed she must be in her twenties, although over the telephone her tiny voice probably made people think they were speaking to a child.

"And . . . oh, here's Keeva," Daniel said. "Keeva Blake, this is Saman— um, Sam."

The middle-aged woman's quick movements gave her a decisive air. She smiled warmly, showing straight, white teeth in an oval face with such pure skin that it obviously had minimal exposure to the dry air and sunshine Sam's own complexion had been tormented by. Her dark hair was pulled up in a clip. She wore a dark blue dress with a tan apron. She set a cardboard carton on the counter and wiped her hands on the apron before shaking hands with Sam and Beau.

"So, you'll be working with us now," Keeva said, as if it were already arranged.

Sam noticed that Ambrose turned his back at the suggestion. Bridget stood with her hands clasped loosely in front of her, looking at Sam expectantly for an answer.

"Well, I . . . I don't know." This was all happening too quickly. "I have a business back home in New Mexico, and a side job as well. I'm a little at a loss . . . But we'll see."

Did she imagine that Ambrose growled deep in his throat?

"So, anyway—" Why was it so hard to put a bright note

in her voice? "Who wants to show us around?"

Beau shot her a look—*us?* She smiled at him and tried to convey, *Just hang in here with me for a little while.*

"Well," said Keeva, "it's pretty much what you see here." She spread her arms and turned to indicate the extent of the shop. "There's a small back room for extra stock, but we haven't much in there at the moment."

"Not much cash in the till, either," Ambrose muttered.

In other words, don't be thinking you'll take an income out of this place. Sam noticed that no customers had come in. Foot traffic outside flowed past the bookshop with barely a glance in their direction.

"Maybe we can put together some ideas for ways to build the business back up," she said. *What am I thinking? I'm in town for two weeks.*

Bridget sent a perky smile her way; Keeva looked as if she wanted to say something helpful but couldn't think of anything; Ambrose grunted and moved a stack of bookmarks from one side of the cash register to the other.

Sam gazed around the room, taking in details she hadn't immediately noticed. Mahogany bookcases that rose nearly to the ten-foot ceiling ringed three sides of the shop. Quality woodwork. Two heavy tables filled most of the open floor space, piled high with books in haphazard stacks. She couldn't discern any labeling system or organization for which titles were located where. A feather duster lay on one of the tables, as if someone had begun to apply it but forgot to finish.

An elderly woman walked in just then and Keeva approached her.

"I'll come back later," Sam said to the others. "We just arrived in town and I need to get my bearings a little bit.

For now, please rest assured that I don't plan to make any drastic changes."

Bridget visibly relaxed but Ambrose just gave Sam a level stare.

The rain had stopped and the sky was skim-milk white, with hazy shadows beginning to show on the cobbles.

"Daniel, we need to talk," she said as soon as they'd walked out of sight of the shop. "Where can we grab a coffee?" Or a stiff drink. She caught sight of a large clock on a tall pedestal—it wasn't even noon.

Beau took her hand. "You two need to talk business. I think I'll wander back to the harbor and check out the boats for awhile. Meet you back at the room?"

She nodded. His parting kiss reminded her that this wasn't exactly how they'd envisioned spending their honeymoon. Her thoughts churned as he walked away.

The lawyer led the way toward a bright green door that stood open. Kelly's Pub was quiet before the lunch crowd came and they ordered coffee and carried it to a table near the windows.

"So." Daniel Ryan tried to make his voice chipper. "We'll have a little paperwork to transfer title of the shop to you."

Sam stared at him—she had at least two million concerns before she could possibly sign anything.

"What on earth was my uncle *thinking*, leaving me a business to run? I have a business back home. I can't be two places at once."

"You have good employees here, Sam. It'll work out."

Deep breath. "I can't just depend on things *working out*. The employees need leadership—that much is clear from the condition of the place. How will I pay them? The store isn't exactly bustling with customers." She felt her voice rise and paused a moment to get control. "I would need to review the financial statements, see if there's any money in the bank to keep operating . . ."

"I'm sure there are adequate records to allay your concerns," he said, picking up his mug.

"Where are they? Can I get to them?"

"I imagine they must be in the shop."

"And who's going to share them with me? Ambrose Piggott? The man clearly wishes I'd never set foot in there."

"Ambrose is an oyster, Sam—tough outer shell but a softie inside."

"Really. Well, you'll have to offer me some ideas on how I'm supposed to break through that tough shell."

He swallowed hard, clearly clueless. Had he truly believed that she would be thrilled with this deal?

"Look, I don't mean to jump down your throat," she said, softening her voice. "I just . . . I need some ideas. I'm due home in two weeks and that's not nearly enough time to solve this. I can't be flying back and forth between countries and letting my pastry shop go downhill while I try to prop up this other one."

"Let me check our files at the firm. Maybe there were additional records or instructions left with my partner, Mick O'Connor. He was Mr. O'Shaughnessy's representative for years before I came along."

It seemed the best he could do. Sam drank her coffee and debated what to do next. When they parted company outside the pub, she started walking. Water had drained off the cobbled pedestrian way and the sun lit some hanging pots of flowers. She strode purposefully until she came to a statue of Oscar Wilde seated on a park bench with another sculpted man. The plaque identified him as Eduard Vilde, an Estonian writer. The two bronze men seemed relaxed and jovial. Sam wished she felt the same way.

Okay, she thought, I can line up some specific steps to take or I can let this whole thing worry me until all the fun is gone out of our trip. *That* was not happening. She wanted to be strolling along the boat docks with Beau right this minute. She made a decision.

Back on Shop Street she stood back and watched the bookshop. *Her* bookshop. Clearly, she needed help with this situation. She couldn't operate a business in a strange town, in a foreign country, with no knowledge of the place. She needed the employees' cooperation and, like it or not, that meant working with all of them, even crusty old Ambrose.

Pedestrian traffic had picked up with the introduction of sunlight and she saw a shopper walk in. Maybe her first impression hadn't been accurate. She crossed in front of a bright yellow woolens shop and a blue storefront selling quality Irish linens, both bustling with customers. Spiffing up the bookstore would help it draw as much attention as these other places were getting.

The door creaked on its hinges as she entered and she was pleased to see that Ambrose was ringing up a sale, while Bridget talked in her high, small voice with two children whose young mother wanted them to choose books. Sam scanned the shelves until the customers finished and left. She realized that all eyes were on her when she turned around.

"This morning's events probably came as a surprise to all of us," she began. "Well, it did for me, anyway. I had no idea that my uncle thought I could handle his store."

Ambrose's heavy eyebrows seemed attached at the center; Keeva scuffed one foot back and forth on the hardwood floor. Only Bridget gave Sam her open and undivided attention.

"Anyway. I think we need to talk, to make some plans. Daniel Ryan suggested that I could find the financial records somewhere here in the shop. I'd like to take a look at them. But I assure you all that your jobs are safe. If Uncle Terry needed you here, then I most certainly do."

The air in the room relaxed a little but no one made a move.

"Ambrose, I will especially need your help. As manager, I'm sure you know more about the business than anyone else, including my uncle. Could you point me in the direction of the files I need?"

He met her gaze steadily. "I'll get them out. When I have the time."

From the corner of her eye Sam could see that Keeva and Bridget were frozen in place.

"Okay. Good enough. I'll come back in the morning— what time do we open?"

Ambrose looked like he planned to say something but, luckily, two women walked in just then so the only word that came out of his mouth was, "Nine."

Sam sent individual smiles to each of her employees, and to the customers, before she escaped to the street again. She tried to get her bearings, hoping she remembered which of the narrow streets led back to the harbor.

The walk calmed her and she found herself noticing her surroundings. Maybe she and Beau would try authentic pub food later, or perhaps look for a nice restaurant. So far, their honeymoon had consisted of a long car ride following a very long plane trip, with airport food and this morning's breakfast, which she barely remembered. Uncle Terry's surprise sort of capped a stressful few days.

She scanned the piers and debated walking the long stretch of dock in search of Beau. They hadn't tried their cell phones here yet, so she wasn't sure hers would work but in any case it was among the things she'd left behind in the room. She decided to go there and see if her husband would be along soon.

It took two tries with the key card to get the door open and when she did, the atmosphere in the room seemed different somehow. Music drifted from somewhere, and the air smelled of honeysuckle. The drapes they'd left open were now closed, making the room dim.

"Beau?" she called out.

"In here. Glad you're back, darlin'."

She pressed the door shut and turned around.

"Surprised?" he said.

Three lush bouquets stood on the nightstand, table and dresser—roses, lilies, daisies and more. The room-darkening draperies were closed, leaving one small lamp and several candles to softly light the space. Although the small bedside radio didn't exactly offer stereo quality, it played soft jazz.

"Beau, what did you do?" She giggled as he stepped over to her and trailed little kisses down her neck. His hair was faintly damp and smelled of eucalyptus shampoo.

"I made us a little love nest. I will put out the Do Not Disturb sign and take the phone off the hook and meet you over there." He tilted his head toward the bed.

She gave herself over to his long and delicious kiss. Now *this* was how a honeymoon should begin.

Chapter 3

Sam stretched luxuriantly. They'd fallen asleep in a tangle of sheets and sometime during the afternoon she'd pulled up the duvet. Beau's arm tightened around her midsection, just a little, as he began to waken. At some point he'd blown out the candles and the light in the room was dim.

"I think I'm hungry," she murmured, "but I can't decide what I want."

He kissed her temple, then her neck, down to the shoulder. "Um . . . I could think of something."

She rolled toward him and they somehow lost track of another half hour.

"What would you like for dinner?" she called out from the bathroom as she aimed the dryer at her hair.

His voice came through but she couldn't tell what he'd said. Silly to ask a question with a noisy appliance running.

She brushed the last few strands and switched off the dryer. A dash of lipstick and hint of blusher and she emerged from the bathroom.

"I'm trying to decide what to wear," she said. "Where would you like to eat?"

He'd donned his standard outfit—jeans and a flannel shirt. "You can eat in that robe if you want to. We're dining in, and it should arrive . . ."

He glanced at his watch but a tap at the door answered the question.

Sam edged aside as the waiter wheeled a linen-draped table toward the window. Beau directed the delivery, set two chairs beside the table, and once again marveled when the man didn't wait around for a tip.

"What's this?" She eyed the covered plates and crystal bowls of condiments.

"Salmon, freshly caught and lightly grilled." He lifted one of the lids. "Potatoes, some sliced veggies . . ."

Sam felt herself salivating. There were crisp salads and something decadently chocolate on separate plates.

"I guessed that a white wine might be the thing," he said, picking up the dewy bottle that the waiter had opened for them.

"Wow. You just might be a keeper." She winked as she took her seat.

The fish was wonderful and the vegetables perfectly cooked. They ate in silence for a few minutes, until Beau set his fork down.

"I could inhale this," he said. "Better pace myself. So, how did things go with the attorney after I left?"

She sipped at her wine. "I think he basically had the impression that he would take me by the shop, get me to sign papers which would transfer it to me, and then he'd be back at his office before lunch."

Beau raised his eyebrows.

"I didn't sign anything. How could I? The place looks like a money pit to me. A dusty, drab *old* money pit. I can't possibly run a store here while I'm keeping Sweet's Sweets going back at home. I'm used to being very hands-on with my business. I'd have to turn it entirely over to the employees here and hope for the best because I know nothing at all about running a bookstore."

"True. Maybe Ivan could give you some pointers."

Ivan Petrenko, the quirky Russian who owned a bookstore next to Sam's bakery in Taos, did seem to manage to keep his little place going despite his complaints that big chain stores and the Internet had drastically changed the world of bookselling since he got into it. Maybe she could get some ideas from him.

"All I know is that I can't put any money into it. If O'Shaughnessy's doesn't at least generate enough to pay the employees and support itself, all I can think to do is shut it down."

"Old Ambrose isn't going to love you for that."

"No. But old Ambrose doesn't exactly love me anyway. Did you see that scowl?" She speared a julienne slice of carrot. "At least I finally understand why Uncle Terrance decided to leave the entire inheritance to only one heir. Can you imagine me trying to divide this with my sister, much less include the cousins? It's a nightmare."

"I suppose you could sell off the inventory and maybe net enough for another trip back here to close the deal."

Sam nodded thoughtfully but that answer didn't feel right either. "I suppose I'll think of something."

* * *

By morning, Sam found herself chafing at the unanswered questions.

"If nothing else, I have to get in there and see the financial records," she told Beau as they took the elevator to the lobby.

"Do you want my help?"

"You don't have to come along, unless you really want to. With luck, maybe there are a few file folders I can bring back with me, something I can go through in the room this evening."

"Maybe I'll look into renting a car so we could take a drive down the coast, or find out what kinds of historic places are around here."

They stepped out into a brisk breeze and zipped their jackets. The boats in the slips were bobbing merrily and Beau slowed his pace to watch them.

"Give me the morning at the shop," she said, "then we can meet up and have a tasty pub lunch and figure out how we want to spend some tourist time."

She gave him a quick kiss and headed across the street. The narrow sidewalks and winding streets felt a little more familiar today, and the absence of rain would—Sam hoped—make her new bookshop look more appealing. By the time she entered Shop Street and located the correct stone building she realized it would take a lot more than good weather to help the old place.

"Good morning, everyone," she said as she walked in.

Bridget's cute smile beamed at her from the back of the

room. Keeva must have just arrived—she was taking off her heavy sweater. Ambrose, behind the sales counter, only grunted.

"Could we have a little meeting before customers arrive?" Sam asked.

The women came forward and Ambrose draped his forearms over the ancient brass cash register, facing Sam.

"I'll admit that I'm not quite sure what to do first," she told them. "Did my uncle spend much time in the shop in recent years?"

Keeva spoke up. "Not a lot, actually. The poor dear had so many troubles. Health, you know. In his last years he . . ."

"Terry came round every week," Ambrose interjected. "Up until his last few months." He stared at Sam. "He cared a great deal for this shop. He loved every book in this room."

"Was business better in the days when he spent time here?"

"Well, aye. Business was better before the recession hit the whole world, better everywhere, as I'm sure you're knowin' from your fancy cake shop." Ambrose's fingers flexed, as if they wanted to curl into fists.

Sam nodded. "You're right about that."

Bridget spoke up. "Our regular patrons, the ones who've come in from times past, they're still comin' around."

The others gave firm nods.

"Mr. Ryan seemed to think that all the business records are here." She slid her gaze over to Ambrose. As guardian of the register, he must surely have access to the bills and receipts as well. The gray haired man looked like he wanted to make some kind of remark but he merely turned toward a short file cabinet to his right.

"And meanwhile, can I help with the dusting or something?" Sam said. "It would help me see what we have in stock."

Keeva motioned Sam toward the back, where she supplied a dust cloth.

"I wish I'd known my uncle better. My mother remembers him fondly," Sam said as the two of them worked on a section of popular fiction.

"He was a good man," Keeva said. "Hard worker in his younger days. He took over this shop under odd circumstances, you know. Won it in a wager."

"Really?"

"Oh, aye. Used to say if it weren't for a jack of diamonds, he'd never've set foot in the place."

That didn't seem like an auspicious beginning.

"He wasn't much of a reader, then?"

"Oh, he became avid. Mostly took out books about the war, got into some heated political discussions, he did." Keeva pushed two Ian Rankin titles closer together to make space for a couple of Ruth Rendell's books.

"Your uncle didn't need book studies to be a smart man," Ambrose called out from the other side of the room. "He had a brilliant mind for business."

Sam smiled toward him but questioned the statement. Obviously, a shop run by someone with a brilliant business mind would be doing better than this one was. She still hadn't seen a customer today.

Almost in answer to that thought, a woman pushed the door open. Walking directly to the counter, she asked Ambrose if her order had come in.

"So anyway," Keeva continued, "the story goes that

Terrance walked in here green as could be and ripped out everything the previous owner had done."

Ambrose's customer had wandered over to the cookbooks so he joined back in on the conversation.

"That's not exactly true, Keeva," he said. "He did change the name of the shop and had his own sign put up right away. That's the one, it's out there now. I was here that day. Me, about Bridget's age and knowin' hardly more."

Bridget gave him a wounded look.

He didn't notice. "But inside the shop, Terry gave us free rein. He knew I read a lot, and the old woman who worked here at the time—former librarian, she was—she knew every writer and every title in this place. Could put her finger on any book a person might want."

Despite the man's hard shell, Sam knew that he would make a valuable ally. If only she could break through.

The customer chose a book from the shelf, added it to the one she'd special-ordered, and pulled out her wallet. While she paid for her purchases Sam gazed at the full shelves—how would she ever learn every book in a place like this?

When the lady had gone, Sam said, "I bet Uncle Terry was really missed around here."

Ambrose's face softened momentarily. He pursed his lips, then said he needed to go out for a smoke. Bridget offered to handle the register if anyone came in. The older man buttoned his jacket and walked out.

Sam watched him cross the cobblestone mall before she turned to the women. "I wonder if there's anything we might do to attract more of the tourists. There seem to be a lot of people walking around out there." How to handle this lightly? "Perhaps more color in the window displays? Maybe a selection of books about Irish folklore? Something like that?"

Keeva chewed at her lip, thinking. "I don't know . . . Mr. Terry didn't always take to buying a lot of new stock."

"Keeva, sadly, he's gone. We have to figure out something."

Sam glanced around the room. "Of course, before we can think of adding new inventory, I'll need to know if there's any money. I don't suppose Terry shared that kind of information?"

Both Keeva and Bridget looked shocked. Of course he wouldn't. Sam would have to find this out for herself.

Outside, she could see Ambrose pacing back and forth across the way. He paused and stared up at the bookstore's sign for a minute, then dropped his cigarette and crushed it against the stones. The open door brought a hint of moisture when he came back in.

"Could you please pull out the financial and sales files for me before I go, Ambrose? I'll look them over tonight and bring them back."

He ignored the request, walking over to a shelf of history books and rearranging them.

Okay, I won't let this become a battle yet. But I am the boss here, like it or not.

Her inner dialog diverted when the door opened once more and pair of women came in. They greeted Bridget and Keeva familiarly. One headed for the disorderly stack of books on one of the tables and began poking through them. The older lady openly regarded Sam with curiosity. Keeva introduced her as Mrs. Flannery. She wore a wool skirt and thick black stockings, with a heavy sweater-coat and a knitted cap nearly covering her short gray hair.

"Sam is Terry's niece," Keeva said. "She's here on her honeymoon."

"Ah, the new one." Mrs. Flannery tilted her chin up so she could see Sam better. "It's fittin' I say. A new business venture always goes hand in hand with a new phase in your life. It's good that you're here."

Sam kept her smile in place, wondering how the woman knew so much about her, concluding that Galway was no less a small town than Taos and word must have gotten around. The other woman had obviously picked up bits of the conversation. She came over and was introduced as Noreen.

"Hi, howarya?" Noreen said. "Enjoying your stay in Galway?"

"We just came in yesterday. I hope to get out and see more."

Noreen regarded Sam critically. "You didn't wear nothin' green at your weddin' did you?"

Puzzled, Sam shook her head.

"And was it rainin' on the day?"

"No, we had beautiful weather . . ."

"Ah, that's good. Very lucky."

Keeva piped up to explain. "There are lots of Irish superstitions, you'll be finding, and a whole bunch of them to do with marriage."

"Ah." Sam nodded slowly.

"You wouldn't want to break a glass that morning, or drop your wedding ring before the ceremony."

Their wedding had come together after a flurry of upsetting events, and Sam couldn't honestly remember if she'd dropped anything before the ceremony. She kept silent and the conversation turned to family. Sam figured out from the context that Noreen was the older woman's daughter and that the two were sneaking away from their household chores to get some shopping done while the nice weather held. Sam left Noreen and Keeva to talk, walking over to the large tables of books to see if she could figure out why they weren't shelved but were sitting there in seemingly random piles.

Meanwhile, Mrs. Flannery had wandered to the other side of the shop, where Ambrose was still rearranging books, stacking some of them to one side while he fiddled around with others.

"Say, Ambrose," she said "Did you ever get rid of that one what was causin' you so much trouble?"

Wondering if the woman might possibly mean her, Sam tuned her ears that direction.

"Well, in case it's a ghost, I brought ya some holy water. Where was he now? Over in that back room?" She rummaged deep into her bag and came out with a stoppered vial about three inches long. "Just sprinkle this around when you get ready to go home for the night. He won't dare enter a room with the power of holy water warding 'im off."

Ambrose turned away and muttered, " 'Scuse me now, I've got some files to locate."

Chapter 4

By noon Sam felt more stymied than ever at the daunting task of learning the store's inventory. She kept telling herself it wasn't important. If she kept the place, she had three good employees whose jobs it was to know all that. If she followed her instincts and bailed out, it wouldn't matter anyway. She gathered the two manila folders Ambrose handed her, along with a handwritten check register and a tall leather-bound ledger, which he claimed would give her all the information she needed.

When she'd inquired about computer printouts or a disk where records might have been saved, he looked at her as if she'd come from another planet.

"Terrance O'Shaughnessy never put any store in trusting machines with his finances, and I don't either."

That, it seemed, sealed the fate of any computer that might have ever worked its way into the business. She fumed at his obtuse attitude but there was no changing it so she would work with what she had.

Bridget gave Sam a sympathetic look, but a shrug told her that's just the way it was. She noticed that the street outside was damp again, so she bagged the records in a plastic sack and pulled out her umbrella for the walk back to the hotel.

In their room, Beau sat in a chair, a scattering of brochures on the desk in front of him.

"How did it go this morning?" he asked.

She rolled her eyes. "About the same. There's dust on every surface, even though Keeva and I worked on some of the shelves. Bridget is very sweet, nice as can be and great with the customers, but I just don't see her hustling about and accomplishing much. Ambrose wants everything to be exactly as it was thirty years ago when he and Terry ran the shop as a team—probably right down to having the very same books on the shelves. I didn't see anything in there that looked new. Even the popular fiction is all four and five years old. In general, the shop is like a ship without a captain and it was all I could do not to jump in and start cleaning and tossing old stuff out."

He sent her a cautionary look.

"A couple of interesting patrons came in, though. I learned that it was lucky I didn't break a glass the morning of our wedding."

He sent her a puzzled look and she recapped the visit of the superstitious woman who'd come into the shop. By the time she got to the part about the holy water warding off ghosts, she was chuckling.

"What would have happened if, say, you had dropped the wedding rings?" he asked.

"Who knows? I grew up in the Southwest. What do I know about Irish superstitions?" But she did know a little something about other unexplainable things. That mysterious wooden box, now sitting in the hotel room safe with her jewelry in it, had shown Sam some things that certainly didn't fit the realm of everyday reality. And who was to say that the old woman who'd given it to her wasn't truly some kind of a witch?

He let that subject go. "I picked up a couple of maps," he said, "and some brochures. There's a little walking tour of the town that we could do this afternoon and—that big park we passed coming in?—it says they have events there all the time. We might catch some music or something."

Sam opened a dresser drawer while he talked, finding a spot to tuck the business files under some T-shirts.

"Lunch first?" he asked.

"I passed a pub on the way back, just a couple blocks from here. Something really smelled good in there. Bring your umbrella—there was a light sprinkle."

They found O'Reilly's, another gray stone building that rose directly from the narrow sidewalk as if it had simply grown up on the spot. Above the stone foundation small, divided windows looked in on a large room of dark woods and glowing yellow light fixtures. A menu was written in chalk above the bar. They ordered Guinness and sandwiches that came piled high with meat on a heavy, dark bread. Sam moaned a long ummm as she took the first bite.

Beau nodded as he pinched off a bite of the bread and stuffed it into his mouth. They didn't manage much conversation for the next few minutes. He went back to the bar for a second glass of the draught and came back to tell Sam to look outside.

"Doesn't look like a long walk or the park will be on the agenda quite yet," he said.

Rain streamed down the windows; she'd hardly noticed it as the pub filled with people.

"So, we'll go back to the room for awhile. I can look over those folders I brought back."

He gave a large yawn. "After this lunch, I think I feel a nap coming on."

They finished their sandwiches, listening to the rise of Irish accents all around. As the laughter increased Sam found her thoughts drifting to the uncle who'd chosen to leave his dilapidated little shop to her and wondering why he'd done that. Nothing about it made sense. He could have left it with the employees and it would continue to operate as it had, probably for another fifty years. Why had his American niece been brought into the picture? And why Sam?—there were surely other relatives closer than she. Beau had stood up.

"Getting crowded," he said. "Someone else might need the table."

Sam gathered her jacket, backpack and umbrella and they started toward the hotel. In the room, Beau immediately pulled off his jeans and stretched out on the bed with the duvet covering him.

Sam brought out the files and turned the desk lamp on low, adjusting the shade so it wouldn't disturb his rest. She hadn't seen a hand-written ledger in ages, surely not since she'd started working for old man Sanchez before she and the other young secretary convinced him to give computers a try. Transferring the ledger entries to their first accounting program had been a lot of work, but after that the reports were much easier to generate and read. She sighed and began to flip through the leather-bound book.

The handwritten headings and numbers might have come out of another century. She had to remind herself that Uncle Terrance was probably in his nineties when he died. He actually had grown up in another century, when penmanship received a grade in school and ciphering was done in neat columns. At a glance, she had to give credit—the entries were neatly done and the math seemed accurate.

However, Ambrose's assertion that the ledger and checkbook would tell her everything she needed to know—that was a little off the mark. According to the dates, months would go by when no sales were recorded. Surely that couldn't be right—deposits were being made into the bank account all along. The ledger entries covered roughly five years, but toward the end it really became sketchy and for the past six months there wasn't a single entry. No wonder Ambrose hadn't wanted to show her this. He'd done no bookkeeping at all since Terrance passed away.

The check register wasn't much better, although he had taken the time to record the balance, apparently from a statement provided by the bank, at the end of each month. Although there wasn't a lot of money in the account, it did seem adequate for the necessities, like paychecks. Surely this wasn't the entire record; next time she talked to Daniel Ryan she would ask him. Perhaps an accountant had a more complete set of records somewhere. After all, certainly Ireland must require businesses to report income and pay taxes like every other place in the world.

She set the ledger aside and rubbed at her eyes. Beau was snoring softly and that bed looked really good. She crawled under the duvet with him and let herself drift into sleep.

When he stirred, bringing Sam out of a muddled dream, she realized that most of the afternoon had gotten away from them. She got up and looked out at the graveyard across the street. The rain had stopped and, for once, there were no heavy clouds roiling in off the sea.

"We're going to have to adapt to this time zone," he said, "or we'll be up all night and sleeping all day." He gave a little eyebrow-wiggle that told her that, in some ways, he wouldn't mind being up all night.

She laughed and tossed a pillow at him.

"It's really nice out now. Let's take a long walk to wake ourselves up."

She slipped her jacket on, picked up her pack and pretended impatience as he took a minute to brush his hair while she waited by the door.

"Be nice to me, wife, or I'll make you buy dinner."

"What—with my huge inheritance?"

She told him about the ledger and checkbook as they rode the elevator to the lobby. A crowd had gathered there, apparently tourists fresh off a bus, who were waiting to receive keys to their rooms. It was a retirement-age group, chatting away with precise British accents.

Outside, the breeze was warmer than before. They turned away from the marina and found themselves on a street bordered on one side by the hotel's parking garage and on the other by a row of warehouses and huge storage tanks. When it became clear that only commercial dock traffic came this way, they reversed course, crossed a street and came out near the entrance to the cemetery that Sam had seen earlier from their windows. A shadowed narrow entry in the high stone wall didn't look terribly inviting so they walked on, soon becoming hopelessly turned around.

"Let's try this again," Beau said. He backtracked until they returned to the open area where the small boat harbor was surrounded by hotels and apartments. The walkway led past some open parks and they could see a pavilion on a wide grassy swale across a narrow stretch of water.

"I think that's the River Corrib," Beau said. "Looking at those brochures earlier, it said there's a water taxi to the other side. They hold events over there. Looks like a little carnival is there now."

Sure enough, a Ferris wheel caught Sam's attention. A pathway on that side of the river was crowded with people and lots of children. It was easy enough to join the flow toward the water taxi and take the short ride. At the park they opted to walk a graveled path along the shoreline while most of the crowd followed their insistent children and headed for the colorful carnival rides. The stroll was an easy one, the grass brilliant in the late afternoon light, small waves lapping at the earth beside them.

At the very tip of the point of land, Beau grabbed Sam's hand and spun her toward him. "I'm glad I met you, darlin'. It's going to be a great life we'll have."

They kissed and didn't care who might be watching.

"Newlyweds, eh?" A short, stooped old man they hadn't noticed had rounded the stone pillar that marked the end of the point. He wore a porkpie hat and a green vest, dark trousers and a pale yellow shirt.

Sam laughed. "How did you know?"

The old man gave her a wink. She smiled up at Beau and when she looked back the old man was gone.

"Tell me I didn't just see a leprechaun," she said, looking all around for the stranger.

Beau shrugged. "My back was to him, I didn't see where he went either. He probably ducked behind that pillar, playing a little joke on us."

"Okay," she whispered. "We'll let him have his laugh."

They held hands and strolled back along the waterway. The water taxi was on the opposite shore, fully loaded.

"There's a bridge just up there." Beau pointed to a crossing a couple of blocks in the distance. "What do you say? We could use the exercise."

Sam agreed. It was pleasant walking past small waterfront houses with gardens of roses and neatly trimmed shrubs. People sat out in their lawn chairs and said hello as they passed.

"It's nice here," she said to Beau. "I'm glad we got out, it was time to think of something besides that dusty bookshop."

"Except that, obviously, you *are* thinking about it."

"Only a little. I promise. I'll figure out something and deal with it tomorrow."

"If it were me," he said. "I'd just hand over the whole place to the employees. I'd bet it's what that Ambrose fellow would want anyway. Probably, that's the reason he's not exactly been a warm and friendly guy toward you."

"I'm sure you're right. And, as usual, you are the voice of common sense. Solves both my problem and Ambrose's." She didn't know why she hadn't thought of it earlier. "I'll call Daniel Ryan in the morning and find out what I have to do. Surely there's some deed I can sign over, right?"

He squeezed her hand. "Yep. Meanwhile, how about some dinner? This place looks pretty good."

The sun set so much later here that Sam hadn't realized it was already past their normal dinner hour. If they were going to adapt to the time change they'd better start eating and sleeping on a regular schedule.

The pub Beau pointed out seemed a popular spot. People stood two deep, in places, at the long bar and many of the tables were filled. But there were a few empty seats and a small band was tuning up in the corner.

They ordered Guinness and the Irish stew, then found a table at the window where they could see the musicians.

"I liked your idea for the bookshop," Sam said. She filled him in with what she'd seen in the written records, until a waiter approached with a laden tray. The stew—steaming, meaty, and delicious—came accompanied by a hearty bread.

"This is definitely the opposite of that lightly grilled salmon we had at the hotel," she said. "But, wow—*so* good!"

The music went into double-time about then, a lively Irish traditional piece and people came out of the crowd and formed up to dance. Four couples paired off, similar to American square dance, and began doing some intricate moves that involved heavy stomping on the wood floor, passes through and under arched arms, and the occasional shout. Obviously, they knew the song and the steps well. Others, gathered at the bar, began keeping time with stomps and claps. Sam noticed that it was a crowd of all ages. Most of the dancers were in their forties or fifties, but several men at the bar looked very young. She mentioned it when the waiter came to bring them more bread.

"Oh, yeah. The legal drinkin' age here is eighteen. But the local ones, they been comin' with their parents all their lives. Most of these is university kids. Lots of Americans study there, and they think it's fun to stand at the bar, get a Stout and act all grown up."

Sam could see the thoughts running through Beau's

head. At home, his department had their hands full with underage drinking, as she supposed happened in a lot of small towns. She wondered if a lower drinking age was a good idea. But at the moment it was easier to become engrossed in finishing her stew.

By the time they'd finished eating, the band was into a fourth song that sounded very much like all the others and the rapid dance steps were beginning to thrum in her head. They agreed it was time to set off for their hotel.

They kept to the well-lighted streets, all of which seemed busy and populated even though it was well after ten o'clock. Police in glo-striped jackets made a visible presence, but no one seemed to be out for trouble at the moment. Soon, the hotel area appeared ahead. A few of the moored boats' owners sat on their decks in canvas chairs, sipping from cans, stretching their legs out. A horn sounded somewhere in the distance.

As Sam and Beau reached the section of boat slips that bordered Dock Road, they felt a change in the atmosphere. Voices went quiet. Someone nearby shut off a loud radio. They looked up to see a Coast Guard cruiser moving slowly into the marina, its movements so still as to barely cause a ripple. Tied behind was another boat, rigged with fishing gear, completely dark, without a soul aboard. It felt eerily abandoned.

The lead boat chugged to an open spot against the dock, near where Sam and Beau stood. As the empty boat came closer, Sam realized that people were quietly drifting over to stand nearby.

"It's the *Glory Be*," someone whispered. It was a good-looking boat—a trawler, Sam thought—with a red hull, modern navigation equipment, wide windows all around the bridge, and a white wheelhouse capped by a matching red roof. She guessed its length at fifty or sixty feet.

"Where's Darragh? This ain't right," came another quiet voice.

She glanced up and saw that a crowd of two dozen or more had filled in behind them. She tugged at Beau's sleeve and they moved aside.

A man wearing the clothing of a boat captain stood close by, staring down at the empty vessel. His face was solemn. "Nothin' good's gonna come of this."

The hair rose on her arms when he said it.

Police arrived within minutes, giving orders and dispersing the crowd. Sam and Beau didn't see any reason to hang around.

"What do you suppose that was about?" she asked when they were alone in the elevator, headed toward their room.

"No idea. But I didn't like the looks of it. Did you notice, near the wheelhouse, those marks?"

She shook her head.

"They looked like blood."

Chapter 5

Sam spent a restless night, remembering people's reactions to the abandoned boat—dark, lonely, spooky—reliving the chill she'd felt. Beau's guess that he'd seen bloodstains on it only added to her disquiet. The heavy meal probably didn't help either.

She lay still in the early morning half-light, trying not to wake Beau. In her mind, she made a plan for the day. One: meet with Daniel Ryan to sign away her inheritance. Two: come back and celebrate with Beau. Maybe they would get a car today and take a drive up the coast. It would be a shame to be in Ireland and confine themselves to seeing only one city. At some point her eyes closed again; when she awakened Beau was facing her, his fingertips toying with the lace on her nightgown.

The touches turned to strokes, kisses became urgent,

clothing fell away . . . and they were too late to catch the hotel's breakfast buffet by the time they got out of their room.

"Good thing I remembered to hang out the Do Not Disturb sign," Beau said, noticing that the maid's cart sat outside the room next to theirs.

They decided to get a brisk walk done before finding a spot to eat. As they passed the marina they noticed that the red and white *Glory Be* was tied up there, but a ring of yellow police tape circled its deck. Beau looked as if he wished he could find out what had happened, but no one was around at the moment. They walked on past it.

Four blocks later they noticed a coffee house that promised a Full Irish Breakfast at a reasonable price, so they ducked in and placed their orders.

"I guess I might as well find out if my cell phone is going to work here," Sam said, digging in a side compartment of her small pack to find it. "Hopefully, it won't cost a fortune for a quick call."

She came up with the phone and Daniel Ryan's business card then spent a few minutes figuring out what sequence of numbers she would need to press to make the connection. When a secretary answered she said that she would like a few minutes with Mr. Ryan as soon as possible. In return, she got an eleven o'clock appointment and directions that depended on being able to locate a certain department store.

"I'm finishing my eggs and sausages before I try to figure out all this," she said when their plates arrived.

Eyeing the silver-dollar sized black disks on the plate, Beau left them alone and cut into his egg yolk.

"Ah, those'd be your puddings," said the waitress who brought coffee refills, at his inquiry. "The dark ones are blood pudding." She breezed away.

Sam took a taste but decided she could pass them up. Beau declared that he was full after two eggs, two sausages, toast, a scone, and a broiled half tomato, so he pushed his puddings aside. By the time they'd finished the food and a full pot of tea she realized it was after ten and they had no idea how long it would take to reach the lawyer's office.

A query to the cashier and they learned that the department store was about six blocks away, fifteen minutes if they didn't dawdle. That was easier said than done—all the shops had enticing wares, and Sam caught herself eyeing gifts to take home and trying to remember where she'd seen each item. Aran sweaters, Irish linens, Celtic knot jewelry and a beautiful greenish marble—her friend Zoë would love one of the worry stones made of that. Beyond the tiny shops they came to the large department store, its windows filled with slim mannequins wearing European styles. The building addresses were a little confusing but when she consulted her notes, she'd written down that the street-level entrance to the law offices was accessed by a shiny black doorway beside a jewelry store. They located it and walked up to the second floor.

Daniel Ryan greeted them warmly and asked Sam how she was enjoying her bookshop.

"Daniel, please. It isn't mine yet. I haven't signed anything. Besides, I've decided to give it away. To the employees."

He had escorted them from the small reception area to his private office and now he closed the door. Indicating the two guest chairs in front of his desk, he waited until they sat down and then took his own seat.

"Sam, I'm afraid it's not quite that simple. I'm sorry but you aren't allowed to give it away."

"What? If it's mine I can do anything I want with it, can't I?"

"Only after two years." He pressed his fingertips together and leaned on his elbows. "It's a provision in the will."

"But—"

"It's the way your uncle wanted it. He felt that you would need time to adjust to owning the shop and to see it become profitable again."

"There's nothing in his records to show that it has been very profitable yet," she said, trying to keep the whine out of her voice. Taking a breath she started over, with the part about how she'd taken the scanty financial records to study last night. "I can't do this, Daniel. I have a life at home."

"Nothing requires you to be on-site at your shop here in Galway," he said. "You can certainly manage it from anywhere you like. Terrance trusted the employees implicitly to handle the daily business."

Was the man blind? Did he not see the shoddy condition of the merchandise, that nothing new had been added in ages? That Ambrose Piggott resented her presence and would surely do everything he could to drive her out?

"Terrance's accountant handled the tax forms and our firm managed all legal matters. It's really only the shop itself that needs your touch." He spread his hands, palms up. "It should be quite simple to keep it going."

Aye. Sam closed her eyes for a few seconds. He just didn't get it.

"But why? I do not see why I can't sign a deed of some

kind . . . we would call it a quit claim deed in the States . . . something that lets me give up ownership. I don't want any money from it."

He fixed his face in an expression of supreme patience. "It's what your uncle wanted, Sam. I don't know what else to tell you."

She searched wildly for an answer but the best she could come up with was to ask for the accountant's name.

Ryan became very accommodating, offering to place the telephone call for her. Tom Mitchell had a kindly voice which grew cautious over the speaker when Ryan explained who Samantha was and that she wanted more information about the bookshop.

"All I can say is that I prepared the required tax forms each year for Mr. O'Shaughnessy, based on the income and expenses he told me about. He kept his own records. I never saw anything more than the totals. I've not received those figures for this most recent year yet, seeing as there was the unfortunate event of Mr. O'Shaughnessy's passing."

Daniel thanked him and hung up the phone. "If Ambrose can't give you more complete records, I suspect it's that Terry kept a lot of the business knowledge in his head."

The head of a man in his nineties. Sam began to feel a wave of despair.

"Come on, Beau. We better leave." Getting out was better than telling Ryan what she was really thinking.

Out on the street again, the sky had become a dark gray, mirroring her mood. She strode purposefully along, making even Beau's long stride work to keep up with her. When she came to the Oscar Wilde statue she paused and stared at the bench he sat on.

"Darlin', let's think about it rationally," Beau said, breathing a little hard.

"What's to be rational about? I've got a business that's failing, it's five thousand miles from home, the employees love the place but are letting it slide into a pile of dusty ruin, and there are no current financial records to be found. I might already be in deep trouble with the Irish authorities and I don't even know it." She clenched her fists down inside her jacket pockets. "God, Uncle Terry, what have you done to me?"

Beau stepped forward and pulled her close to him as fat raindrops began to pelt them. "Let's get out of the rain. Something will come to you."

She let out a rueful laugh. "Yeah, the last time someone said something was coming to me it turned out to be a surprise I didn't exactly want."

He kept one arm around her shoulders and steered her toward the awning of a nearby music store. A display of fiddles, guitars and flat drums reminded her of the lively music they'd heard last night, of the fun atmosphere and friendly people. She couldn't let the drab bookstore and gloomy weather dampen their honeymoon. It was her attitude that was ruining the trip, and she determined to turn that around.

"You're right," she said. "I have to make the best of this. Somehow."

Beyond the awning, the downpour drilled at the autumn flowers in their baskets and water splattered in the puddles that rapidly formed in low spots in the uneven stone paving.

"We didn't bring our umbrellas, did we?" said Beau with a little chuckle.

Sam patted her backpack, but she knew the answer.

She shook her head. Suddenly the whole situation seemed ridiculous and they both started laughing. An old woman wearing a heavy headscarf hunched under her black umbrella and hurried past them.

Ten minutes went by and the torrent became merely a pour.

"The bookshop is closer than the hotel," Sam said. "And I really need to go back and see how things are going today anyway. Shall we head over there?"

She tucked her pack under her jacket and they dashed to the next shop that had an awning. Half a block at a time, they made their way to O'Shaughnessy's Books and stepped up to the door. Shaking off as much water as they could, they went inside.

Keeva stood at the register. "It's bucketing down out there," she said when she saw Sam's wet jacket. "And you, did you just leg it over here?"

From the back room Sam heard Ambrose utter an expletive, followed by the sound of something hitting the floor. She hurried to the doorway and saw him stooping to pick up a massive dictionary.

"You all right?" she asked.

"Aye, just lost my grip on it," he said with a wince as he stood up straight.

"Can I help you with it?"

"No, no. I've got it." He pushed past her and carried the large book to one of the cluttered tables, where he edged a stack aside and set the dictionary down.

"Ambrose, I need to talk to you about the shop's finances."

He sent her a wary look and turned back toward the storeroom. She followed, noticing that Beau was standing at the shelves and seemed to be keeping himself busy.

"I went through all the receipts and the ledger you gave me yesterday," Sam told Ambrose. "But they don't begin to cover it. There are no entries at all for the past six months. I spoke with the accountant and he says he never received the tax information he needs for the current year."

"Well, that ain't my doin'. Your uncle took care of it all."

"Okay." She took a very deep breath, working to think what Ivan Petrenko might do with this place. "Okay. It is what it is. But now I have to deal with it. We can probably think of some things to boost the business back up. Can't you give me a little help here, Ambrose?"

She may have only imagined that his expression softened. He turned to an open box and began fiddling with something inside, his back to her.

"Terry left us all a bit in the lurch, didn't he now." His voice came out soft and low. "He was gettin' frail, we all knew that. But we dinna think he'd go so sudden-like. And then we didn't even get—" He cleared his throat, gathered a stack of books into his arms and pushed past her, back into the sales area.

Sam turned, caught something like worry in Keeva's expression, saw Ambrose's gnarled hands working over the books on the messy table, without really changing anything. She sighed. Obviously, she would only get information out of him in tiny doses.

Keeva tilted her head toward Sam, motioning her over.

"I could show you the register and how we ring up the sales. If you'd like." She looked over toward Ambrose. "Hey, if you want to take a little break, Sam and I can handle things here for a while," she called out.

The older man stood up straighter, tugged at his

cardigan and walked toward the door. "I could do with me lunch break now."

He walked out without another word.

"Sorry he's giving you such a hard time," Keeva said. "We all understand what you've gotta do. It's just been especially hard on him—losing Terry and all."

"Are you saying that they were . . ."

"Oh, I'm not sayin' they were a couple or anything like that," she said, almost a little too solidly. "But, you know, Ambrose did love your uncle. Worked here together over forty years. Ambrose was fairly young when he started working here. Terry, being twenty years older kind of took him in, became like a dad. He's takin' this hard."

Sam felt a tug. Maybe she had come on too strong.

"It was rough, watching Mr. O'Shaughnessy slippin' in the last few years. Me, I've been here only ten years but I saw it, the difference in 'im from when I started."

Sam nodded. She might have to resign herself to the lack of written records. If her uncle had kept everything in his head, and then his faculties began to slip . . . well, there might not be anything to do but pick up with what she'd been handed.

She glanced around the shop. "I just realized—where's Bridget today?"

Keeva neatened a small display of notecards. "Oh. Ambrose said she called earlier. Told him she'd be a bit delayed. I'd expect her soon, though."

As if in answer to the thought waves, Sam spotted Bridget crossing the street, heading toward the shop with a drag to her step. She seemed smaller, if possible, bundled into a tan raincoat that was a couple sizes too big. Ignoring the rain, which had settled to a steady light patter, the young woman pushed the door open slowly.

"Morning, Bridget," Keeva said.

When the girl looked up Sam saw that her pale complexion was mottled and her eyes were red.

"Bridget?" she said. "What's the matter?"

Bridget's lip trembled. "Family stuff. Me dad's terrible upset and we're all real worried."

Keeva came from behind the counter and put her arm around the girl's shoulders. "What's happened, doll? What's going on?"

Sam noticed that Beau had gone still, although he kept his back turned. So like him, ready to come to someone's aid if needed, but not wanting to intrude if this was what he would call 'girl stuff.'

Bridget sniffled loudly and Keeva reached into her apron pocket and came out with a neatly folded tissue.

"Here now, wipe your nose and tell us what we can do."

Bridget wagged her head back and forth as she squeezed at her nose with the tissue. "It's my Uncle Darragh, me dad's brother." To Sam's ear the name sounded like Dye-ra. "He's gone missing."

Keeva looked concerned. "Was he out? On the boat?"

Bridget nodded. "A charter. Yesterday. The police are lookin' into it. They're just not telling us anything."

Beau set down the book he'd been browsing and walked over to where the women stood.

"Excuse me," he said. "I heard. Bridget, was your uncle's boat the *Glory Be*?"

She nodded miserably.

Sam saw Beau's mouth go into a straight line. He was thinking of the blood stains.

Chapter 6

Bridget gave a loud, hiccupping sob and blew her nose. She straightened her shoulders. "I can't think what to do and I'm no use at home. It makes more sense for me to be working but I wish I knew what was happening down there."

"Would you like me to see if I can learn something?" Beau offered.

Sam explained that he was in law enforcement. Maybe out of professional courtesy the local police would at least speak with him about the case.

Bridget actually smiled. "I'd be ever so grateful. My family, we know no one in the Garda and I don't think Dad wants to be a pest."

"Let me see what I can do," he said, turning to Sam and letting her know that they would meet up later at the hotel if he didn't get back to the bookshop before closing time.

Sam watched him walk away in the direction of the docks.

"So. In the meantime, teach me everything you can about the shop," she said to the two employees.

Keeva understood that what Sam really needed to see were the areas that Ambrose guarded like a bulldog.

"While he's away, here's where the files are kept." She pulled open the top file drawer and Sam thumbed through the worn manila tabs.

There were account files for the wholesalers from whom the store's inventory was purchased, and a quick glance indicated that no one had bought new stock in months. But then, Sam had pretty much already figured that out, just by looking at the shelves. A folder labeled 'Paid Bills' was filled with aging copies, pages with dates in the last decade. It appeared as if Ambrose really had given her the most current records after all.

The bottom drawer of the cabinet was filled with book catalogs. Layered in dust, there wasn't a current one in the whole place.

"Is there really a reason to keep all these?" Sam asked, looking up at Keeva.

"Can't really think of one, no."

"I won't throw them out, but I'd like to drop a strong hint to Ambrose that eliminating clutter is a good way to get organized and boost everyone's morale. This drawer might be a good start."

"And himself is always complainin' about having no storage space. I'll give him the hint, Sam."

"Maybe we can think of some other suggestions, too," Sam said. "I don't want to hurt anyone's feelings, and I know that I'm new at this. But, really, a visitor's first impression of this shop, from the street, is that it's either out of business or in a severe decline. It just doesn't come across as a winner."

Bridget walked over from a shelf of romances, nodding vigorously. "I agree. I've tried to say it to Ambrose. Mr. O'Shaughnessy would have listened, I think. He was a nice man, but he spent no time here in the last year or two."

Keeva piped up. "He's afraid of change, Ambrose is. Wants everything to be as it was in the old days. The shop thrived when it was only Ambrose and Terry operatin' it. He just wants it to be that way again."

"I understand. This has been hard on him," Sam said.

"But we'll lose the shop if we can't get the business to make it stay open," Keeva said.

"Exactly." Bridget had perked up now that she had something new to think about. "I have some ideas about it."

"First, we better figure out how to get Ambrose on board," Sam said. "Nothing will happen if he's fighting us every step of the way." Had she actually said *us*?

"Let me think about it a day or two. There has to be a way." Keeva glanced up. "Here he comes."

Sam pushed at the heavy file drawer full of catalogs until it closed.

There was more spring in Ambrose's step as he crossed the street and mounted the step to the shop's front door. Even his expression seemed lighter. His eyes scanned the room and he spotted Bridget.

"Heard about Darragh," he said. "Sorry. He was a good man."

"*Was?*" Bridget's face went to a paler shade of white.

He shuffled and reached out to straighten a book that lay at a tilt on one shelf.

"What did you hear, Ambrose? They told my family he'd not been found." She strode over to him and stared into his face.

"That's all I heard, Bridg. Really. Sorry, I didn't think before I spoke."

"So they still haven't found him?"

"No, I don't think so."

Bridget turned around and went back to her romances. Keeva was studying Ambrose, wondering, probably, if this would be a good time to discuss changes in the store. Sam found herself watching all of them and thinking she would rather be with Beau right now.

When a lone customer walked in a minute later, the employees drifted into their normal spots. By two o'clock Sam decided she wasn't accomplishing anything. She could only wait it out, let Keeva find the best way to broach the idea of an overhaul of the shop whenever she felt the timing was right. Sam slipped her coat back on and left with a quick, "See you later."

She walked the same route back toward the hotel and docks that she and Beau had taken earlier, reasoning that if he were headed back this is the way he would come. By the time she got to Merchants Road she could see a small crowd gathered dockside. The bright red roof on the wheelhouse of the *Glory Be* was visible above their heads. She crossed at the traffic light and made her way toward the restless mass. Striped sawhorse barriers marked a perimeter, with yellow plastic tape strung between them to mark off an area close to the boat.

Above the heads of the civilians she caught sight of Beau. He seemed to be in earnest conversation with someone, a black-haired man in his forties wearing a tweed jacket and dark slacks. Beau spotted Sam and apparently asked the man if she could come behind the barrier. The guy nodded and motioned her over. Aboard the boat, she could see several other people, probably crime scene evidence collectors, studying the trawler and picking things up with tweezers. They wore black jackets with glo-green stripes, Garda insignia and latex gloves.

"Detective Joe Lambert, this is my wife, Samantha." Beau said. "She has helped me on several of my own cases at home."

Lambert sent a quick smile her way. He had intense blue eyes, a high forehead and straight nose, with weary creases near his eyes and mouth. She had the feeling he didn't smile all that often.

"So, this is Darragh O'Henry's boat?" she asked, trying to get the pronunciation right.

"It is. Beau says his niece is an employee at your shop." Joe Lambert's voice was soft and cultured, what she would imagine more from a poet than a cop. She didn't try to explain the complexity of her ownership of the bookstore; instead she merely nodded in response.

"But Mr. O'Henry himself? He's not turned up yet?" Bridget and her family should be the first to hear of it, Sam hoped, before word got out among the crowd.

"Not yet. We're still piecing together what might have happened. Darragh's a professional charter captain, well respected around here. He'd not have abandoned his craft willingly." He pronounced craft with a slightly rolling 'r', as if the word had two or three of them.

"Was he out with a charter yesterday?" Sam asked. "Sorry, you've probably been over that already with Beau."

Lambert nodded but answered anyway. "He was. We

have an officer speaking with his dispatcher now."

Beau spoke up. "We should let you get back to it. Let me know if there's anything I can do."

Lambert's parting nod seemed to say that he was sure they had the situation under control. Sam knew, from watching Beau at work, that sometimes lawmen appreciated input from outside sources but most of the time they simply wanted to be left alone to investigate and process their evidence. Beau took Sam's elbow and guided her past the barrier and through the crowd.

They received inquisitive stares from several onlookers who clearly wondered what two obviously-American tourists were doing speaking with the police. Sam kept her eyes forward; Beau didn't talk again until they'd cleared the area and he was sure they were alone.

"Want to grab some lunch?" he asked. Rather than heading straight for their hotel they'd circled the three-block-long commercial dock.

"Food? Again?" She thought of the weight she'd lost before their wedding and how she'd hoped to keep it off. That wasn't happening on a diet of Irish potatoes and full breakfasts. On the other hand, she was starting to feel a twinge of hunger. "Something light," she said.

They walked a few more blocks, until they spotted a sandwich shop that appeared to be open. The clouds had broken up, showing wide patches of blue, so they opted for an outdoor table. They'd missed the prime lunch time and their waitress informed them that there was no more brisket or chicken, and Sam couldn't bring herself to eat more potatoes, cabbage or stew. They opted for a salad and decided to share it.

"If we do this and skip dinner tonight, I *might* still fit

into my jeans by the end of this trip," Sam said. She settled into her seat and let the sun warm her face. "So, did you learn anything useful from Detective Lambert—anything that would help Bridget?"

He glanced around, making sure they were alone.

"The stains I saw last night were definitely blood—human blood. There wasn't enough to prove a fatality—I mean, not a large pool of it or anything. So, the evidence is still being collected and they'll soon see what they can learn from that."

He paused while the waitress approached with cups of tea. When she'd gone back inside he said, "On the other hand, they do know a bit about the boat's activities yesterday. While I was talking with Lambert, an officer came up and gave a quick rundown. The charter business consisted of the one boat, Darragh as captain, a crewman named Sean Bareth, and an office employee Deirdre Athy. The officer had spoken with her."

He stopped again as their salad came, courteously divided between two plates. They spent a couple of minutes shuffling flatware and taking tastes.

"According to Ms. Athy, the *Glory Be* went out yesterday with Darragh, Sean and some Americans who'd chartered the boat for the day. They'd told her they wanted to go along the coast a little way and do some fishing. She says the area they wanted to go to isn't exactly the best spot for fishing and that Darragh tried to talk them into another place. In the end he told her he would go where they wanted. The customer is always right, kind of thing."

"So, the men got mad that they didn't catch anything?"

"Deirdre Athy told the police that Darragh doesn't keep in touch continuously when he's out on a charter. Usually just radios in when he arrives at the location and again when he heads back home. Since there was a little disagreement on where they would actually catch any fish, she wasn't surprised that she didn't hear from him. At least until it started to get dark. Says he would have been on the way back and would have radioed that fact to her. That's when she got concerned and called the coast guard. Lambert told me they found the boat abandoned and towed it in."

"Was it out of fuel? Maybe the men were stranded and had to leave it."

"Well, the lifeboat *is* missing," Beau said. "But why wouldn't Darragh have radioed for assistance? A captain isn't going to leave his boat in those circumstances. Plus, Lambert said the *Glory Be* is equipped for long trips. She could have sailed to England on her normal fuel load. His men started the engine this morning and the tanks were nearly full. The boat was found only ten miles or so down the coast, and the fuel used was about right for that."

Sam mulled that over while she chewed a forkful of lettuce.

"So, a boat goes out with several men aboard and comes back with nothing but some bloodstains."

"That's the gist of it," he said.

"How many Americans were there? I wonder if their whole party went out on the boat or if there's someone here in the city who's worried about them."

"There seems to be a little confusion over that question," he said. "Deirdre Athy said two men came in to book the charter. Gave their names as Smith and Jones, but they didn't show any ID or give addresses."

"That seems odd. Darragh O'Henry would have asked for that, though, wouldn't he? The men would have needed fishing licenses. Maybe he wrote down more information on his copy of the paperwork and it's somewhere aboard the boat."

"Possibly. Based on what Lambert told the younger officer who reported to him while I was standing there, they hadn't found any manifest at all aboard the boat."

"Hm." Sam popped the last bite of her bread into her mouth.

"There's more. Deirdre Athy said that the men's gear didn't look like the typical things guys take fishing. They had a suitcase, like you'd carry on an airplane."

"So, maybe they never intended to do any fishing at all. Maybe they wanted the trawler to take them to another destination."

"That doesn't make a lot of sense either. They could have rented a car to go down the coast. Right now the police don't have enough information to rule out anything."

Sam glanced at her watch. The waitress had cleared their empty plates, but without pressure to vacate the table it was pleasant and tempting to let the afternoon slip by.

"Maybe we should stop by the bookshop," she suggested. "Bridget was nearly frantic for news of her uncle. I suppose you could tell her a little bit of what you learned, without messing up the police investigation."

Beau seemed reluctant to say anything about another jurisdiction's case, but she could tell he was intrigued about the mysterious abandoned boat. Perhaps he could learn more than he gave away by talking to the family of the missing captain.

Chapter 7

Bridget seemed apprehensive when Sam and Beau arrived at the shop and asked if they might speak privately.

"Is there news of Uncle Darragh?" she asked when they'd stepped into the storeroom.

Beau shook his head. "Not much. I've seen the boat."

"I know my mum and dad would want to know whatever you have." Bridget's small voice seemed almost frail when she talked of serious subjects, Sam noticed. "Please, could you both come to our house and speak to them?"

Without really waiting for their answer, Bridget picked up her coat and purse. Ambrose gave Sam a long stare but he didn't comment on Bridget's leaving early. She led the way, a confusing series of turns for several blocks, before she came to a plain yellow door on a rather modern three-story building.

Her key opened the street-side door and they stepped into a tiny vestibule. A hallway led toward the back of the building but Bridget headed for the stairs at her right. She didn't say anything as they climbed to the third floor. They passed numbered doors painted in primary colors, mainly red or blue or yellow, made two additional turns and she came to a bright turquoise one and unlocked it.

"Home," she said.

They stepped into a small, rectangular living room, made tighter by a large sofa, two overstuffed armchairs and a coffee table. A television perched atop a little cabinet full of DVD movies, and an end table held a reading lamp and a bud vase with a red silk rose. A framed photograph of two men stood beside it.

"They're twins," Bridget said, handing Sam the photo. "Dad and Uncle Darragh."

The two smiling faces were nearly identical, even in their forties. Sam set it back in place and glanced around the apartment.

To the left, off a tiny vestibule, two bedrooms were visible. A third door was closed. On the right a dining table was set with three places, and Sam could see into a tight kitchen with appliances that would be small compared to their American counterparts.

"Mum? I've brought someone home with me," Bridget called out. A plump woman peered around the kitchen door. Her blond hair was faded but otherwise she was simply an older version of her daughter.

"Where's Dad? Mr. Cardwell here may have some information for him."

"Oh, lord, is it about Darragh?" She came forward, drying her hands on her apron.

In answer to Bridget's question, they heard a toilet flush behind the closed door and the doorknob rattled as a man stepped out. He seemed a little flustered to find two extra people in his home.

Bridget made quick introductions—Maeve and William.

"Come in, come in," Maeve insisted. "I've just put the kettle on for a cuppa. Have a seat."

William O'Henry was nearly as tall as Beau, with a bit of a belly on him, and he greeted them with the same hospitality as his wife. He, too, immediately asked about his brother. There was something about Beau—people recognized his authority and trusted that he had answers.

William waved them toward the sofa and took a seat in one of the armchairs. Maeve stood near the kitchen door.

"I'm afraid there's no real news," Beau said, "as far as locating your brother. The police have talked with the woman who works at his office, trying to piece together who all was aboard the boat when it went out. None of them have been seen since." He filled in the few details he'd already told to Sam.

"Sean's family must be half-frantic," Maeve said.

"If you know anything about where he might have gone," Beau said, "his favorite fishing locations . . . I'm sure the police could use any information."

William rested his forearms against his knees, staring at a spot in the middle of the room. "He's got his favorite spots, for sure. Darragh's a brilliant man. Born at the stroke of midnight, he was. I came fifteen minutes later. Darragh keeps his fishing secrets guarded well, not wanting the other captains to crowd him."

"Does the boat have some kind of navigational equipment that records where he's been?" Sam asked. "I don't know much about this stuff—is there anything that maps his route and transmits it back?"

William shook his head. "They make equipment like that but Darragh, he couldn't afford it. He's got the basics, that's all."

"Detective Lambert said the boat was found adrift near the shoreline. He mentioned some cliffs on the north side of the bay," Beau said.

"Oh, saints preserve us!" Maeve said with a small cry.

William's mouth went tight. When he spoke, it was with fear in his voice. "It's a dangerous stretch of the coast. Without power, the *Glory Be* would have been dashed to pieces at the next high tide or if the wind come up. Darragh wouldna' have chosen it for fishing."

"Maybe that's the answer, then," Bridget said. "Their engine quit and they all had to take to the lifeboat. They've made it to a safe spot but haven't been able to get word to us."

The teakettle whistled, distracting Maeve and Bridget. William continued to contemplate the center of the carpet.

Sam glanced at Beau. He hadn't mentioned the bloodstains or the fact that the boat's engine had started right up for the police this morning. He gave a tiny shake of his head. Let the family hold on to hope, at least until the police decided to share all the facts.

Maeve came back, carrying a tray with steaming cups of tea, pots of sugar and milk, and a plate of cookies. She set it on the table in front of them.

"How're you findin' Ireland?" she asked, after Sam commented on how tasty the cookies were.

"It's beautiful," she said, "The rain is something to get

used to. We come from a very dry climate."

"Ah, yes. It's where all the green comes from." Maeve gave Sam a warm smile. "I'm understandin' that you might have your hands full with the bookshop, though."

Bridget spoke up. "You know, Mum, trying to get Ambrose Piggott to try anything new could take donkey's years."

Maeve nodded in agreement.

Beau set his empty cup on the tray. "We'd best leave you to your evening."

"Please, Beau," said William, "If you get any further word on Darragh . . ."

Beau nodded. "I will. And I'm sure the Garda will be in touch as they learn anything new. We're very sorry for your—for this worry in your lives right now."

Out on the street, Sam reached for his hand. "It's nice of you to try to reassure them."

"I didn't have much to say. The authorities here certainly don't need to share any information with me."

"At least we can offer support. The sooner this gets resolved, the sooner I'll have Bridget's full attention at the shop. I have the feeling she's my one hope for turning the place around with some modern ideas and a fresh look."

They worked their way back toward the shopping district, more by instinct than by remembering the winding route they'd taken to reach the O'Henry's apartment. They found themselves at a corner where each of the four streets had a different name.

"Let's go across that bridge and make a bit longer walk out of it," Sam suggested, pointing to their right. "I need to work off those extra potatoes. And don't let me stop in at a pub. Another of those dark brews would not do me any favors."

Beau laughed and checked the traffic before they crossed. Standing in the center of the bridge, watching the river rush under their feet, made Sam a little dizzy.

"Okay, ready for steady ground again," she said.

They cleared the bridge and were debating whether to take the next lane and double back toward their hotel or to keep going forward. At the moment Sam couldn't say for sure where they were—it seemed that waterways were all around them. As she looked around to get her bearings, a familiar figure walked down the steps of a nearby building and turned toward them.

"Look, Beau. It's Detective Lambert." He had on an overcoat now, but otherwise was dressed exactly as he'd been at the dock earlier in the afternoon.

Lambert spotted them.

"Sheriff Cardwell," he said to Beau. "On your way home?"

Beau returned the detective's smile. "In a roundabout way, I guess. We aren't quite sure where all these streets lead."

Sam noticed that the gray stone building Lambert had just left sported a distinctive blue glass lamp with the local Garda insignia on it. The police station.

"You're working late," she said.

"Ah, it's not done yet for me." His voice seemed weary. "When I start a day in the wee hours, like today, doesn't mean I get away earlier in the evening. Just takin' a little dinner break now. Care to join me?"

She almost refused, but Beau spoke up quickly. "We might grab something light."

Very light, Sam thought as they ducked into a pub two doors away. Like a glass of wine and some information for Bridget. Lambert rattled out something quick and unintelligible to the barkeep, which translated to drinks for the three of them. They settled at a corner table.

"We saw Darragh O'Henry's brother and family this afternoon," Beau said. "I think I had mentioned that the brother's daughter works in Sam's bookshop."

Lambert nodded, his dark hair falling across his eyes.

"They, of course, are nearly frantic with worry about Darragh," Beau said.

"Yes, as they would be. I wish I'd some better news for them."

"Has he been located?" Sam blurted out.

"No, there's really no news," Lambert said after taking a long pull on his Guinness. "I put the crime scene investigators right to work and the lab will get the evidence processed as quickly as they can."

"The blood—it's definitely human?" Beau said.

"It is. We knew that from the immunochromatographic test at the site. We've got loads of fingerprints. Have to rule out those of the two crew and see if we can come up with identities of the Americans. It doesn't seem likely that 'Smith' and 'Jones' were their real names, and Ms. Athy admits that she didn't ask to see any identification."

"What if they were? If Smith and Jones were really their names?" Sam asked.

"We'll still have to identify them. It's a bigger job but if they've vanished we have to find out who to notify." He looked up as the waiter delivered a large bowl of stew for Lambert and a small plate of fried potatoes to Beau, who set the plate between them and indicated that he intended for Sam to share them.

Sam speared a small chunk of potato, thinking of what Lambert had said about the men. Someone back in America would be worried if their relatives went off for an Irish vacation and never came back.

"Someone's got to answer for that bullet casing, as well," Lambert was saying. "We only found the one, which makes me wonder if there were more and someone picked them up. Might have just missed that one."

"That doesn't sound good," Sam said. "Sounds like you definitely think there was some sort of foul play."

"Can't think of a logical reason for Darragh to carry a .45 caliber pistol aboard his trawler. Especially since we found no gun."

"That wouldn't even be legal here, would it?" Beau asked.

Lambert scoffed. "Legal? No. Possible—you know very well that illegal gun ownership is possible nearly anywhere. Private ownership was curtailed a few years ago, but it doesn't mean that everyone registered theirs when the new law passed or that all the guns are legal hunting equipment or small caliber weapons. If someone wants one here, they'll find a way to get it."

Sam regarded him carefully.

"But do I think Darragh O'Henry had an illegal gun? Not really. The man has no record of trouble. Seems a law-abidin' sort all around." He focused his attention on his dinner for the next few minutes.

"So, it seems more likely that one of his passengers brought it aboard," Beau said.

Lambert shrugged. "We're checkin' out the mate, too. Sean Bareth. Young hothead, that one was."

Sam felt her eyebrows rise.

"I've got someone checking the records. I don't recall anything recent with him. But you know, he had his share of scuffles and fights. I remember bringin' him in for boxing with one of the Traveller lads—the fight got out of hand and we thought young Bareth was gonna be done for."

He wiped his mouth with his napkin and stood up.

"I'd best be back at the job. Stay in touch, Sheriff." He picked up his overcoat from the back of his chair and walked toward the door.

"Interesting, about the gun. And about the crewman's record," Sam said.

"Interesting, and not something we should be sharing with Bridget's family. From now on, anything they learn needs to be given to them through the police."

Sam drummed her fingers on the table top.

"Sam? I'm serious."

"I know. I won't say anything. I'm just thinking . . . about all of it. You don't suppose Sean Bareth might have caused some trouble aboard the boat—gotten into a scuffle with either Darragh or the passengers—do you?"

"I'm sure Detective Lambert will be investigating all possibilities." He stood and held up Sam's jacket for her. "Come on, you. Let's figure out how to get back to our own neighborhood."

A chilly breeze came off the water as they made their way back across the bridge and through the crowded streets. As they neared the docks they saw that people were crowded around the area where the *Glory Be* was still moored. A single Garda officer stood by, making sure no one attempted to board, but the bustling work from earlier in the day had concluded.

Sam knew too well what it was like to wait around for lab results and had watched as victims and families anticipated news from a crime scene. She hoped the O'Henrys would get good news, and soon.

Settled into their room at the Harbour Hotel, she calculated the time difference and placed a quick call to her daughter's cell phone. It went to voice mail and Sam could envision Kelly in the middle of bathing some reluctant dog at Puppy Chic. She left a message that all was well in Ireland.

If only it were completely true.

A second call, this time to her own business, the bakery which had been her lifelong dream. She said a quick hello to Becky, her decorator, who told her that everything was going just fine. At the insistent quizzing about her inheritance, Sam would only give the barest of clues.

"You'll have to keep guessing until I get back," she teased. "It's too expensive for lots of cell calls from here, so text me if there's something I absolutely need to know."

Before she got home she still hoped to figure a way out of owning the musty bookshop. Much as she loved having a great book to read in her spare time she didn't want a room full of them, and there was no way she wanted to be responsible for a business clear across the Atlantic.

Beau had stretched out beside her on the bed while she talked and now he seemed intent on removing her clothing with his teeth. As the top button on her blouse gave up its hold on the buttonhole, she ended her phone call with a giggle.

"I'm giving you one hour to stop that," she said.

Naturally, it was an empty threat. She'd unbuttoned his shirt and peeled it off his muscular shoulders in under a minute. The rest of the hour melted away and soon the lamp was out and they lost themselves in the warmth of each other and the deep pile of blankets.

When Sam next became aware, there were flashes of blue light hitting the ceiling in the room. She realized that they hadn't closed the heavy drapes before they fell asleep. The clock showed that it was nearly three in the morning. She rolled over and got up, thinking she would close the curtains but realized that Beau was already standing there, staring down at the harbor.

"Something's going on," he said. "A coast guard boat roared in awhile ago. Two Garda vehicles and an ambulance met them at the dock."

Sam stared down at the commotion.

"They've put one person onto a gurney and loaded him into the ambulance. The police seem to be taking the other one into custody."

An officer climbed into the ambulance and it pulled away. Before it was out of sight, a car pulled up and a dark-haired man in a tan overcoat climbed out. Flashing a badge toward one of the officers, he was waved through.

"That looks like Detective Lambert from here," Sam said.

"Yeah, I think so."

"So, either this has something to do with the *Glory Be*—"

"Or he's really got his hands full this week."

Motion on the water caught their attention. Another coast guard vessel came slowly abeam of the first one. In a pile on the open deck lay a massive orange thing.

Beau squinted and leaned forward. "I can't read the print on it. But it looks to me like a deflated lifeboat."

If this was the missing one from the *Glory Be* and the two men they'd just seen were the only ones aboard, it looked like at least half of its complement was gone.

Chapter 8

Sam went back to bed and Beau soon joined her but it was a restless night. She could tell that he wanted to go down to the dock and see what was happening—law enforcement types tend to want to solve everything. But there was the touchy subject of being too nosy around someone else's investigation. She snuggled in close to him and drifted into an uneasy sleep.

By six o'clock they were wide awake. While Beau showered, Sam pulled her wooden jewelry box from the safe to look for a different pair of earrings. The gloomy-looking wood brightened at her touch and she held onto it for a minute. In the past the box had helped her with a variety of things—from boosting her energy to fine-tuning her investigative senses. She had no idea how it worked; the special powers had come to her soon after the box was given to her by an old woman believed by some to be a witch. Sam had never bought into that; she only knew the effects the box had on her.

Beau emerged from the bathroom as she was tucking the box back into the safe.

"Ready for breakfast?" he asked.

Downstairs, over coffee and scones—both of them managed to pass up the full buffet—Sam told him she wanted to check in at the bookshop.

"I really feel pressed to get things settled," she said. "Yesterday, I put the idea in Keeva's head about making some changes so the place doesn't simply settle into a pile of old stones and papers. I'll be interested to see whether she's talked to Ambrose about it. Plus, I'd like to be sure Bridget's okay."

"I think I'll wander by the police station," Beau said. "Maybe I can find out what was going on last night."

Sam smiled at him. That was what he'd wanted all along.

Outside, they could see heavy clouds scudding in from the sea. Sam dug into her pack and handed Beau one of the umbrellas.

"Come by the shop if you get the chance," she said. "If I get ready to leave before I see you, I'll text you and set up a plan."

At the corner, he gave her a kiss and headed the opposite direction. By the time Sam got to the bookshop a light mist had enveloped that part of the city.

"Ah, it's a fine soft day, it is," said Keeva when Sam paused at the door to close her umbrella.

"I see you've started to rearrange things," Sam said, eyeing the two large tables in the middle of the room, which were now empty.

"T'wasn't I," Keeva said. "And the others don't claim the work either."

Confirming that, Bridget shook her head.

"Where did the books go?" Sam's glance darted around the room.

Keeva pointed upward. At the very top of the bookcases that circled the entire room, haphazard piles of books leaned outward over empty space. The slightest touch would send them crashing to the floor. Ambrose appeared from the storeroom just then, pausing in the doorway.

"Be careful," Sam cautioned. "Don't walk near the shelves."

He started toward the sales counter and as he passed, one stack of books toppled and hit the floor.

"Who put them there?" Sam felt a sharp edge in her voice.

The three employees looked at each other, then at her. "None of us," Keeva said. "It had to be the mischief of the faeries."

Seriously? Faeries? Even in her head she mimicked Keeva's pronunciation.

"Ah yes," Bridget said. "When they get angry they'll destroy your things. Sometimes they even steal babies."

Sam looked at Keeva, who was nodding in agreement. She took a breath. "Okay, let's say that this was done by faeries. What's made them angry? Why would they take it out on the shop?"

"Well, ye can't be sure," Keeva said. "Could be they're unhappy with one of us. Maybe with your uncle. Maybe someone ate an egg and didn't destroy the shell. Bridget, check the waste bin. Faeries love to live in empty eggshells," she said by way of explanation to Sam.

Okay. She'd heard that the Irish were superstitious but never dreamed the extent of it.

She gazed back up at the shelves, but saw no mystical explanation for the tippy stacks of books. She saw only a lawsuit waiting to happen if a customer happened to be smacked by a tumbling pile of them.

"Let's get to work bringing them down," she said. "There must be a stool or stepladder here somewhere."

Bridget fetched a short ladder and Sam climbed to reach for the first stack.

"As long as we're moving them, let's try a different arrangement for these," Sam said, handing down four hardback books. "Rather than just piling them on the tables again."

Ambrose gave her a hard stare but she ignored it. The man seemed determined to disapprove of her ideas, no matter what they were.

"How about if we designate one table for items that we can price at a discount? It seems to work for other bookshops, brings the customers in to look for bargains."

She'd often seen her neighbor, Ivan, set up a sale table out on the sidewalk; however, that tactic would only work in a dry climate. Here, they would have to get people into the shop to discover the bargains.

"Keeva, can you locate some poster board or art paper and design some signs? Ambrose, you know the stock better than the rest of us. Choose the titles that have been here a long time, gathering dust, and we'll mark them at the greatest discount."

Gathering dust, indeed. Everything in this place had been gathering dust for a century.

Ambrose shuffled forward to take the books Sam handed to Bridget, grumbling something under his breath. Sam ignored it, focusing on the surge of energy that coursed through her as she worked. She remembered handling the wooden box this morning and decided she better tone down the energy before the others became suspicious.

"Sort them as you set them down," Sam said. "Please? I want—um, let's try putting only newer stock into the bookcases, sale items on the one table, and maybe we can create a theme or special display for the other table."

The faeries might have thought they were creating havoc in here, but it could turn out to be just what Sam needed to move the staff off center and get them thinking of new ideas. She reached for another stack, handed it off, then moved the ladder farther along the wall.

She and Bridget developed a rhythm for moving the books along, and Keeva had found construction paper and markers. She seemed pleased with her first effort at a sign that said BOOK SALE. She taped it to the front window and started on another.

Ambrose moved like molasses, but he'd managed to sort the first dozen books Bridget handed him into three piles. Sam hummed as she approached the next section, hoping a cheery mood would be contagious.

The door opened and a white-haired man came in. "There's a sale on books?"

See? Sam wanted to say. Instead, she said, "Ambrose, could you show the gentleman the ones we're marking down to half price?"

He looked a little startled but the customer perked right up. "Half price? That's a bargain I'll take."

If the pricing in Ireland worked the same as in the States, Sam knew that selling at half price meant taking a loss on the item. She'd once listened to one of Ivan Petrenko's rants in his peculiar Russian/French/American dialect, the gist of which was that his discount from the list price was nowhere near enough. But, she reasoned, O'Shaughnessy's faced an extraordinary situation. They simply had to clear some of the outdated stock to make room for new things that would draw in more business. And if giving away some of the junk was the way to do it, then fine.

She'd finished removing the precarious stacks from one long wall and was moving to start on the next by the time the customer left with a sack full of books, only two of which had come from the bargain table.

Keeva closed the cash drawer and said, "This might work."

Ambrose continued to shuffle along like a turtle but Sam and Bridget didn't slow down. Within thirty minutes they'd removed the immediate danger.

"Help Ambrose go through these," Sam suggested to her young assistant. "Keeva, what do we have that would make a good window display?"

"Children's books? They're bright and colorful."

Sam pondered. "Are there any about Halloween? It's coming up in a month, and kids love it." She thought of the hundreds of cookies and cupcakes she moved through the bakery during October.

Keeva brightened. "I like that idea. I'll find them."

The only thing going for the children's section of the shop, Sam discovered, was that someone had thought to shelve the books in the lower spaces so kids could actually see them. She joined Keeva and started pulling everything out, sorting by age group as she went. They pulled a few classics that Sam remembered reading to Kelly as a child, along with an assortment of picture books that had especially bright covers.

"I think we should clear everything out of the front window and fill it with these," Keeva said. "What if I make a sign that says 'Children's Book Week'? We can create our own occasions, can't we?"

Thank you! Some fresh ideas.

Sam let Keeva work on the window while she rearranged the children's book section, placing the covers facing out on as many books as possible and grouping them by reading level. She was nearly finished with them when she felt a presence behind her.

"They look nice," Keeva said. "Your uncle used to do little things like that. I suppose we all grew to depend on him for ideas and when he could no longer stretch and bend as he once did . . ."

"You will find lots of new ideas, yourselves," Sam said, loudly enough for all to hear.

"I thought you had no bookshop experience," Bridget said, walking over to admire the new arrangement.

"It's not so different from a bakery, when you think of it. We display the things with the most eye appeal, make new items according to the seasons and holidays—you know, that sort of thing."

Keeva's new signs were getting some notice and soon two young mothers were browsing the children's books while another customer worked her way across the expanse of discounted titles. Even Ambrose's surly expression had relaxed into something that nearly resembled a smile.

Sam put the stepladder away and discovered a teakettle

in the back room. She filled it with fresh water. Treating someone to a cup of tea was as well accepted here as at home, she'd discovered.

"Speaking of bakeries," she said when Keeva walked in, "is there one nearby? I'd like to have some fresh cookies on hand. People will stay in the shop longer if we give them a treat."

She put on her jacket and followed Keeva's directions to a tiny place one street over. While she pointed out shortbread, jam thumbprints, and cutouts tipped in chocolate she also had the clerk add a few of their more unusual varieties—research for some new things Sam could include at Sweet's Sweets when she got home.

Back at the bookstore, she'd begun to rummage for the tea in the storeroom when she heard a familiar voice.

She peeked out into the shop to see Beau greeting the staff. Bridget looked a little nervous, perhaps sensing that he brought news of her uncle. Ambrose warmed up when Beau took a moment to compliment him on the neatness of the table display.

"Hi, sweetheart," Sam said when he walked toward her. "I'm making tea. Did you notice the new window display?"

"I did. Three kids were standing there, faces to the glass, so I guess it's working."

She made a show of crossing her fingers. The kettle whistled and she switched it off, lining up the cups on the shelf they used as a worktop.

"So? Was Lambert willing to talk to you?"

"A bit. The fuss down at the dock was what we thought. The lifeboat from the *Glory Be* was brought in. He said it had some abrasions on it and was taking on water. One of the American men was treated for mild hypothermia—he'd gotten dunked in the water and it was pretty cold out there."

"Any word about Darragh O'Henry?" She lowered her voice to a mere whisper.

"I should speak privately to Bridget about it."

"Oh, no. He's—"

"Not been found. But that may be the good news."

Sam gave him a puzzled look but he didn't say more. "Let me get her."

She picked up two cups of tea and carried them out for Keeva and Ambrose, then signaled Bridget to join her. Beau found two folding metal chairs and motioned the young woman toward one of them.

"Your uncle hasn't been found yet," he began. "So there's still hope. The Garda are contacting your father right now, and I offered to tell you what's being done."

She swallowed hard and nodded.

"Last night they located the lifeboat from the *Glory Be*. Two American men were aboard, cold and miserable, but alive."

"The passengers Uncle Darragh was to take fishing."

"Yes. That's the story they gave. They also gave false names when they arranged the trip, so the police still have a lot of questions for them."

"So they're being held in custody?" Sam asked.

"That's right."

"Where's my uncle?" Bridget's normally small voice became even quieter.

"We still don't know," Beau told her. "That's why the Garda are holding the Americans. The two of them . . . well, they're claiming that Darragh and Sean took them out to sea and abandoned them."

Sam stared at Beau. Were her suspicions about Sean true then?

Bridget's face went white. Then her lip began to tremble. "They're saying Uncle Darragh left them for dead? It can't be. He'd never do that!"

Chapter 9

Bridget stood abruptly, knocking the metal chair backward. Sam grabbed for it before it clattered to the floor. The young woman's eyes flashed. "My uncle would never harm anyone!"

Sam tried to wrap her mind around this new possibility. Of course the O'Henry family would stand behind Darragh, no matter what. They might even think that Beau would automatically believe the Americans, although Sam knew that Beau didn't automatically believe anyone. His nature and his profession taught him to find out the facts before making assumptions.

"Bridget, calm down. Let's think rationally about this." Sam looked up at Beau and got a little nod of verification. "No logical person would believe that a boat captain would abandon his own boat and turn two strangers out in the lifeboat. I mean, where would Darragh have gone? It doesn't make sense."

She kept her voice reasonable and calm and found Bridget responding in kind. Sam set the chairs in place and suggested Bridget sit, but she was still too keyed up.

Beau reached into his coat pocket and brought out some folded sheets of printer paper. "The detective made copies of some pictures and asked me to show them to you. He's showing them to your parents too."

Bridget took the pictures and held them apart, shaking her head after a few moments.

"Do you recognize them?" he asked.

"No. I've never seen either of them."

She started to hand them back to Beau, but Sam reached out and took them.

The two men hardly looked like the types who would be buddies off on a fishing trip. The younger one was a black guy, probably in his early twenties, with close cut hair and chocolate eyes. He looked scared in the photo, as if he were completely surprised at being held by the police.

The other mug shot showed a white man who might be anywhere from thirty to fifty, with the rough complexion that comes from long experience with smoking and drink. His head was shaved; there were silver studs in both ears; the short-sleeved jailhouse jumpsuit revealed heavily tattooed arms. He stared at the camera with an expression that said he wasn't worried—he'd beaten other raps and would beat this one too.

Neither photo had a name attached.

"Smith and Jones?" Sam asked.

"Presumably. They didn't have ID on them and so

far they aren't talking. The younger one was taken to the hospital for hypothermia but was being released a little while ago. Lambert felt pretty confident that they would get him to talk. He doesn't seem to have the same worldly indifference as his cohort. Their prints were taken and I'd bet money that it won't be long before there's a match."

Sam studied the photos for another minute. Something seemed familiar but she couldn't pin it down. She handed the pages back to Beau.

"Beau, you said that the Garda were talking with my parents?" Bridget's voice had become tiny again. "I should call them and be sure they're all right."

Sam nodded. "Take the afternoon off if you want to."

The girl sent a grateful look toward Sam, pulled on her coat and left.

"So, what next?" Sam asked Beau.

"You look pretty busy here," he said. "So if it's all right, I think I'll go back to see if the detective could use my help."

Sam smiled. She felt very certain that the Galway police could adequately handle their case, but she knew that Beau was at loose ends. He almost never took time off work; law enforcement was in his blood. Lambert would send Beau away if he didn't want the help. And who knew? Maybe having an American lawman on their side could open some doors when dealing with their American suspects. She assured him that she could stay occupied for a few more hours, then sent him out the door.

She arranged the bakery cookies on a plate and carried a tray of tea things to the other room.

In the sales area Keeva was happily drawing more signs. "I thought we might try labeling certain of the books as

Staff Choices," she said, holding up some small cards she'd designed.

Sam complimented her on the idea.

Ambrose had just completed a sale and Sam was pleased to see that he actually wished the customer a good day as the lady walked out.

"How are things going?" she asked.

"Steady." His mouth did a little twist. "Actually, it's been a better morning than we've had in awhile. Terry would have been pleased."

"I wish I'd known my great-uncle. I know my mother has fond memories of him." She leaned against the counter, toying with one of the bookmarks that some publisher had provided as promotional items.

"He was a kind man. A good sense of humor. Sometimes, though, he'd put you to the test."

"I suppose we all do that sometimes. You worked for him so many years. It must be hard to see things change."

The old man's expression softened a bit, as if he appreciated her acknowledgement of his feelings. "It is."

He cleared his throat and opened the cash drawer to put a credit card receipt inside. Sam sensed that the moment of openness had ended. She stood straight and walked over to help Keeva with one of the display tables, pleased to see that the books were now dusted and set out so the covers showed well.

Apparently, the bright children's books in the front window were doing their job. Two young mothers, each with two kids, came in and asked about specific titles. Keeva stepped over to assist and Sam took over dusting and setting up books on the big table.

She found her mind drifting back to the situation with

Darragh O'Henry's abandoned boat. Whose blood was on that wheelhouse? And the two men whose photos Beau had just shown her—why did they look vaguely familiar?

She and Beau had barely reached Galway before the silent trawler was towed in, so it didn't seem logical that she'd seen the men here in town. With Bridget in the room awhile ago, Sam hadn't gotten the chance to ask Beau if the men looked familiar to him. She would have to do that.

She stayed in the bookshop long enough for Keeva and Ambrose to each take a lunch break, then made her excuses and set out to meet Beau. His text message had said: hotel or lunch? She'd replied with: meet at dock 2:00. So that was where she headed now.

She spotted him, half a head taller than most of the other men on the sidewalk, walking toward the bench where she'd decided to sit when she arrived first.

"Hey, darlin'," he said, his familiar smile grabbing her heart.

"I'm guessing that you have some good news," she said.

"We got the identities on the two Americans."

By the way he said 'we' Sam could tell he was enjoying the fact that Lambert was letting him in on the local case. She spotted a hot dog vendor about a block away and suggested they grab a snack since they'd both worked through the lunch hour. They set off in that direction.

"So, the black guy's name is Hank Greenlee. Age twenty-one. One conviction for participating in the armed robbery of a convenience store in New Jersey. He was nineteen at the time and the judge went pretty easy on him. Two years, part of it suspended, and a little time off for good behavior in Rahway."

And he ends up in Ireland, hiring and then abandoning

a fishing trawler? She pondered it while they ordered hot dogs and the old man behind the counter handed them over. They carried their food to a bench that faced the water.

"The guy with all the tattoos is Ted "Trucker" Furns. Thirty-two years old, born in Brooklyn," Beau said through a bite of hot dog. "He has a long rap sheet—the guy's been in trouble since his teens. Served two simultaneous sentences for bank robbery and got out six months ago."

"Did Hank and this Trucker guy meet in prison?"

"The US authorities are still checking on that. At first glance it wouldn't seem as if they served time together, but you never know. Guys like that gravitate toward each other. They might have been in a holding cell somewhere, or maybe they just met up on the streets."

Sam nodded. She took a bite of her hot dog. It wasn't the best she'd ever had, but it would tide her over until dinner.

Beau scarfed his down, probably without tasting. "Get this. During the interrogation, Hank said something about a third man, a guy named Quint. Naturally, when Lambert asked Trucker about this Quint, he wouldn't say a word."

"But still—"

"Birds of a feather and all that . . . yeah. It's quite possible that the three know each other. The New York police are checking a variety of databases to see if there are warrants out on any of them."

"So maybe Hank Greenlee gave a good lead?"

"Could be." He wadded up the hot dog wrapper. "We should be able to piece it together soon."

"We?" she teased. "So Detective Lambert is hiring you?"

Beau made a face at her. "Let's just say he hasn't kicked me out yet. I actually think I've been of some help to him.

The New York jurisdiction seemed more willing to work with a small town American lawman than a small town Irish one. For whatever reason."

"You're having fun at this!"

"Well, yeah. It's good to see how another department works. I'm learning things too."

She grinned at him.

"But I'm not going to work through our honeymoon," he said. "As long as you don't."

She was not going to allow this to become a controversy between them. Even though she had to devote some time to the bookshop, if only to figure out how to get rid of it, she had no plan to spend all of her days there.

"Tell you what," he said, draping an arm across her shoulders. "Let's get that rental car and check out the countryside. We have the rest of the afternoon and evening for a quick trip somewhere. Then tomorrow we'll plan a full day away."

She answered him with a kiss.

The concierge at the Harbour was happy to get them a car, which was delivered almost as quickly as Sam and Beau gathered a few things from their room. The man provided them with maps and directions for a few sights along the way.

"The coastline is spectacular," he told them. "Take the N67 to the R478 to get to the Cliffs of Moher. The view is spectacular. From there you can go through Doolin, get on the 477 and follow the coast for miles. Or you might want to circle back, just so," he said, drawing a line on the map, "and visit the Burren. People are always astonished when they see it. Just be careful—some of those tour buses are quite large and places in the road are fairly narrow."

Beau spent a few minutes getting accustomed to the right-hand drive controls before he pulled out into traffic. Shifting with his left hand and watching for traffic from the right kept him alert, and Sam pressed tightly into her seat until they'd cleared the tight streets of the middle of Galway and made their way to the first of the highways where traffic moved as quickly as on any American interstate. By the time they'd reached the open countryside they had both relaxed into simply enjoying the vivid green scenery.

A little more than an hour later they began to emerge on the rise that revealed the stark gray-brown cliffs, which dropped more than seven hundred feet to the sea. They parked and walked to the viewing area. A visitor center with gracefully sloping windows peeked out from the hillside behind them, a building nearly hidden in the earth. In the distance Sam could see the Aran Islands and a ferry boat heading toward them. Heavy gray clouds hung low over the horizon and a brisk wind came off the sea. Up the coast toward Galway waves crashed against the massive rocks.

Standing at the barrier at the edge of the cliffs, Sam was struck by the sheer force of the ocean and the vast length of the coastline. Whatever had happened aboard the *Glory Be*, there were literally hundreds of miles of open water where the crew and passengers might have ended up.

Beau placed an arm around her shoulders. "Wow, huh?"

She had a feeling he was thinking the same thing about the fate of the small trawler.

They walked toward the visitor center where they found comforting cups of tea. "I wish we had time to stay and explore all the displays," Sam said as they carried their paper cups to the car. "Maybe on another day, before we go home."

Inside the car, Beau studied the map while they sipped their tea.

"I think there's time to get around to this Burren area before dark," he said. "Shall we?"

Sam found herself wishing they had more time to see everything. Of course, Beau could ignore the fact that he'd become involved in the case of the *Glory Be* and completely turn tourist, but how could she walk away from the bookshop her uncle had willed to her? She really needed to resolve that situation before she left the country.

Beau put the car in gear and they started east toward Doolin, a charming crossroads town of B&Bs and hostels, with the bragging rights of being the capital of Irish traditional music. With no time to check out that attraction, they made a southeasterly loop, following a road that took them directly north.

"Somewhere along in here is a dolmen called Poulnabrone . . ." he said, scanning the sides of the road. A small car-park appeared with only one other vehicle in it. "Out there, I think."

The sun was low in the sky behind them as they walked across the flat, rugged landscape that made up most of this area known as the Burren. A lone shaft of light came out of the clouds, illuminating the rock dolmen ahead of them. Two upright stones held a larger, flat one on top, as if the structure were a giant's trestle table.

"According to the brochure, this was excavated in 1986 and they discovered the remains of about twenty adults and six children. None of the adults had lived beyond the age of forty," Sam said, reading from the pamphlet he'd brought with them. "I imagine that was an eerie find."

While they stared at the gray rocks, clouds again

obscured the sun, almost in answer to her observation.

"Can you imagine how hard a life it would have been here?" Beau said, surveying the miles-wide expanse of flat, rocky ground.

A chill wind came from the north and they felt the first spatters of rain. They made their way back, noticing tiny purple and white wildflowers that struggled in the small cracks between the rocks. Back in the car, they turned the heater on and started north. Rain pounded the windshield and it was slow going as darkness set in on the narrow road. Beau visibly relaxed when they came to the main highway again and he turned toward Galway.

"Want a little break from driving?" Sam asked. "Ballyvaghan is just ahead. We might grab something to eat."

The tiny town seemed to consist of restaurants, hotels and gift shops, with a sprinkling of homes for the local people. Its location was apparently the ideal spot to catch everyone who'd spent a day hiking the cliffs or walking the rugged Burren, and a signpost with multiple arrow-shaped markers directed drivers toward various sights, shops, and nearby towns. They quickly found a pub that didn't look too crowded and within minutes were settled at a table near a cozy fire.

"I know I said that I had to cut back on the meat and potato meals," Sam said, looking at the menu. "But there's something about that shepherd's pie that sounds irresistible."

"You're right—I'm having it. I guess all that fresh air did a number on my appetite." Beau went to the bar and ordered the pies.

Outside, darkness had fallen, creating blurs of light as

rain streamed down the windows and bounced reflections from passing vehicles. Their meals arrived and they lost themselves in the enjoyment of the hearty food.

"I love it, but I can't finish all this," Sam finally said. She glanced over at Beau's plate. He didn't seem to have the same problem.

A lively band was tuning up in the opposite corner but Beau suggested they get back on the road. They probably had at least another hour to drive.

"Luckily, the rain has stopped," Sam said as they walked toward the car. They'd discovered it was tricky enough negotiating the roundabouts in clear daylight; many of them didn't have a lot of information posted.

Beau stopped in the middle of the sidewalk and pointed toward an open field about a half-block away. "Look at those."

Under the protection of a large tree sat a wagon of some sort. It looked like a big round barrel set upon a square wagon bed with large wooden-spoked wheels. A set of wooden steps led up to a door, which had a small curtained window near the top and a round metal knocker in the center. The whole thing was painted bright red, with decorative wavy lines done in white, and yellow trim around the roofline. Sam's first thought was *carnival attraction* but as she watched, a little girl came out, pushed the door shut behind her and raced over to another, similar wagon, this one painted yellow with blue trim.

"They're like old-fashioned campers," she said.

"Those'd be the Travellers," said a passing woman. Her tone turned derisive. "Gypsies. Tinkers." She hurried on, away from the small encampment.

Sam looked at Beau with raised eyebrows. Obviously, these Travellers weren't always well regarded, even though their homes were quite picturesque.

Beau tilted his head toward their rental car and they were soon on the road again. By the time they reached the outskirts of Galway, Sam was nodding in her seat, waking every few seconds and wondering if Beau was feeling the drowsy aftereffects of their comfort-food dinner in the same way. He located the hotel's parking garage and guided Sam toward the elevators.

In their room she took time for a hot shower before bed, wondering where those Travellers normally stayed. Maybe nowhere specific—it was probably why they were thought of as gypsies. While Beau showered, she hung their clothing in the closet and got her wooden box out of the safe so she could store her earrings and bracelet.

As she opened the lid of the box, a scene flashed before her—a crowded place with announcements over a PA system. Two men standing in a nearby line looked familiar. She squeezed her eyes shut, trying to hold the vision but it rapidly began to fade. As the scene blurred she focused on the faces, but the man's tattooed arms stood out. One of them was almost certainly the American suspect from the picture Beau showed her earlier in the day—"Trucker" Furns.

Chapter 10

Sam's cell phone rang while they were eating breakfast. She immediately recognized Bridget's childlike voice.

"Sam, are you coming to the shop this morning?" her voice was shaking.

"I can." Sam looked at Beau. They had talked about driving toward Dublin today, but hadn't set a time to leave. "What's up?"

"I think there has been another visitation. The things we did yesterday are all in a mess."

A visitation? From faeries? Sam held her comment back.

"I can be there in a half hour. Don't clean it up yet. I'd like to see just what happened."

She clicked off the call and passed along the information to Beau.

"They trying to pull some kind of leprechaun-sneak on you?" he said with a grin.

"I don't know. It could be something like that."

She hadn't told Beau yesterday how she suspected that Ambrose was behind the mischief. As the day went on she'd almost gotten a feeling of acceptance from him. The manager seemed to run hot and cold, though, and she had no idea how far he might go to get Sam to give up on the business. If only it weren't for that clause in the will, about Sam keeping the shop for two years, Ambrose would get his wish immediately.

"I guess I should get over there," she said, laying her napkin across her near-empty plate. "I'll try to make it quick, so we can still do our tour."

He signed the meal tab and stood up. "Don't worry about it. We've got time."

She gave him a kiss. In truth, she would bet that he would get in touch with Detective Lambert to see what was going on with the mysterious *Glory Be* and the two American suspects. She'd tried last night to recreate the vision of the man, Furns, and figure out what it meant, but nothing had come to her. She hadn't mentioned it to Beau.

The first thing she noticed at the bookstore was that the new front window display was completely gone. Behind the small glass panes a bare wood shelf greeted the eye. She found Bridget and Keeva inside, staring despondently at a large trash can filled with books. Some of the dust jackets were ripped and brown liquid that looked like coffee had been spilled over them.

"What's this?" Sam demanded.

"It's what they've done this time," said Keeva with a sigh. "We found them like this when we arrived."

"They're the books we'd placed in the front window," Bridget said. "All those lovely little children's stories."

"Where's Ambrose?" The question came out more sharply than Sam intended.

"I'm right here," he said, emerging from the storeroom with a mug of tea in hand.

"Who came in first this morning?" Sam asked. "Who found the books?"

"I did," said Keeva, "followed shortly by the others. We were all here within five minutes of opening time."

"Sorry. I didn't mean to sound critical or to place blame," Sam said, massaging her forehead. "Just trying to figure out what happened. Does anyone else have a key to the store?"

"I do," Ambrose answered, with a challenge to his voice.

"Terrance had one," said Keeva. "Mr. Ryan probably gave it to you, Sam. And I do."

"I wasn't issued one," Bridget said, "but there was no need. The others are normally here first before me anyway."

"Aside from this destruction being caused by *faeries*, does anyone have any ideas?" Sam bit her lip and forced her sarcasm back.

Ambrose shot her an angry look but Keeva and Bridget only shrugged. She fought back a wave of hopelessness. It was bad enough that the shop wasn't in good shape; she really didn't need the employees pulling pranks against her, too.

"Okay. Let's get this cleaned up. Bridget, see if any of the books are still clean. Pull them out, wipe off the dirt and . . . whatever that is." She pointed to the brown stains. "Put them into two groups—those that are in new condition and those we might be able to sell at a discount." She turned to Keeva. "Make new signs for the window. We can't let it sit empty all morning. We all saw how a better window display brought in more business. We have to do it over."

The women set about their tasks. Sam stepped over to the counter where Ambrose was sitting on the stool behind the register, sipping his tea.

"It seems that someone other than any of us has a key to the shop," Sam told him, keeping her voice even. "I'd like to have the locks changed."

"There's only the one door," he said. "It should be an easy matter."

Well, at least he didn't argue against the idea or go into a snit, thinking she was accusing him.

"Would you mind calling someone? Tell them we need the job done right away."

"Certainly." He pulled a telephone directory from under the counter and opened it.

Sam left him with that task and walked over to the large table where Bridget and Keeva had dragged the heavy trash can and were pulling books from it.

"Most of them should clean up just fine," Keeva said. "The brown liquid looks like it's mostly been taken up into this paper toweling. I'll get busy re-making my signs."

So whoever poured it might have done it only for effect, not to actually ruin the books. Sam dampened some clean paper towels in the bathroom and brought a stack of dry ones to the table. Together, she and Bridget had the books sorted and most of them cleaned up within an hour. It looked like only six books were damaged badly enough to warrant discounting them.

The locksmith arrived, installing a new deadbolt quickly and asking how many keys they wanted. Ambrose stared defiantly at Sam.

"Four," she said. "Please." She returned Ambrose's gaze.

When the workman left she handed out keys to each of her staff. "Now we know that no one other than any of us can get inside. There can't be a former employee, a ghost, or a faerie with access to this shop."

Keeva looked as if she wanted to say something about faeries not needing keys, but she closed her mouth again. Ambrose's expression had warmed a tad. Sam wondered how long it would stay that way.

"Okay, then," she said with as much brightness as she could work into her voice. "Let's continue what we were doing yesterday, rearranging shelves and displays so the inventory looks fresh and new."

The women went right back to their tasks but Ambrose's face was again a mask. It wasn't the first time she'd felt his moods go icy. She was weary of walking on eggshells around him.

"Could you help me in the back room?" she asked him, walking that direction without waiting for a reply.

When they were alone she turned to him. "Ambrose, what *is* it? Aside from the fact that I showed up here, unwanted, and that I'm trying to see the shop get back on its feet again—what is bothering you?"

He stood with arms folded across his chest, staring at the toes of his shoes.

"Terry's dying has obviously caused you a lot of pain," she continued gently. "You cared a great deal for him, didn't you?"

"Of course I did. The man was a mentor to me, almost a father. I've missed havin' him here each day."

"But he hadn't been coming into the shop for months before he died. You've had time to adjust to that. So there's more." She waited for a dam of some sort to burst, an outpouring about how unfair it was that Sam got the shop.

"There's something fishy about all of it," he finally said. "Ask that lawyer. Where did Terry's house go? His personal things? No one ever said."

Sam took a breath. "Mr. Ryan mentioned some sort of charitable trust. I'm afraid I don't know any details."

"Exactly. And where is that trust? And who *does* know the details? If you're the heir, you should have been told all that."

"So it isn't me that you're angry with?" Sam ventured.

"Get over yourself, as they'd say in America," he said, his eyebrows fiercely pulled together again. "This is about Terry and the rest of his estate. What's happened to it?"

Sam took a mental step back. What was he talking about?

"Are you saying that the lawyers have pulled something? Done something illegal?"

"I'm saying I don't know. The funeral they held for Terry was nothin'. It was like someone said 'ah, just stick 'im in the ground'. And the wake—a paltry thing. And Terry, him bein' a solid gold member of this community. I'm sayin' it was all wrong." His arms gestured wildly and she noticed his brogue got heavier the more excited he became.

"You mentioned his house. I've never seen it," she said. "No one has said a thing to me."

"He'd a lovely home, in a nice part of the city. No castle, mind you, but a large place. I'd been there a few times. We all had. Terry hosted us and our families for Christmas dinner. Keeva's sister even worked as his caregiver in his final months. Was she just given the boot, I ask? I cannot imagine it." His face had become flushed as he spoke, but now he simply leaned back against the small worktop where the teakettle sat, as if the energy had left his body.

"Ambrose, I promise you, I will look into this. I agree. You are entitled to better answers than you've gotten so far." She patted his arm and started toward the door. "I'd like to have those answers too. I have a feeling my uncle would have wanted you to know."

She walked out, leaving Ambrose to collect himself.

In the shop Keeva was ringing up a sale at the register while Bridget arranged books in the front window, making today's display even more enticing than what she'd done yesterday. Sam glanced around but couldn't see anything that required her immediate attention. She decided to pay a surprise visit to the offices of Ryan and O'Connor.

A mist had moved in during the morning and Sam found it a bit challenging to locate the law offices that she'd only visited once before. But eventually she came to a familiar intersection, with the jewelry store that she remembered. She opened the shiny black door at the street level and climbed to the second floor.

Daniel Ryan was busy with a telephone call, according to the secretary who occupied the desk in the small reception area. When he finished, she would be happy to announce Sam.

Magazines about finance, business and the computer industry lay in a neat row on an end table and gave Sam a pretty good idea of the types of clients represented by Ryan and O'Connor. She picked up one on business and idly flipped it open, wondering if there were articles about how to revive a very dilapidated, very old retail store.

Before she found the answer to that question, Daniel Ryan opened the door to his private office and invited her inside.

"Come to get the paperwork out of the way, then?" he asked, reaching into a drawer and pulling out a folder.

"No, actually. Not quite yet. I still have questions about the financial state of the store—"

"Which, as I mentioned last time, has nothing to do with the fact that it *is* yours."

"Yes, you did say that." Sam put on as gracious a smile as she could muster. "There are other things. You mentioned that certain items in the estate went to some kind of charitable trust—including my uncle's home?"

"Yes, that's true."

"What's the nature of this trust?"

"Well, I'm not really at liberty to say." His gaze traveled across the desk.

"I suppose what I'm asking is whether this trust, or whatever organization it is, actually occupies the house. Or, are my uncle's possessions still in it?"

Ryan fiddled with the pages inside the folder some more. "I'm not sure I can say."

"It's just that some of Terry's friends here in Galway . . . well some have expressed—how do I say this?—reservations, about the way his funeral and wake were conducted. It's led me to be concerned about who, really, has taken over his house and his other things."

"Oh, that. Well, I can assure you that everything was done in accordance with your uncle's wishes. A nice service, a quiet burial, a small wake. He was a man of simple tastes. He didn't want there to be a big fuss over him. At the end."

Sam watched his face, the slight twitch that grabbed at the corner of his eye.

"I would like to visit my uncle's grave," Sam said. "My

mother asked me to do that." It seemed like a reasonable request, even if it weren't true.

"I'll take you there," Ryan said. "Soon. Um, I'm afraid I have appointments the rest of the day now. Maybe in a day or two? I could call you."

The lawyer's words made sense, but why was there such discrepancy between what were supposedly Terrance O'Shaughnessy's wishes and what his close friend Ambrose Piggott believed them to be? Sam thanked him for his time and said she would wait for his call.

Out on the street the mist had broken up, leaving everything glistening with damp; the clouds were high and white and unthreatening. She felt the last of the style go out of her hair. A walk in the cool air might help clear her head, she decided, so she set off toward the hotel.

Who was right about Terrance's final wishes—Ambrose or the lawyer? She asked herself why it mattered to her— this was something that had happened months ago and couldn't be changed—but for some reason it bothered her. Maybe it was simply that if she had to take ownership of the bookshop, as Daniel Ryan stated, she wanted to have a decent working relationship with Ambrose. Plus, there had been the man's emotional connection to her uncle. She tended to believe him.

Down by the dock sat the *Glory Be*, alone and still in the same berth where the police had left her. Sam wondered if Beau had been in to see Detective Lambert again today. She ducked out of the pedestrian traffic and sent a quick text to him. Are you in the hotel?

Almost immediately she got his response: At police station. Can head back now.

She replied: See you in 20 min.

She stared at the boats for a couple more minutes, debated going inside and having a glass of wine in the pub while she waited for him.

Across the street from the hotel she noticed the high stone wall and remembered that they could see over it from the third floor. There was a graveyard behind that wall.

Maybe she could save Daniel Ryan the trouble of taking her to visit the grave if she could find it herself. She crossed Dock Street and followed the rock wall around the corner where a doorway-sized entrance led to the grassy area beyond. She climbed the steps past a wooden sign that said Forthill Graveyard and a plaque written in Latin with a rather graphic skull and crossbones on it.

The place was as quiet as, well, a graveyard. Vivid green grass covered the ground between a variety of headstones— white stone crosses, round-shouldered gray mossy ones, a few that leaned at angles. She looked around the enclosure that was probably an acre or two at most, not spotting any graves that looked obviously newer than the others. She began to walk among the stones, which weren't exactly in precise rows anymore, picking out names.

At one side she noticed that an equipment shed stood with the door open. Fifteen minutes until Beau would be back, and reading every gravestone in the place would take hours. She called out, "Hello!"

A man in dungarees stepped out. He had a wicked looking blade in his hand and Sam found herself taking a step back, although she was still a good twenty feet out of his reach.

"Hi, I wonder if you could tell me where a particular grave is?"

"Might. I been working around this same bunch for a long time now." He chuckled at his own joke.

"Terrance O'Shaughnessy."

"There ain't no such."

She gave him a puzzled look.

"Most of 'em's the graves of those men from the Spanish Armada. Executed after they tried to invade England in 1588, they were. Buried right here."

"So there aren't any recent graves here?"

"No ma'am, you've got the wrong place."

Sam was nearly certain Daniel Ryan had said her uncle's grave was there but maybe she was mistaken. One of them certainly was.

Chapter 11

Sam left the cemetery and crossed the street to the hotel. Beau's familiar shape had just passed through the heavy glass doors that led to the elevators so she picked up her pace and caught up with him just as one of the elevator doors slid open.

"Hey," she said.

"Hey. How did it go at the bookstore?"

It took her a minute to shift mentally, past the graveyard and the visit to the attorney's office. She described the nuisance of the destroyed window display and the fact that she'd had the shop's locks changed.

"If another incident in the night happens now, it's got to be one of the employees," she said.

He smiled down at her as the door opened to the third floor hallway. "It pretty much has to be anyway, don't you think?"

"Unless you believe in faeries, sprites or leprechauns. At least they'll all know that I'm keeping closer tabs on them." She sighed. "I don't know what to think about this whole thing, Beau."

She told him about the lawyer's cagey manner whenever she tried to ask him questions, and the visit to the cemetery, which had left her completely puzzled.

"I think Daniel Ryan is hiding something from me. He sure is eager for me to sign those papers, but when I ask questions he manages to divert the conversation another direction."

"So, talk to his partner?"

Sam had nearly forgotten about the other one, since she'd never met him. She pondered Beau's suggestion. "That makes sense," she finally said. "He's the older partner, was probably the one who worked with my uncle for a long time. Maybe I'm being unfairly suspicious of Ryan. Maybe he just doesn't know that much about the estate."

She rummaged in her bag and came up with the business card she had stashed there. "I'll set up an appointment and then *we* can take the rest of the day off and go do something fun."

As it turned out, the only time both attorneys would be in their office was that afternoon, as O'Connor was leaving for London in the morning.

"I'm sorry, sweetheart," she said when she'd hung up the phone. "If I want to talk to Mick O'Connor it has to be today."

"I'll come with you," he said.

"Thank you. Maybe they won't give me such a runaround with your big strong presence in the room."

He laughed. "More likely, they'll just feel that it's twice

the reason to get the deal finalized and get rid of us."

At the law office, the secretary led the way to the senior partner's private office, where they were greeted by a florid-faced man in his sixties. His hair was white around the edges, nonexistent on top, and blue eyes twinkled under thick white brows. Add a red hat and you might be shaking hands with Santa.

Sam returned his smile but didn't let herself become distracted from her mission.

"I don't mean to cause problems," she said, "but I feel like there is so much I don't know about this bookshop I've inherited. I don't want to sign anything until—"

"Completely understandable," O'Connor said.

Daniel Ryan had joined them in his partner's office, his eyes darting back and forth between the others.

"Your uncle spoke very fondly of his American family," O'Connor said. "Terrance and Maggie never had children. He thought of your mother and you as the family he never had here."

"Mother remembers him fondly, too. It's just that the news of this inheritance came completely as a surprise. None of us expected anything like—"

"Oh, I know. That was a big part of your uncle's nature. Generosity, surprises, watching people's reactions—he loved doing nice things for those he cared about."

Sam suppressed the impulse to argue. Surely there were people right here in town that he cared about more than a faraway relative he'd never seen.

"I've looked over the financial records for the shop, and there's hardly any information. Wasn't there more, somewhere? If I'm to operate this business from another continent I need to have some idea what to look for in sales."

A glance passed between the two lawyers.

O'Connor didn't answer immediately. "It's possible that some of the records would be in Terrance's home. He did keep a room there as his study."

"May I go there and have a look?"

The lawyer's eyes narrowed as he thought about it. Sam felt as if she were pulling teeth to get to the heart of the situation.

Finally, he spoke: "We could probably arrange that."

Some kind of signal went between the partners and Ryan left the room.

"We shall make sure the place is tidy and that no one from the trust is using it at the moment."

"What *about* this charitable trust? Isn't there some way I can leave the bookshop to it as well?"

"Well, I'm sorry to say, no. It's a matter of how the estate was all arranged."

She bit back a surge of frustration as Daniel Ryan opened the door and gave his partner a nod.

"Well, then, that's set," Mick O'Connor said. "Shall we go now? My car is just downstairs and, well, because of my meetings in London this week, today's the best time."

He stood up, not really making it an option unless Sam chose to miss out on the opportunity altogether. She noticed that the younger lawyer had vanished behind the closed door of his own office.

The car was a silver Mercedes, spotlessly clean, and Sam almost got into the driver's seat before realizing she was on the wrong side of it. Beau took the back seat directly behind Sam. O'Connor drove carefully through the narrow lanes until they'd left the congestion of central Galway and began to see individual house lots and places with small gardens out front. The route was completely unfamiliar to Sam and she guessed they were going north, although there was nothing to really tell her so. She suspected that Beau, with his internal navigation sense that she'd often teased him about, would know exactly how to repeat the trip.

Gradually, the size of the homes and the land they occupied grew larger, and when the lawyer turned onto a lane and slowed, Sam saw that her uncle's neighborhood was a nice one. O'Connor brought the car to a stop in front of a Tudor-styled house surrounded by mature trees and a neatly manicured lawn. Unless Terrance O'Shaughnessy had been an avid gardener until his dying day, he'd hired help with this place.

Dark half-timbers delineated sections of the second floor, with four evenly spaced windows across the front and it appeared at least an equal number along the sides of the structure. The ground floor façade was bisected by a small portico in front of a leaded glass door, where identical topiary plants stood sentinel on either side. Wide mullioned windows balanced the appearance.

"Uncle Terry's home is certainly in much better condition than his business was," Sam commented as they got out of the car in the circular driveway in front. A side drive led to a large old carriage house.

"Oh, yes. There was a full time gardener and a housekeeper. The house itself was something Terry acquired after making some very successful investments on the continent. Years ago. He and Maggie chose this home and made it their own."

"When did the bookshop come into the picture?"

"Ah, well, that was Terry's passion—books. He bought the shop from an old woman who couldn't run it anymore and then created the legend that he had won it in a poker game. He had a fondness for Western novels, you see. He loved being in the store, watching the new titles come in, recommending books, matching his customers' tastes to the books he thought they would like. Ambrose is much the same, you know."

Sam nodded but didn't say anything. So far, the only soft side she'd seen to the grumpy manager was when he talked about Terry. But she had to admit that she'd not spent enough time around Ambrose to know him yet.

O'Connor pulled a small key fob from his pocket and used the single key on it to open the front door.

They stepped into a wide, dim foyer with glossy hardwood floors. Beyond, she could see a formal living room with windows that showed gardens behind the house. A staircase rose to the left, carpeted with a floral-patterned runner and bordered by a heavy railing and balusters. Other doors along the foyer were closed.

"Beautiful," Sam commented. "May we have the full tour?"

"Oh, no. The charity, you see. If your shop records exist, they'll be found in the study anyway. No need to bother with the rest of it." He opened the first door on the right and ushered Sam toward it.

She bit back a retort which, she had to admit to herself, was half based on envy anyway.

Terrance O'Shaughnessy's study revealed itself to be a real man's room. Dark wood paneling, leather chairs, heavy red drapes, and a massive desk. The latter held a telephone and blotter with a matched set of pens in a stand. Otherwise, the top was bare. Bookshelves lined two walls, but they were hardly jammed with rare editions. Most of the titles seemed to be about real estate investment, economics and politics. Between the books were a variety of little collectible objects, all tucked behind glass doors with locks on them. A small fireplace in one corner looked as if he had used it regularly.

Sam felt another twinge of jealousy. Why had she, as the favorite niece, been left a crummy old store in severe decline, while the real value of the estate had gone to some charity that no one would name? She stopped herself. She certainly didn't begrudge the charity anything that would help them, and she couldn't very well lay claim to her uncle's possessions when she hadn't even known he existed until a few weeks ago.

"Now just here," O'Connor was saying, "in these drawers would be the business records."

He pulled open one of the four file-sized drawers, running his thumb through the tabs. "No, this one appears to be household bills."

The next drawer revealed what he was looking for, so he left that one standing open and indicated that Sam could sit in Terry's leather swivel chair and take a look. On the mantel, a clock ticked—the only sound in the room.

Sam sat down and pulled out the first folder from the drawer. O'Connor bustled about, getting Beau to sit in one of the leather chairs, then he took the other one—the one closest to the door. Sam suppressed a sigh and directed her attention to the contents of the folder. The top page contained a list of the bookshop's furniture and fixtures, something Sam could have almost produced herself after a day in the shop. It was dated a year ago. Behind that sheet she found others, each dated December of the preceding year, each nearly identical but for the addition or subtraction of an item or two.

The next folder in the drawer had an inventory of the books, but as it was dated nearly two years earlier there was no way it could be very accurate now. Another folder held a sizeable stack of paid bills—two years' worth. Since he had owned the shop close to forty years, there must be boxes of such receipts in storage somewhere—perhaps in the attic of the house—unless older ones were destroyed after the passage of some time.

At last she came to a folder of financial records, standard profit and loss reports prepared—judging by the signature line at the bottom—by Tom Mitchell, the accountant she'd spoken to. She scanned to the bottom line. The little business had netted less than ten thousand euros per year, after expenses, for its entire existence.

Sam glanced up at the men, who were quietly conversing about fishing. Apparently, O'Connor was right—Terry had owned the store because of a love of books, certainly not for the income.

One thing was certain, she couldn't justify even so much as one trip to Ireland per year to keep the shop going. The weight of the obligation settled over her.

"Mr. O'Connor?"

He chuckled at Beau's last comment and looked up at Sam.

"Since the business is mine, I assume these records are too?"

"Absolutely. The minute you sign the papers accepting title to it." He reached into his jacket and pulled out a small folded sheaf.

She sighed. This question just wasn't going away. She nodded. "Okay. Give me the documents so I can study them thoroughly tonight."

She began stacking the files on top of the desk.

"I can't release these—"

"We can come back for them tomorrow, if it's that important."

His mouth twitched for a second. "I'll locate a box. The files will be at my office."

The moment he left the room, Sam looked at Beau. His eyebrows flicked up and down a couple of times. He mouthed the word 'later.'

She turned away, noticing for the first time some of the items inside the glass-enclosed bookcases. A wooden object caught her attention but before she could get out of the chair and take a look, O'Connor was back.

"Here we go, then," he announced. He set a large cardboard carton on the floor beside the open drawer. "Load up whatever you need."

What I need is to know how I'm going to operate a no-profit business without actually being here. But she tamped down the thought and began stacking manila folders into the carton. At least this was a start on figuring out what to do. When it came time to sell the business, after her two-year sentence was up, she would need these records.

The lawyer watched her but didn't offer to pitch in. When the carton was full he stood back so Beau could pick it up, then he herded them out of the study, out the front door (which he locked immediately) and down the stone front steps to the car. He opened the trunk and watched Beau set the carton in.

"All right then," he said as he started the engine once they were all safely inside. "Where can I drop you? Bookshop? Hotel?"

Sam felt the long day weighing on her. "The Harbour Hotel, I suppose."

They got out at the curb and watched the silver car pull away.

"You're pooped, darlin'," Beau said, rubbing at the back of her neck. "Do you want to go straight to the room or grab some dinner first?"

"Once I sit down I'll never want to get up again."

"I spotted a little Italian place, about a block from here," he said. "We could try that. Or I would be happy to order room service while you're in the bathtub, if you'd rather."

He was so considerate. She dithered for a second. "You know, a walk would do me good. I've been inside my head too much today. It would be good for me to clear it before I have to sit down with this document."

She tucked the pages O'Connor had handed her into her pack and they set out. The scent of tomatoes and oregano wafted out of the restaurant before Beau opened the door. Inside, the place was tiny—eight small tables— but the patrons seemed happy and the food in front of them looked wonderful. Within minutes they had a bottle of red wine and had placed their orders.

"This afternoon was a little weird, didn't you think?" Sam asked after they toasted each other.

"Those lawyers are hiding something. Holding back access to the records, pushing you to sign the papers, and then not even showing you around your uncle's house."

"Yeah, what's with that?"

He bit at his lower lip. "I don't know. I wish I had some way to do background checks on them. It's hard. I'm used to having a lot of resources at my fingertips. Here, it's not so easy. This charitable trust, for instance—did you see any mention of it among the paperwork you looked at today?"

"Not a thing." She fiddled with her silverware. "I don't really have a concrete reason to believe this whole thing is shady. I mean, we did check out the law firm through the American attorney who first notified me about the inheritance. On the other hand . . ."

He nodded. Their waiter showed up with steaming plates—lasagna for Beau, ravioli for Sam. At the first bite, Sam nearly wilted with pleasure. The sauce was exquisite.

"I know," Beau said. "I just can't figure out why all the tippy-toeing around."

"Maybe it just seems that way because things are done differently here."

"Or maybe because neither of us ever had an inheritance. We don't know what the procedure should be. It just feels odd."

She grinned at the truth in that. The wine and good food were relaxing her.

Above the small bar at the back of the restaurant a television set had been broadcasting the Irish news, the volume muted. Sam glanced at it once in awhile, happy to have other topics break her constant train of thought on the lawyers and the bookshop. Her ravioli were perfectly cooked, the cheese melting in her mouth with each bite. She gave one of the pasta disks to Beau. When he didn't immediately respond she realized that his attention had drifted to the TV.

"Huh," he said. "Look at that."

The written dateline showed New York, and the running commentary at the bottom read: Jewel theft believed to top $14M.

Sam realized her plate was empty and the wonderful meal had settled her into a tranquil cloud. She drained her wine glass and watched Beau finish his lasagna, then they strolled back to the hotel. With every intention of studying the papers Mick O'Connor had given her, Sam stretched out on the bed but it only took moments before she drifted off.

Chapter 12

The next morning Sam was already seated at the room's small desk when Beau emerged from the shower. The sheets of legal paper were spread out in front of her.

"It looks pretty simple," she said, enjoying the view as he dressed. "I agree to accept ownership of the bookshop for a minimum of two years. I'll receive no operating money other than what the store generates, and I relinquish any and all claims to any other part of the estate."

"Which could leave you with a giant money drain if you can't make the store profitable."

She nodded slowly. "That's the thing . . . from the quick glimpse I got of the profit reports it looks like the store has always made a small profit. My guess is that while Terry was there to oversee things, it was a popular place. I just can't figure out why Ambrose hasn't kept it up. He's been there long enough to know what to do."

Beau reached for the document she'd been reading. "This looks like something that was drawn up by the law firm, but your uncle's signature isn't on it. It's almost like anyone could have written this up and asked you to sign it. At the very least there should be a reading of the will or you should get to see a copy of it, to be sure these terms are definitely what your uncle had in mind."

Good point. She refolded the sheets and placed them in the room's safe, searching her jewelry box for a pendant while she was there, and locking up after everything was stashed away.

He continued, "Last night I was thinking about Ryan and O'Connor and wishing I could get more background on them. Well, since I've got a connection now with the police department, maybe we should pop by there. Lambert might let me do some research with their computers."

"I like it. Let's go."

They decided to stick with the lighter offerings at the breakfast buffet this morning and to walk the six blocks rather than take their car. Sam noticed her jeans becoming harder to button each day while Beau, as always, had no trouble with his. She growled a little as she put an apple and dry toast on her plate.

Forty minutes later, they were on Bridge Street, crossing the Corrib, with the Garda station in sight. When Beau asked for Detective Lambert they were told he would be out of a meeting in a few minutes.

"Place seems to be buzzing this morning," Beau said under his breath.

True, Sam sensed the energy in the air as plain-clothes detectives and even the uniformed officers bustled about with purpose in their steps. Joe Lambert came out of a room at the far end of the corridor and ducked into another. After five minutes he came out and headed their direction, giving Beau a weary smile as he approached.

"It's fair hoppin' here, I'll tell you." He held out a hand to Sam.

She noticed that the skin around his blue eyes seemed puffy, as if he hadn't slept.

"C'mon back," Lambert said, turning to lead the way.

They walked into a situation room where the energy zipped through the air. White boards on the walls were filled with scrawled notes, and photographs were tacked alongside. One board seemed devoted to the case of the abandoned *Glory Be*. Sam noticed photos of the boat, the missing Darragh O'Henry and his crewman, plus the two suspects who'd been found drifting in the trawler's lifeboat.

Another wall, it seemed, was becoming the focus for a new case. Fewer notes, no photos, yet a half-dozen men and women—detectives, Sam assumed—milled about, taking notes from the information on the board, talking among themselves. A younger man, dressed similarly to Lambert in dark slacks and tweed jacket, approached with proper deference. He had a plain face with ruddy cheeks and abundant blond hair combed back from his forehead and tucked behind his ears.

He handed a sheet of fax paper to Lambert, who introduced him as Sergeant Aiden Martin before stopping to read the page. When Lambert looked up he turned to Beau.

"Bit of excitement in America in recent days," he said.

Sam went blank for a moment but Beau remembered. "The jewel robbery? We saw the headline on TV."

"The media are all over it," Lambert said, "but the police in New York are trying not to let all the information get out. What they're saying is that a diamond wholesaler, Jacob Goldman, was nabbed on the street and forced to let the robbers into his shop to open his safe for them. The thieves had enough information to know what time to do it so that the time lock wouldn't keep them out. Completely cleaned out the poor old man, beat him badly and left him for dead. His son, who's a business partner, was away at a trade show and didn't discover the robbery until he got back to the city that night. The senior Mr. Goldman is in hospital now, still unconscious."

"And what they're not saying . . .?" Beau asked.

"These guys were good. The robbery happened days ago and police still don't know for certain how many thieves there were. At least two, possibly three or four. They left precious little trace evidence. They got away with millions in diamonds and other gemstones, plus a lot of cash. The number that's being bandied about by the reporters doesn't come close. The total take was probably over twenty million dollars."

"Marked?"

"Unfortunately, no. The firm had just made several large transactions and hadn't logged the serial numbers on the cash. According to the son, Richard Goldman, his father was taking the cash to the bank that morning as soon as he arrived at the shop. Richard says he's been trying to get his father to switch to electronic fund transfers for their sales but the old man is very old-school in his attitude about those things. We'll hope that doesn't prove fatal for him.

"The other thing they're not saying on the news is that there was one crucial piece of evidence. A tiny piece of latex glove. And a blood stain on the doorknob. The blood wasn't Mr. Goldman's. It belongs to one of the thieves."

"So they'll have DNA evidence to convict the guy if they can just catch him," Beau said.

"Precisely."

Sam wondered why the Galway police were even following the case but Lambert seemed to have read her mind.

"There's more. A partial fingerprint was taken from the piece of latex glove. It's only a wee bit but they hoped to match it." He held up the fax page. "That's what this is about. The print is about sixty percent certain to match a known felon named Quinton Farrell. Farrell is in his fifties, last known residence is New York, and he tends toward high class stuff like financial fraud and he is known to travel internationally."

Beau glanced around the room. "You think he may have come to Ireland?"

"Possibly. Farrell has family in Ireland, so we've been put on alert throughout the republic that he might contact them."

Lambert laid the fax on his desk and reached for a stained mug. "Oh, sorry. Terrible manners. Would you like a cuppa?"

Sam and Beau both declined.

Aiden Martin, the young sergeant, rushed over as the senior detective was setting his tea mug down.

"This just came by fax," he said a little breathlessly. "Shall I put it on the board?"

Lambert reached out to take what Sam could see was a photograph. He studied it a moment and handed it over to Beau.

"That's him. Quinton Farrell."

Sam edged closer and looked at it. There was something vaguely familiar but she couldn't place the man with the ruggedly handsome face and dark hair with touches of gray at the temples. It could simply be that she watched too many Robert De Niro movies. Beau handed the sheet back and Aiden carried it to the wall where information on the new case was slowly being fleshed out.

Beau started to tell Lambert the real reason they'd shown up this morning—to see if he could use a computer to run some background verification on the law firm representing Sam's uncle—and Sam found herself drifting in the direction Aiden Martin had taken. The collection of information about the jewel heist was still skimpy but filling out as information specialists added new tidbits that came in.

In contrast, the boards with information on the abandoned *Glory Be* had quite a lot of forensic information, along with the photos of the trawler and the lifeboat, maps showing where the two craft had been located, and the shots of the two survivors who'd been picked up. Were they innocent fishermen who'd somehow been caught up in a boat trip gone wrong? Or did they have a hand in the disappearance of Darragh O'Henry and Sean Bareth? A close-up shot of the blood on the wheelhouse attested to the probability that there wasn't an innocuous explanation for the fact that the boat's captain and crewman had never come home. Sam thought of Bridget and her parents, the worry on their faces.

Behind her, she heard Beau's voice; he would be at Lambert's desk using the computer. As she turned toward him, something else caught her eye. Quinton Farrell. Hank Greenlee. Ted "Trucker" Furns.

She had seen these three *together* somewhere. Her eyes darted back and forth, scanning the three images on the walls. Where?

She stared so hard and so long that the memory began to blur. It was like trying to remember a name that was on the tip of her tongue, with the same frustrating result—the mind went blank.

She faced away from the walls and watched Beau, sitting at a desk, his face scrunched in concentration. A tingle started in her fingers and a flash-vision of her wooden jewelry box came to her. When she closed her eyes she saw the three men standing in line at an airport check-in desk.

"Beau! Detective Lambert! I've remembered something." She kept her eyes closed, working like crazy to keep the memory from fading.

"Sam? What's the matter?" the detective's voice said.

She pretended to take a snapshot of what she was seeing. Memorized it. Opened her eyes. Gathered her thoughts to present it logically enough that Lambert wouldn't think she was a nut.

"I've seen those three men together," she said, pointing toward the two areas of the crime-wall. "The two that you found in the lifeboat, they were with the other one—Farrell—at the airport. In New York, when we were checking in for our flight. They were in the other line, buying tickets." She paused a moment, searching for additional details. "Wait a second—they didn't actually buy their tickets together . . . They were at the entrance to that place where you line up, you know, where the sign says to enter."

She and Beau had paused to figure out where they

needed to be, unfamiliar with the process for flying first class.

"The older man—Farrell. He was pulling cash out of a thick wallet-thing he got out of his jacket. He gave money to the others. Once we found our own line to join, I saw that the three men weren't together. They were all in line, but not together."

"And . . ." Beau said. "didn't one of your suspects drop the name Quint?"

"Possibly the same?" Lambert looked excited. He turned back to Sam. "You've quite the memory."

This probably wasn't the best time and place to admit to having tingles and visions that came from handling an odd wooden box. "I guess I noticed because so few people pay with cash these days," she said with a shrug.

Beau, bless him, stayed quiet. He'd witnessed a few of her insights, and even though he wasn't much into supernatural beliefs he'd learned to trust that she wouldn't be making this up.

"We know these two ended up here in Galway," Lambert said, pointing at Furns and Greenlee. "They're still in our custody. But what about the other, Quinton Farrell . . . Which airline were they checking in with?"

"That's just it. Aerlingus." Beau spoke up while Sam searched for anything else she could remember. "We were on the direct flight from JFK to Shannon."

"I think they were, too," Sam told them. "Once we'd gotten through security and were walking toward the gates, I saw them together again. They were sitting in a bar directly across from the gate where our plane would leave."

"Did you actually see Farrell on the plane?"

Beau explained that they'd been in first class, boarding

separately and waiting in the club lounge before the flight left. Lambert gave him an appraising stare, and Sam felt obligated to explain about the inheritance and the free flight. She couldn't have him wondering how a small town sheriff and a baker had managed the expensive tickets.

The detective nodded and she could see him processing all the new information. He got Aiden's attention and motioned the younger detective over.

"I'd like to have Greenlee and Furns brought to interrogation rooms. Separate ones." To Beau he said, "Now that we have Farrell's name, this could get interesting."

Beau glanced around the big, open room. "There aren't any American authorities here to question them?"

"Not yet." He said it politely but the inference was there—he'd only learned of the possible connection between the three men, just minutes ago.

"Sorry," Beau said. "Didn't mean to—"

"No, actually . . . Would you like to interview them with me?"

A smile spread over Beau's face.

"You see where I'm going with this," Lambert said.

"Absolutely."

"Sam, you are welcome to watch from the safety of the side room," Lambert offered.

"Thank you, I'd like to." She was intrigued to see what might happen next.

Chapter 13

Sam stepped into the room where Lambert instructed her to wait with Aiden and watch on a video monitor. Lambert entered the room where Hank Greenlee sprawled in a chair, posed nonchalantly although his fingers drummed on the table with contradictory nervous energy.

"Mr. Greenlee, good morning."

The young black man answered with a chuff.

"It's customary to say good morning here," Lambert said.

Greenlee's posture stiffened almost imperceptibly. "Morning. When'm I outta here?"

"Well now, I suppose that depends."

A ridge deepened between his eyebrows. "On what?"

"What can you tell us about Quinton Farrell?"

"Say who?"

"The man who gave you cash to purchase your plane ticket to come to our fair country."

"Don't know whatcha mean."

Lambert turned on him, slamming his palm onto the table top with a *whap*. Greenlee flinched and pulled his own arm tighter to his body but he gave Lambert a disdainful stare.

"You and your friend Trucker came to Ireland with Quinton Farrell, accomplices to a very large robbery. You're in for some very serious prison time, you little punk. Don't bullshit me." Lambert hovered over the suspect, his hands balled into fists.

On cue, Beau tapped at the door and walked into the interrogation.

"Detective, the sergeant needs you for a minute," he said.

Greenlee watched him with hooded eyes, clearly wondering.

Beau waited until Lambert had left and closed the door before turning to Greenlee. He acted relieved to be left alone.

"They treating you all right?" he asked.

Greenlee shrugged. "Not really. Who're you, anyway? You sound American. You like a ambassador or somethin'?"

Beau didn't directly answer the question, simply took the other chair and leaned in toward the prisoner. "I'm trying to find out the truth. With any luck we can get you out soon."

"I ain't done nothin' and they can't be holding me here, can they?"

"They said you and your friend hired a fishing boat. Next thing anyone knows the boat is drifting at sea, the crew is missing and you two are floating around out there in the lifeboat. Sounds pretty cold and scary to me."

The younger man said nothing about the fact that he'd been taken to the hospital with hypothermia.

"Look," Beau said. "They just need to know what happened. This guy, Quinton Farrell, he's really behind all this, isn't he? He paid for the plane tickets, probably the charter boat too. He's the one they really want. Tell them that and you'll probably be out of here pretty quick."

Hank's eyes shifted back and forth. The offer was tempting.

"Look, man, I don't know nothin'. I don't like fishin' so I just sat down in the back and I fell asleep."

Beau let a long moment go by. "Uh-huh. And the next thing you know you're out there in the dark in that lifeboat, freezing your ass off and you have no idea how you got there? Did Farrell go out on the boat with the rest of you?"

Greenlee's eyes shifted then he sat back and sighed deeply. "Quint—he's smart. Way smarter than Trucker, way-way smarter than me. I don't know what all he done. He said he'd give us a share of all this money if we'd help get some diamonds or some such shit from some old man in Manhattan. I just needed me some cash and that's all I signed on for. Man, I just want my money and to see the other side of this damn building."

Beau nodded, as if agreeing with that sentiment.

"So, where's Quint now? The police really need to find him."

"Hell if I know." He sat back in his chair and crossed his arms across his chest.

Lambert came back in and exchanged some kind of

signal with Beau, who left the two alone. When Beau stepped into the viewing room, Aiden asked, "Do you believe him, then?"

"Parts of it are probably true. Parts are clearly a matter of his saying what he thinks we want to hear."

Sam offered him a bottle of water she'd been sipping and he took three long pulls on it.

"Guess I'm up next in the 'Yankee-cop-Euro-cop' game with the other guy, Trucker," he said. "You don't have to hang around here, darlin'. I can meet you somewhere later, if you want."

Aiden busied himself by setting up a second monitor and bringing up a camera in the room where Trucker Furns waited.

Sam thought about going to the bookshop to see what was happening but felt torn. Until she fully committed to signing the papers and accepting that she would own the place for the next two years, she couldn't work up the enthusiasm to put in long hours there. "I'll stay here," she said to Beau. "I came to Ireland to be with you."

He put his arm around her shoulders and pulled her close. "I'm sorry, darlin'. I don't have to be here. We can go get the car and take another drive."

She turned toward him and gave him a quick kiss. "You are loving this. A big case that's made international news— you don't get the chance to get in on that every day. Go. Interview. When you're finished you can take me shopping for gifts to take home to everyone."

He pulled out a chair for her. "You can watch again. You always come up with good ideas—partner."

Once again Sam found herself seated in front of a

monitor, watching Beau walk in and confront a suspect.

Ted Furns—Trucker—sat in a metal chair at a metal table, casually grooming his nails by scraping under each one with the zipper pull on the jailhouse jumpsuit he wore. The tattoos on his arms were a vivid mix of fantastical myth and what Sam supposed were prison gang symbols. Skulls seemed to feature prominently. He didn't look up when Beau entered.

"Mr. Furns," Beau said, taking the seat across from him. "I just spoke with Hank."

"You American?" Finally, Trucker looked up.

Beau nodded. "Your partner says Quint Farrell planned this whole thing, talked you guys into going along with it."

Trucker regarded him coolly. "I don't know no Quint."

"You were all seen together in the airport. We know you were on the same flight."

A shrug. "Lot of people on them big airplanes. I don't know them neither."

"True."

Sam felt a shiver go up her arms. They'd been on the same plane. What if either of these bad guys remembered them? Recognition could work against them as well as in their favor.

"Your buddy Hank says he fell asleep on the fishing boat. Doesn't know what happened to the captain and the mate. You weren't asleep. What did happen? Where are they?"

"I want a lawyer." He dropped the zipper pull and folded his arms at the edge of the table.

"This isn't America," Beau said.

"It's a civilized country. They got lawyers."

"You don't have any rights here. You're not a citizen." Beau let the air fill with silence. After a full three minutes he said, "I suppose I could call the American embassy for you. Get you a quick ticket home on a Con Air flight."

A flicker of uncertainty crossed Trucker's face. He quickly masked it and stayed quiet.

"It's okay. The police here are liking you for piracy and murder in Ireland. They really don't want to send you back across the Atlantic anyway."

Beau stood up and walked out of the room without looking back. The instant the door closed, Sam saw Trucker's face twist into a mask of fury. He slammed his fist into the palm of his other hand.

"You got to him with that last part," Sam told Beau when he walked into the observation room a minute later.

Beau looked at the interrogation room monitor but Trucker glanced up at the camera mounted high on the wall, gave a tiny smile and settled back into his seat. Detective Lambert walked into the room where Sam and Beau were standing.

"I'll let himself cool his heels for awhile, let him think we're printin' out his entire history, then I'll get in there with more questions. Would you both like to pop out with me for a little lunch?"

Beau glanced at Sam. "I promised my wife that I would take her shopping this afternoon."

"Unless you need him here," Sam said. "He'll certainly have more fun grilling your suspects than he would looking at sweaters with me."

Lambert chuckled. "It's your call. I don't mind your bein' here, though. You've a better feel for how the American criminal mind works."

The words were hardly out before he realized how they sounded. Beau assured the detective that he understood what was meant—and agreed.

"How about this? While you're having lunch we'll hit the shops. Then I can come back. Sam can do whatever she wants . . . more shopping, the bookstore, the hotel . . ."

As it turned out, Sam found everything she wanted in two places. She came away with thick Aran wool sweaters for her daughter, Kelly, and friends Zoë and Darryl Chartrain; they loved to cross-country ski. Beautifully woven scarves worked perfectly for Jen and Becky at Sweet's Sweets, for her friend Riki and her buddy Rupert Penrick who had helped her out of more than one scrape in her life. Julio, her one male employee, would like the black stone beads with the Harley Davidson emblem (okay, not really Irish), and she would get Ambrose to recommend something in the shop for her bookstore-owner friend Ivan.

They dropped their packages off at the hotel and went by a fish and chips stand where they got food to go and nibbled at it as they walked back to the station.

"If you're serious about wanting my help, I'm here," Beau told Lambert when they found the detective staring at the computer screen on his desk.

"I do. Never made it out for any lunch," he said. "There's a new case, out toward Salthill, and now I've got the pressure from above to wrap up this one."

Sam handed him the paper wrapper of fish and potatoes she hadn't finished. He reached for it and ate while he talked.

"If I could only get these two to admit something about what happened to Darragh O'Henry. We've got their fingerprints all over the boat. There's the blood, which doesn't match either of theirs. And that one shell casing.

But no bodies."

"Darragh's family say there's no way he would willingly abandon the *Glory Be*," Sam offered.

"Aye, that's true enough," said Lambert. "Me own dad was a sailor. He'd have never surrendered his ship without a fight."

The detective performed a few mouse clicks and a printer across the room began spitting out pages. Among them were photographs, apparently from surveillance cameras at JFK airport, which showed the three men together and a printed list of names.

"Farrell traveled under his own passport," he told them, "but we aren't sure what names the others used. I want to get that information out of them."

"Let's switch off our good-cop, bad-cop roles and see what happens," Beau suggested, taking one set of the printed pages with him.

Once again, Sam watched as Beau entered an interrogation room. Hank Greenlee rested his head on folded arms at the table, and it seemed he'd fallen asleep. Beau kicked one leg of the chair, sending the young black man to attention.

"What's that for, man?" he grumbled.

"I want the whole story, and I want it now." Beau's voice went hard, a tone Sam had never heard before. "Start with the robbery of that diamond wholesaler."

Greenlee stuck out his lip, debating. Beau flashed the sheets of paper in the suspect's face, nearly ruffling his eyelashes with them.

"Now!"

The belligerent attitude receded. "I don't know what you want, man."

"I want to hear what happened to Jacob Goldman in New York, and I want to hear what happened aboard that fishing boat here in Galway." He jerked a metal chair into place across from Greenlee; it clattered to a standstill and Beau sat and stared.

"I don't know nothin' about the dude in New York. Quint and Trucker went in there. I waited in the car outside. They come running, I take off. Quint yells out what to do. I go to this parking garage."

Beau jotted notes and continued his silent stare.

"In the back seat, Quint's putting stuff into bags—I don't know what all. Then we get outta that place and suddenly he's all, like, now we gotta go to Ireland. What's with that? But he's taking us out to the street, grabbing a cab, then we're at the airport buying the tickets and he's got passports all set for us and everything. So then I figure we'll get here and get our money, but then he's all, 'okay now we need to get this fishing boat'."

"How did he get the gems and cash through airport security?"

"No idea. He had all that stuff with him. Trucker and me, we just had suitcases with, like, some clothes and stuff."

"What about a gun? Did you see one?"

"In a airport? Hell, no."

"Okay, you get on the flight with a fake passport. What name was on it?"

Greenlee rubbed at his temples. "I don't remember . . . I show it a couple times at the airport, then to some uniform dude when we get here . . . then Quint takes the passports back from us after that."

Quint must have some darn good connections to get fake passports, Sam thought. A lot of planning had gone into the jewel heist—a lot more than Greenlee was letting on.

Beau spoke again. "So you get to Ireland. Did you check into a hotel? Where'd you stay?"

"Nowhere, man. We ride some bus from the airport to here. Quint's making phone calls right and left. Like, he's trying to reach some uncle or somebody. I don't *know*." His voice rose in a tired whine.

"Did he say a name?"

"Prob'ly. I don't remember. Can I just get some sleep?"

"No. Not until we finish. Tell me about renting the fishing boat."

"Quint sends me and Trucker into that little office place of theirs and we're supposed to say that the two of us want to go fishing. I'm so beat after the plane flight that I don't know if I even said it right. But there's this boat captain— wearing some stupid-shit hat—and he says he can take us out right away. You know, the kind of guy you can just smell desperation on him."

Sam remembered that Bridget had said her uncle's charter business had been slow.

Beau gave Greenlee a steady stare.

"So anyways, Quint's waiting outside and when we all go to get in the boat he comes up like he don't know us and asks this captain can he go along. He flashes some cash and it's a done deal. He didn't like it that the guy wanted to give his name to the secretary, or whoever that lady was. Quint distracted him with somethin' else."

"So the boat heads out with all of you onboard. How did you get the captain to go the opposite direction from where he wanted, away from the good fishing spots?"

Hank shrugged. "Don't know, man. Once we get outside

that little marina, or whatever it's called, Quint takes over, starts ordering the guy around. He pulls out a gun. Trucker's all, grrr, actin' tough, getting the guy all intimidated, buttin' heads with the smartass crew kid. Me, I'm freaked. This wadn't supposed to be about hurtin' nobody. Quint just said he wanted to get to some other town where his cousin was meeting him."

"Who fired the gun?"

"Trucker. Quint's pushed the two dudes into a corner and he takes over driving. Tells Trucker to keep 'em under control. We go . . . I don't know how far . . . maybe like a half hour or more. Quint slows the boat down a little and tells Trucker to get rid of the two guys. Just like that. Just shoot 'em."

"What were you doing during all this?"

" 'sides freakin' out? Just watching the bags, man. Quint tells Trucker to shoot me if I let any of those bags go overboard. So I'm, like, watchin' them like a hawk—that guy's crazy, I'm finally figuring out."

Beau scribbled more notes. "You went out to sea? Along the coast?"

"Kind of along the coast, I guess. We was pretty far out there, but we could see the land all the time."

"Go on."

"So, like after he slows the boat down and tells Trucker to get rid of the guys, he just—bam! Kills 'em. Pushes 'em both over the side. Then we get the hell out of there."

"Who pulled the trigger?"

"Trucker."

"Then what?"

"We get a little closer to the land, but we're prob'ly still a few miles out. Quint's got the gun back by now. He pulls a bunch of plastic bags out of the suitcase—leaves the cash in the big bags, puts the baggies full of diamonds into one of them zipper pouch things you can strap on—a fanny pack. He makes me and Trucker pull the thingy that inflates the lifeboat, tells us get in it, then he roars off in the bigger one, the fishing boat."

"Any idea what time of day that was?"

Hank's face twisted as he concentrated. "Not really. Late afternoon, maybe. Didn't seem like no time at all and we was out there in the pitch dark."

Sam tried to imagine the feeling—alone and cold on a dark, roiling sea. Beau left the suspect with those thoughts and stepped out of the room. Back at Detective Lambert's desk, the two men compared notes.

"Ted Furns says that Quint was the shooter," Lambert said.

"Logical that both of these guys will deny it," Beau said. "But they were all present and all part of the crime. At least that's how it would be prosecuted in America."

"Yeah, here too."

"Did Trucker offer any information about how Quint might have gotten away?"

"Other than agreeing with what you just told me about Greenlee's information—that Quint took off in the trawler alone—not really. When I told him the trawler showed up here, empty, he speculated that maybe it ran out of gas and Quint abandoned it."

"But that doesn't work with the evidence, since your forensics people were able to start the boat right away."

"Right."

"So, we know more than we did, but somebody's lying."

Each trying to save his own skin—of course they were lying.

Chapter 14

Sam left the men to parse the interviews, telling Beau that she ought to check in at the bookshop at least once today. For all she knew, some elfin prankster might have painted the whole place purple or something.

But everything seemed to be in good shape when she got there. The front window display now held a variety of cookbooks in addition to the children's titles; two women browsing them stepped inside as Sam watched. Bridget was with an older woman, one Sam remembered from the day she learned that she'd inherited the place. Ambrose had two customers at the register, and Sam found Keeva in the back room.

"Look at this," the middle aged assistant exclaimed. "I'd quite forgotten we had these." She held up two paperbacks.

On the floor an open carton was filled to the top with new books.

"Don't know what I was thinkin'," Keeva said. "There seemed no room for more stock, I suppose, so this box got pushed to the back. By the receipt, I'd say they've been here more than six months."

Six months ago these were new releases in the US, Sam realized. But what did it matter? They were popular authors and would sell now.

"Let's get them on display," she said, picking up an armful and feeling a twinge of excitement.

In the sales room they cleared an end of one of the big tables. Sam found some small easels and propped up the top-name authors' books.

"I'll make another sign," Keeva said, rushing off to get her markers and poster board.

Sam stacked books and made sure the front covers showed well from across the room. Bridget sent her customer to the register, then she walked toward Sam.

"Could I have a word?" she asked.

Up close, worry was still evident on her face. Sam nodded and they walked together into the storage room.

"It's me dad," Bridget said. Her fingers twisted together in a painful-looking tangle as she spoke. "The oul fella's near frantic with worry. He's callin' the police every day for word on Uncle Darragh, but no one's saying. He doesn't eat and by the look of him I don't think he's sleepin' either. Does your husband know what they're doin' about this?"

Sam debated. She and Beau had not been following the local news and she had no idea how much information was being released.

"What have you heard?" she asked.

"Two men were in the lifeboat from the *Glory Be* . . . I guess the police have them now?"

"Yes, that's true. They are questioning the men but I don't know . . . I haven't heard anything that would lead to finding your uncle."

"But, is there any news at *all*?"

Sam wasn't about to get into the connections with the jewel heist in the States. She had no idea which bits of information Lambert was releasing and what he was keeping back, in hopes of pinning the suspects with their own admissions.

She sent Bridget a regretful look. "I'm afraid not. I'm sure the detectives will contact your family the minute they know anything."

"Darragh is my dad's twin, you know. It's killin' him, thinkin' the worst."

Sam reached out and took Bridget's hands, to offer comfort and to keep her from twisting her joints to shreds. "I know, hon. I'm so sorry I don't have a better answer for him."

Bridget drew a ragged breath and stood straighter. Her mouth clamped tightly, then released as she exhaled. "Thanks, Sam. If you learn anything new . . ."

"Sure." She squeezed the young woman's hands and released them. "Just take care of your dad in the meantime."

Bridget nodded and went into the tiny bathroom in back. Sam thought over the morning's interviews with the suspects but couldn't honestly come up with anything that would reassure the O'Henry family.

She busied herself rearranging the second display table while Keeva made lively looking signage to pull customers' attention to the products they most wanted to move.

"The place is looking quite good," Keeva said, as they

stood back and admired their handiwork awhile later.

Even Ambrose issued a grunt that almost sounded like approval.

"I was tellin' my sister, yesterday, about how the shop is coming along," Keeva said. "She said Mister O'Shaughnessy would have been proud. That's what Anna always called him—Mister O'Shaughnessy."

"He would, wouldn't he?" Sam mused, secretly happy that those who knew her uncle were approving of the changes. Well, maybe everyone but Ambrose. The jury was still out on that.

"You should invite Anna here to see for herself," Sam suggested.

"I will. Can't imagine how, but she seems busy as ever these days, even since Terry passed. You'd think she'd have all sorts of free time. I'll put the bug in her ear to come see how fine it all is now."

She set another poster in place. "For now, I'm going to put the kettle on. Are you up for a cuppa, Bridget?"

Bridget's petite heart-shaped face brightened and she followed Keeva into the back.

"What do you think, Ambrose?"

Sam watched the old man's expression soften just a touch. Somehow, some way she needed to break through that crusty exterior and get him on her side. She walked over to the counter where he sat in his usual spot at the register.

"I think my uncle would be very proud of you for keeping his business going." She said it quietly enough that the others wouldn't hear. "I'll need your help, you know. I have to leave in a week and, until I can figure out a long-term solution, I really need you to keep the business afloat."

He gave her a direct look. "I'd never do anything to sully Terry's memory."

"I know. I'm glad." She started to reach out to pat his arm but thought better of it. Ambrose still wasn't exactly a touchy-feely type.

Keeva saved the moment by appearing with a tea tray holding four mugs of strong black tea, a pitcher of milk and a plate of thin wafer cookies. Ambrose took a mug, declined the cookies and went back to adding up the credit card receipts for the day.

Sam finished her tea but found herself glancing at the time. Beau had hinted that he planned to put the romance back in their honeymoon with something special this evening, and she'd noticed him at the police station, making a couple of secretive phone calls.

Rain pelted her as she turned the corner, driven by a fierce wind off the sea. She grappled in her pack and realized she'd left her umbrella in the room this morning. Ducking her head, she concentrated on trying not to be run down by other pedestrians. By the time she passed the docks, the storm was a full-on gale and she was soaked to the skin.

"Ohmygosh!" she said with a huff when she got to the room. "I can't believe how fast this storm came up."

"Darlin', you should have called. I would have driven over to pick you up," Beau said, helping her out of her jacket.

"It wasn't this bad when I left the shop. It's okay. I'll dry off."

But he was already in the bathroom running a tub full of steaming water and dumping the tiny bottle of bath gel into it. She peeled off her clothes and climbed in, reclining with a sigh.

"Afraid my big plan for our romantic evening is getting messed up," he said from the other room.

Sam smiled anyway—it wouldn't matter, really, what they did.

"So, I've changed the location but kept the dinner plan," he said.

She could tell he was moving around in the room. At one point, a clatter followed by a mild curse made her smile.

"What's going on out there?"

"A surprise. Just hold on—I'll bring your robe." He leaned around the doorjamb, the collar of her robe dangling from his fingers. "Dinner's almost ready."

"That's good, because I'm almost a prune." She laughed as she stood up and reached for a towel. "Let me dry my hair and I'll be right out."

Five minutes later she walked into a transformed hotel room. She just wasn't quite sure what it had been transformed into.

The lamp from the desk glowed softly from the floor in one corner of the room, an orange piece of fabric, which looked suspiciously like one of Beau's shirts, draped over it. Otherwise, the room was in near darkness with the heavy curtains drawn. The bed had a woven throw tossed over the pure white duvet and a wicker basket sat in the middle of it. She caught the silly grin on his face.

"Beau?"

"It's our first date all over again." He patted the impromptu picnic blanket and she crawled onto the bed and sat cross-legged. "Except we weren't indoors, on a bed."

"We watched the sunset at the edge of the Rio Grande Gorge."

He pointed toward the orangey glow of the lamp. "Your sunset, madam. Afraid the bed has to represent the cliffs—the weatherman didn't cooperate on that little detail. But I think I've got the rest of it pretty close."

He reached into the picnic basket and pulled out a bottle of wine and some plastic containers.

"Beau! How did you get guacamole and tortilla chips here? And your special chile?" She peered into the containers and saw that everything was just as he'd made it for her the first time. Her eyes grew misty.

"A little combination of sneaking some items into my luggage and convincing the hotel chef that the recipe wasn't that hard to make." He opened the wine and handed it to her. "No glasses—remember, I forgot them the first time—we have to drink it right from the bottle. Okay, at least the first swig. Then I'll get you a glass."

"Beau, I love it. You are so . . ."

He pulled two wine glasses from the basket and poured.

"Samantha," he said, raising his glass, "you are the most wonderful woman I've ever known. You are pretty and smart and energetic and you've brought that energy into this perfect relationship, and you've made me a better man. A year ago I had no idea how good my life could be. I love you with all that I am and all that I have."

She blinked back the moisture in her eyes. "Beau, I—Saying 'me too' is way too simple, but it's how I feel. I've never been happier."

He held her gaze as their glasses clinked and they sipped at the woodsy red wine. She exclaimed over the chile (yes, it was wonderful and the chef did it *almost* as well as Beau). The guacamole and corn chips were a delightful treat, and soon he pulled her back against the pillows and made jokes about how that sunset in the corner just never seemed to end.

And although their first date didn't end naked in bed, this one did.

* * *

Sam woke the next morning feeling thoroughly satisfied—until the previous day's unanswered questions started to nag at her. She filed away all thoughts of the bookshop and of the interviews at police headquarters, snuggling instead into the perfect curve of Beau's arms.

Eventually, though, they both began to be restless so they showered and went downstairs for breakfast. The hotel's buffet had closed already so they ordered from the menu and sat at a table near the front windows in the nearly empty room.

Outside, a man in overalls swept up leaves and small branches ripped from the potted plants and hedges that fronted the property. It seemed the only evidence of the violent storm that had raged through the night. Otherwise, the deep blue sky boasted a brilliant sun which had already baked away the moisture from the sidewalks.

Against the far wall in the restaurant a television set was on and a newscaster's voice came through to Sam. She pointed toward the screen and Beau turned to see it.

"*. . . on scene now, as Search and Recovery personnel begin the arduous and dangerous job of bringing the bodies up the treacherous cliffs near Doolin.*"

Sam felt her breath catch. They'd driven right through that area.

A second voice chimed in, apparently the reporter at the scene. *"Yes, Janelle, and it will be quite some time. Police are on the scene but they are not saying whether they have any information about the deaths of the two. We've only been told that the victims are two males, and at this point we don't even know their ages."*

"Tragic, certainly, and it is perfectly understandable that families must be notified before names are released."

The on-scene reporter began to wind down, with promises to come back with new developments, when a familiar figure passed behind her. Detective Joe Lambert.

"He said there were new cases coming in every day," Sam told Beau as soon as their waiter set their plates down and moved away.

"I wonder. I think I'll give him a call later."

Neither of them said it, but both were thinking of Darragh O'Henry and Sean Bareth. They ate breakfast quietly and Sam could tell that Beau was impatient to learn what Lambert knew. When they went back to their room and Beau reached the detective's cell phone, Beau waved Sam over to listen so he wouldn't have to repeat all the information. It seemed that Lambert was happy to talk about it after he verified that the remains found on the rocky shore were indeed the two missing men from the *Glory Be*.

"The bodies are quite battered. Not a good sight for family members to come and identify," he said.

Sam thought of Bridget's father, Darragh's twin brother, and how hard this would be for him.

"However," Lambert was saying, "they both have gunshot wounds and the caliber seems to match that of the casing we found. Only the coroner can say if the shots were fatal or if the men died from the elements. Either way, there will be an inquest and it's murder charges for our two suspects. Leaving a man for dead out in the sea is as good as firing the fatal shot."

"What about the third man, Farrell?" Beau asked. "Isn't the FBI still after him?"

"I'm sure they would accept our help, but we're understaffed. The man might not even be in Ireland by now. He could have hijacked another boat and got his way to England or the Continent by this time." Lambert gave a frustrated sigh. "Right now my Chief Superintendent is pressing to charge the two we have and get on with it. Greenlee already said in questioning that Furns shot the captain. Furns may turn on Greenlee before it's all said and done, but I'm ready to put paid to the whole mess. Either way, doesn't matter who actually fired. They'll both go to prison and I'll have the time to work some of the other cases that are stackin' up on my desk."

Sam thought about the missing cash and diamonds and felt disappointed—she had pictured what it would be like to come across a bag of gemstones and open it to find all that dazzle.

Chapter 15

"I better call Bridget," Sam said when Lambert had hung up.

Before Sam found the listing among the thousand or so O'Henrys in the directory, the room's telephone rang. Bridget's small voice seemed tinier than ever.

"Beau and I are so sorry about your loss," Sam said. "Is there anything we can do?"

"Thank you. We'll get through it. Mum and Dad are at the funeral home now, making arrangements. The removal will be this evening. It's something like a viewing or a visitation in America, I think, if you'd like to come."

She gave the name of a funeral home and its location, which seemed easy enough to find. Sam promised to be there and ended the call with reassurances that Bridget not worry about taking a few days off work. She placed the receiver in its cradle and turned to Beau.

"So. Now what? The police are content with their suspects. And I'm not especially in the mood to go to the bookshop."

Beau had been shuffling the sightseeing brochures that had lain all week on the desk. "It would be a shame to waste a sunny day. Take a drive?"

They ran through some of the itineraries but most were day-long trips and they were already getting a late start. Getting back in time for the visitation might be tough.

"How about this walking tour through the city's historic areas?" she suggested. "It wouldn't hurt us to learn more about the town."

"And a charming old cathedral or fort would be more interesting than a police station."

"Well, I wasn't going to say it." She laughed and reached for her pack.

Beau pulled out the brochure and they oriented themselves, discovering that they could walk the two long blocks toward the train station and large park known as Eyre Square to start where the brochure's author suggested they should.

Most of Galway's population seemed to have the same idea about the beautiful day. The sidewalks were crowded and every restaurant that could eke out a space for outdoor tables had done so. They came to the popular square ringed by vendors with food stands and bright flags fluttering in the light breeze. Beau read from the brochure—the area had once been the public market and in medieval days was the site of public hangings. Over the years it was renovated many times and, in 1965, had been officially renamed for John F. Kennedy. They took a moment to read a plaque at the site of the old gallows before walking on.

"Watch ahead for a bank," Beau said, checking the brochure again. "It was actually a castle that dates back to the 1300s."

It was easy to spot and, once inside, Beau became fascinated with a series of panels that described the castle's history, but Sam found herself thinking again about her inheritance as they got closer to the shopping district.

"So, now that it appears the police are done with the mysterious *Glory Be*, I guess the other pressing thing is for me to decide what I'll do about the bookshop," Sam said as they left the bank and walked side by side along the wide pedestrian mall. "I brought the papers the lawyers want me to sign, but for some reason I haven't brought myself to do it yet."

"Isn't that their building?" Beau asked, pointing with his brochure toward the glossy black door beside the jewelry shop.

Sam stopped, regarded the door, felt disgusted with herself for being so indecisive. Even more so, she felt impatience with the whole situation and the lawyers for being so cagey about it. "Let's pop in," she told Beau. "I feel like a confrontation with Mr. Ryan."

"Good idea." He led the way and they walked into the law offices to find Mick O'Connor talking on the phone at the front desk. The receptionist was nowhere in sight.

"I'll call you back later," O'Connor said to whoever was at the other end. "Samantha, good to see you again."

She thought it came out much the same way he might tell his dentist he was happy to arrive at an appointment.

"I thought you were in London," she said.

"I was, and I'm due back there in the morning."

"I need to talk to you," she said with a glance toward the hall that led to the private offices.

"Sure, sure." O'Connor motioned for them to precede him. When they'd seated themselves he spoke again. "Now, what may I do for you?"

"I still want the copies of the shop's financial records. I should have the right to examine them in detail before agreeing to accept ownership."

The lawyer tented his fingertips and smiled warmly. "All the records will be yours, Samantha. It's no problem. But one of the provisions of the will is that you sign the agreement before taking possession of any of the assets. Those records are one of the assets. I am truly eager and willing to help you with this."

She felt her frustration rise again. "Mr. O'Connor— Let me donate the shop to the charitable trust my uncle set up. I don't need it for myself, I would be happy to help out a good organization . . ."

Beau piped up. "I'd like to know more about this charitable trust. You haven't even told us the name of it— what charity it benefits. There's no valid reason I can see to withhold the name and certainly no reason not to let Sam donate her portion of the inheritance to it. It's charity, for pete's sake."

It crossed Sam's mind that there might not be a charity— what if the lawyers had found a way to split the house and property away from the rest of the estate? But that didn't make sense either. They could have stolen it all without ever contacting her in the first place. She certainly would have never known the difference.

"All will be revealed, in time," O'Connor said, his friendly smile turning oily.

"There isn't much time," Beau said. "We leave Ireland in a few more days, and I'm pretty certain that my wife doesn't want to travel back here to haggle over this any further. If the estate has to go into some sort of court process, well, so be it."

For the first time, the lawyer's smile slipped a fraction.

"Good day, Mr. O'Connor," Beau said, rising.

Sam stood and they saw themselves out, ignoring the half-hearted sputters from the lawyer.

"He's definitely hiding something," Beau said once they were out of the building. "Did you see the way he put that smile quickly back in place but there was worry behind his eyes? He doesn't want to see the thing go to court, but he's under some kind of pressure to get you to sign those papers."

A band of steel tightened around Sam's head. "I need a coffee. Can we get something and just continue our walk?"

Nothing about this inheritance made sense, she thought as Beau went into a small café and ordered two takeaway coffees. Either the laws were very different here—a possibility—or her uncle's lawyers underestimated the American drive to understand what they were getting into. Or, perhaps Terrance O'Shaughnessy didn't have much of a head for business and really thought that his American niece would be so thrilled with the bequest that she wouldn't mind signing anything they asked of her. At any rate, the whole thing made her head pound.

"Here we go," Beau said, handing her a cup. "You okay?"

"Just a headache. Nothing that this coffee, three aspirin and being done with the bookshop wouldn't cure."

He steered her toward a bench in a shady spot near a

candy shop. "Do you have pain pills in your pack? I can go back in and get some water."

"I'll be all right. I should have known that I wouldn't get anything out of O'Connor. It's not like I haven't already tried that. I'll have to decide—maybe I should just sign the stupid papers and deal with the consequences later."

"I don't know . . ."

"Don't worry. I'm not doing anything rash. As you said, those guys want this thing finalized way worse than I do." She sipped the strong brew and felt her tension ease. "Let's finish our walking tour. Maybe there will be time for a quick nap before we have to change clothes and go to the funeral home."

By the time they'd seen two cathedrals and finished a nice lunch on Quay Street Sam's head was much better and she almost felt relaxed.

"Let's just head back to the hotel," Beau said. "The only thing on the walking tour that we haven't done is to walk out Nimmo's Pier." He pointed. It was the area where they had walked a few nights ago, this time teeming with people out to enjoy the wide grassy areas in the sunshine.

By the time they reached the Harbour, Sam felt her feet dragging. She pulled the drapes to darken the room, crawled under the duvet and was out almost immediately, leaving Beau to watch some kind of action show on TV with the volume turned to nearly nothing.

She awakened to a quiet room, Beau snoring softly beside her and she realized with a start that the viewing at the funeral home would begin in a few minutes. She rolled over to give Beau a gentle kiss before she got up and headed for the shower.

* * *

Funerals were so difficult. Sam cringed, all her life, every time she had to attend one, and it wasn't only the various church services that set her teeth on edge. Call it a funeral, memorial, wake or removal—it was the whole process of saying goodbye to someone you loved dearly or, as in this case, watching others stricken by grief.

A small crowd stood outside Hardiman's Funeral Home, mostly salty men with sun-creased faces who chatted in low tones and smoked cigarettes. Beau nodded to them as they passed through the group and walked up two stone steps into a room of dark wood paneling and plush carpet. Sam spotted Bridget and her mother, greeting newcomers and pointing them toward a side room where she caught a glimpse of a closed casket and several rows of padded chairs.

Bridget hugged Sam and shook hands with Beau. Maeve offered her hand and gave a stoic smile. "Dad's with Aunt Ava, in there," Bridget told them. "Sean's family are gathering in the other viewing room."

Sam's gaze followed the tilt of Bridget's head and she saw another space, identically set up. Beside the closed casket she could see a large framed photograph of a young man who looked barely out of high school, with blond hair and sparkling blue eyes. An innocent, after all. Sam felt a momentary twinge for having briefly suspected him.

"We'll go in and pay our respects," Beau said to the women, taking Sam's elbow.

"Thank you for coming," Bridget said.

William O'Henry's face had settled into a basset-hound arrangement of deep creases in recent days. His eyes looked puffy, more so than Sam remembered from their first meeting. He rose from his chair beside the casket and shook hands with both of them, thanking them for coming.

Next to him, a thin woman swathed in black introduced herself as Ava O'Henry. Darragh's widow's face clearly bore the ravages of recent days—waiting through days and nights when he was missing, to receiving the awful news yesterday. She raised tired eyes and accepted their condolences quietly.

Sam noticed that the other mourners would walk over to the polished wood box—some placing their hands on it—and pause for a few moments of prayer or silent thought. She followed suit, hoping during her private moment that those responsible for the fisherman's death would be brought to justice.

A girl of about thirteen pointed toward a side table where tea and sandwiches were being served. Sam accepted a cup of tea and when she spotted Ambrose, seated in a chair near the back of the room, she walked over to join him.

"Closed casket," he said with a jut of his chin toward the front of the room.

"I understand the body was—a little roughed up by the elements," she said under her breath.

A wrinkle formed across his forehead. "Wouldn't otherwise do it this way, would they?"

"Did you know Darragh O'Henry?" she asked.

"Not well. Only through Bridget and her father, really. But it would be an insult to the family if I hadn't at least stopped by." He popped the final bite of sandwich into his mouth. "The same for you, I imagine."

Sam nodded.

Ambrose carried his plate away and left without saying

anything more to Sam. He was out of sight by the time she thought that she might have asked him more about her uncle's funeral. Sam glanced around, realizing she'd lost track of her husband.

The viewing room had become crowded so she set her tea cup on a table full of empties and set out to find him. In the lobby Bridget and Maeve continued to greet newcomers. Sam spotted Beau near the door to the other viewing room, the one where Sean Bareth was laid out, speaking with an elderly man in a dark suit. By the white flower in his lapel and the discreet gold-tone name badge, she guessed he might be the funeral director. She walked over to join them.

"Ah, here's my lovely bride now," Beau said. "He noticed that we are American and asked about our stay in Galway. I'd just told him you were here because of an inheritance from your uncle."

Sam and Mr. Hardiman shook hands.

"You may have handled his funeral," she said. "Terrance O'Shaughnessy."

He blinked quickly. "Ah, yes, and his dear wife Maggie. He purchased a double plot so they would rest side by side, you know. She was a lovely woman, very active in the church I attend. She passed more than twenty years ago. Very sad for him."

"Where is the plot?" she asked.

"Kew Gardens, I believe." He sounded a little unsure.

She thanked him and they took a moment to express condolences to Sean's family before leaving.

"I want to go out to that cemetery," Sam said. "Let's drive out there."

Beau looked at the evening sky. "Wouldn't tomorrow be

better? By the time we find out where it is and then negotiate these streets, driving on the wrong side of the road . . .”

She saw the sense in waiting—a quiet evening at the hotel did sound inviting—but it was difficult to tamp down her impatience until morning.

Luckily, the good weather held and since Beau had spent part of the evening locating the graveyard on a map and plotting out the route, they arrived while the birds were still chirping a daybreak song from the many trees that rimmed the grassy area. A stone wall enclosed the few acres of neatly placed headstones, and a small building of the same material housed a little office. Sam tapped at the door and was almost surprised when it opened.

“I’m interested in locating the grave of a relative,” she said after they introduced themselves to an efficient-looking man in a suit and tie. Evidently, he dressed to impress the mourners more than the residents in perpetual rest.

When Sam gave Terry’s name, the man turned to a very modern metal filing cabinet and opened a drawer.

“Aye, it’s here. Mr. O’Shaughnessy purchased a double plot when his wife passed. He planned to occupy the other half when his time came.”

“Which was about six months ago,” Sam said.

He wagged his head back and forth. “I don’t have that in my records.”

“What do you mean?”

“The file here doesn’t show that we buried Mr. O’Shaughnessy.”

“Could he have changed his mind and opted for cremation?”

“I suppose it’s possible, but it’s not very common here.

Older people, especially, they're rather traditional in their
thinking, you know."

Sam thanked him somewhat absently as her mind was
reeling with the new information. No wonder Ambrose was
chafing over the treatment he felt Terrance had gotten at his
funeral. What kind of scam were the lawyers trying to pull
with her uncle's estate?

Chapter 16

Back in the car, Sam pulled out her cell phone. She had to get to the bottom of this. She punched in the number for Ryan and O'Connor, made her requests, hung up frustrated.

"Mick O'Connor is back in London," she told Beau. "Daniel Ryan is supposedly in a meeting. You heard me ask that he call back. Any bets on whether he will?"

He grinned at her and started the engine. "I'm not touching that one."

"Beau—do you think you could find Uncle Terrance's house again? Someone is caring for the place, or someone from the trust might be there. Maybe we can just bypass the lawyers and get a look around."

He'd started to back out of the small parking area at the cemetery but he pulled back into his spot and picked up the map.

"I remember that the street name was Woodgrove Lane. Seems the address was a low number . . . four hundred something, maybe?" She edged over to get a look as he ran his finger over the part of town that they remembered from their one trip there with Mick O'Connor.

"There's Woodgrove," he said. "It's not far from here."

He traced the route with his finger and put Sam in charge of navigation once they got on the road again. Some of the intersections on the map were roundabouts that were not well marked. After taking a wrong turn at one of them and asking a cyclist for clarification, they found themselves on Woodgrove Lane about thirty minutes after they set out.

Beau cruised slowly along, trying to spot house numbers, until Sam recognized the Tudor. He rolled to a stop at the curb.

"Look!" she said. "A car just pulled into the carriage house."

Sam leaped out of the rental car and made a dash, calling out as she approached. "Excuse me?"

The dark-haired woman stopped at the open garage door, a cloth bag over one arm and a plastic one in hand. Inside the old carriage house Sam saw another parked car, in addition to the one the woman had driven. The walls were lined with garden tools and expensive riding gear, all neatly hung up and organized. The woman looked up at Sam with a quizzical expression. Sam came up short—this surely was Keeva's sister.

"Are you Anna?" she asked, working to breathe normally after her little sprint. "I'm Samantha, Terrance O'Shaughnessy's niece. I've been working with your sister at the bookshop."

"Oh, yes," Anna said in a neutral tone. She glanced

toward the house but turned her back on it as Sam spoke.

"I was here the other day, with Uncle Terry's lawyer, looking for the business papers on the shop. I guess you weren't here at the time."

Anna continued to look at her.

"I told the man I wanted to see the rest of the house, but there wasn't time that day." Sam hoped she was fudging the truth well. "So . . . could I see it now?"

Anna's eyes darted back and forth as she searched for an answer. "I'm really not supposed—"

"Certainly. You want to keep the place clean and in good condition for the trustees, I'm sure. But I'm a relative and I was named in the will. I can show you my identification."

"That's all right. I believe you. It's only that . . ." Anna's thought trailed off and she finally gave a what-the-heck shrug. She thumbed through the keys on the ring in her hand and aimed one of them for the lock on the back door. "Follow me."

The door opened into a service room, lined with wood shelving that held packaged household goods and large cooking pots. From there they entered the kitchen, modern by 1960s standards. Anna set her packages on a worktop and turned to Sam and Beau.

"Well, I'm not certain what there is to see. It's never been a grand house, by any means. I believe it was built around the 1930s and updated sometime later, when Mr. and Mrs. O'Shaughnessy bought it. I understand they never had children, so it was a somewhat large place for the two of them. I never knew her, myself. Only came to work for the mister here near the end."

"Thank you," Sam said. "On behalf of our family, we're grateful that you were here for him."

Anna actually blushed. "Well, here's the kitchen, as you can see."

She opened a door into a large, formal dining room and let them take a peek. "These are the back stairs," she said, turning to a smaller door at one end of the kitchen, "up to the bedrooms."

Sam started up them and Anna quickened her pace to lead the way. A long hall spanned the house.

"These doors were always kept closed," Anna said. "They go to bedrooms and bathrooms. A nursery that was never used."

Sam opened a door and peered in, seeing an average-sized room furnished with quality furniture as a guest room.

"They're all about the same. Quite nice, but not grand." Anna opened a linen closet and showed them a small sewing room. "Ah, here we are at the main staircase."

She clutched the newel post, ushering Sam and Beau toward the stairs. A series of botanical prints lined the wall on the way down and they found themselves in the foyer where they'd entered on their previous visit, facing the leaded glass front door.

Anna waved an arm in each direction. "Formal parlor, there. Dining room, just there. And at the back, a garden room—I suppose the English would say it's a conservatory. It leads out to the gardens in back. Of course, by the time I came here Mr. Terry wasn't well enough to go out much."

"What do you think the trustees of this charity will do with it?" Sam said.

"Oh, I've no idea. Don't know much about that at all. I'm just to keep the place dusted and tidy until someone comes along, I suppose."

They passed the closed door to Terry's study on their

way to the front door. Sam stopped and opened it.

"There was something in this room that caught my eye the other day," she said to Anna. "May I take a look?" She headed for the bookcases without waiting for permission.

She hadn't imagined it. There, behind glass, was the box. Carved of wood in a quilted pattern, with small stones mounted at the intersection of each X in the carving. It was about double the size of hers—the box given to her by the old woman in New Mexico. Otherwise, the two were nearly an identical pair. Sam felt the breath go out of her.

The old woman had told Sam on her deathbed that the box was destined to be hers. That with it she would be able to accomplish good things. When she'd first handled it, though, the thing had sent something akin to an electric shock through her. And her life had not been the same since. Had the Irish uncle, about whom she'd known nothing, also been destined to receive one of these? The hairs on her arms prickled.

"Can you open this glass door?"

"Sorry, I don't have a key," Anna said, looking as if she wanted to herd Sam out of the room.

"Maybe there's one in the desk." Sam started to turn toward it but Anna was in the way.

"I've never seen one in there."

Sam edged past and pulled the center drawer open. Pens and pencils, an eraser, a notepad, a small calculator. She pawed through the drawer and the one adjacent to it. No key.

"Sam?" Beau's voice caught her attention from across the room. "Maybe we better be going and let Anna get back to her work?"

The woman *was* looking a bit flustered and Sam realized

that she'd probably come on way too strong.

"Sorry. Of course. We'll let you get back to your day."

Beau and Sam walked out to the car. "You were awfully quiet in there," she said as he opened her door.

"Just taking it all in."

"Did I get out of line in the study, trying to get into that bookcase?"

"You were pretty enthusiastic," he said with a chuckle. "What was in there anyway?"

How could she explain being drawn to a carved object and the possibility that it could contain the same kind of magic as the one she already owned? More to the point, since she didn't especially want the responsibility of the wooden box she had now, why on *earth* would she want another?

"Just a keepsake," she answered.

"Well, I suppose if we can ever find out who to contact with this charitable trust, you might ask if they would trade their keepsake for a cute little old bookshop."

She laughed because he expected it, but she felt oddly drawn to the suggestion.

"Look at that," Beau said, aiming a finger at the dashboard clock in the car. "What time is the funeral?"

Sam had forgotten her promise to Bridget that they would come to the wake, which was being held at Darragh's home. What had she been thinking? Now they were locked into the Mass and burial as well, since they had no idea where the O'Henry home was or how to get there unless they followed the other mourners. The series of remembrances started at two o'clock.

Beau steered back toward the hotel, where they quickly changed into their only somber clothing and they left again, heading for the cathedral across the river. After the formal service, the graveyard seemed full of quiet weeping as William O'Henry gave an emotional eulogy honoring his twin, not shirking the fact that Darragh had died before his time, at the hands of violence. Sam found herself holding her breath in hopes that he wouldn't talk about how it was Americans who'd killed him. He didn't.

Keeva edged near to Sam at the adjoining cemetery. "If you'd like to ride with me to their home, you're both welcome."

Sam glanced at Beau, who suggested they could follow Keeva in their own car. Relief. At least they could leave on their own schedule.

Darragh's and Ava's third floor apartment demonstrated to Sam exactly how alike the twin brothers had been. Similar floor plans and furnishings, even a familiar smell to the place—furniture polish and lavender. Sam had noticed the resemblance between their wives when she met Ava at the funeral home but now, seeing the two talking quietly in one corner of the living room, she realized that they even chose the same style of clothing.

Beau had remained behind to say hello to the men who'd gathered outside the front door, so Sam signed the guestbook for both of them. The home exuded mourning—draperies drawn shut, mirrors covered in black cloth, hushed voices. Women in the small kitchen were organizing sandwiches on platters and slicing cakes that had apparently been brought in by neighbors.

Keeva had walked upstairs with Sam and she spotted her sister across the room. Anna walked over to join them.

"I wanted to thank you again," Sam said, "for being my uncle's caregiver. I know you must have been a comfort to him. And thanks for showing us around the house earlier. I'm sorry if I said the wrong things, there in the study."

Anna gave a sideways glance toward Keeva.

"It's not a problem. Mr. O'Shaughnessy has always been a pleasure to work for. A fine man."

Despite her words, she seemed a little uneasy around Sam. Or maybe it was simply a restless energy that had the woman bouncing slightly on the balls of her feet. She excused herself the minute Bridget walked up.

"Sam, thanks for coming," Bridget said. "It means a great deal to my family."

She edged her eyes toward her father who seemed eager to get out of the houseful of women and join the men downstairs.

Sam offered one of those standard platitudes—if we can do anything to help—but felt completely inadequate in the presence of their grief.

"He'll be wantin' his stout—I'll be right back." Bridget went into the kitchen and emerged with a bottled drink that she handed to her dad.

Sam made her way over to say hello again to Ava and Maeve, the two brothers' wives, who were standing near the laden dining table although neither of them had a plate or cup for herself. Maeve pressed Sam to accept tea, but then Sam found herself hanging at the fringes of the room, knowing only a handful of people in the crowd and unable to escape until she'd finished the beverage.

"There," said Bridget. "He seems more at ease with the men." She'd obviously walked downstairs with her father and come back up. Her petite features were flushed pink.

"Dad seemed a bit put out with Deirdre Athy, however. I hope she— Oh yes, there she is," Bridget said, craning her neck and spotting a blond woman who'd come into the living room. "Have you met her?"

Sam recognized the name of Darragh's office employee from the information that Detective Lambert had passed along to Beau.

"No, we haven't met," she told Bridget. "Introduce us?"

Bridget signaled Deirdre over and performed the niceties. Sam registered a woman in her forties with coppery blond hair and features hardened by weather and perhaps a bit of a rough life. The smell of cigarette smoke wafted off her clothes as they shook hands.

"Your husband the tall chap outside?" she asked. "The one workin' with the Garda?"

Sam nodded. "I guess they've caught their suspects already. I hope that's good news for everyone."

Deirdre asked Bridget for a bottle of the stout and when the younger woman had left she told Sam. "I hope so. I tell you, I'm not looking forward to giving evidence in court. But I know I'll have to. They tell me I was the only one to see them when they hired the boat. Well, aside from Darragh and Sean, of course."

Her voice was a little too loud and Sam noticed that Ava's mouth tightened.

Sam sent a weak smile in her direction and turned the conversation to the fact that the weather had been very nice the past couple of days.

Deirdre accepted the bottle Bridget brought her, and went into a little lament about how she expected that she would need to start looking for a job now.

Maeve and Ava were both staring in their direction now.

"Deirdre, would you like to walk downstairs with me?" Bridget offered. "It seems a bit stuffy in here."

Sam wished she'd thought of that sooner. She set her teacup down and followed them. When they reached the sidewalk, Bridget steered Deirdre down the street, pleading the need for a walk.

William O'Henry's voice caught her attention. "How can they let the third man get away?" he demanded. Sam noticed he was talking to Beau, but a half-dozen others milled around.

"One of the suspects they have in custody has already named the other as the one who fired the shots."

"And I'd like to know how those Americans got a gun into the country anyway," said another man, one Sam didn't recognize.

That led to some back-and-forth about how nearly all the guns in Ireland were hunting rifles, few handguns, so the Americans must have somehow brought theirs with them. A good question, Sam thought as she stood at Beau's side, listening, but she also thought it was a little naïve to think that a criminal couldn't get hold of a gun anywhere if he really wanted one.

William O'Henry let the others go off on that tangent; he pulled Beau aside and spoke quietly.

"Please help us," he said, his voice tinged with desperation. "Even if they put the two away, we know there was this third man and we know he was aboard the *Glory Be*. He was involved. He should be brought to justice, too. It just isn't right."

Chapter 17

"What could I tell him?" Beau said that evening as he pulled his boots off in their room at the Harbour. "I tried making the point that I don't have jurisdiction here or the time to really pursue this case."

"And then he begged . . ." She teased, reaching into the safe and putting her bracelet and earrings into the wooden box. A quick memory of its larger twin flashed by.

"He did. And then when we went back in the house and the widow—"

"Ava."

"Yes. She came up and thanked me because William said I would be trying to gather more information that the local police were ignoring."

"Did you set her straight? Or did you actually agree? I didn't hear that part of the conversation."

His expression said it all. He was never one who could ignore someone in need. But there was something else, some little thing she couldn't quite read.

"Beau . . . what's the rest of it?"

He pulled on pajama bottoms. "Well, the office employee. Deirdre, I think was her name?"

Sam nodded.

"She was getting a little drunk there near the end, didn't you think? Well, she said something that I'm not sure anyone else caught. She'd been yammering on about what she'd seen on the local news, about how there was still an unknown suspect out there who might be tied to a big jewel robbery in America."

"I didn't realize they'd released the connection." Sam crawled between the sheets.

"Me either. We've stayed pretty busy without watching much TV news." He gave her a little leer.

"Beau—on topic."

"She was rambling on, but what I picked up from it was that these gypsy groups that move around the country— what did that other lady call them?—the Travellers? Anyway, Deirdre made it sound like common knowledge that they're involved with fencing stolen property at times."

Sam remembered the brightly colored wagon they'd seen after their drive down the coast.

"Anyhow, a few pieces slipped into place—Quinton Farrell supposedly having relatives in Ireland, needing a source for fencing the jewelry he's carrying around with him . . ."

"And you don't suppose the FBI has figured this out yet?"

"Most likely they have. But who knows? Maybe I can do

a little checking and give them the tip that would help break the case open."

"Tomorrow, though—not tonight."

"Not tonight."

She rolled toward him and slid her fingers around the waistband of his pajama bottoms. "Okay, *now* we can change the subject."

* * *

Beau woke the next morning and declared that he would like to talk more with Deirdre Athy while they had the chance. Not exactly the ideal follow-up to their tender night, but Sam had to admit that she was also curious what Darragh's former employee might have to say. They found her only a couple of blocks from their hotel, at the offices of O'Henry Fishing Charters, loading a cardboard box with her personal items, a lit cigarette dangling from one side of her mouth. There were puffy bags under her eyes but she seemed otherwise unaffected by the quantity of liquor she'd consumed at the wake.

"Hi, Deirdre," Beau said, leaning in through the glass door he'd pushed half open.

"Well, hello yourself, handsome sheriff." A tendril of smoke went straight into her eye so she set the cigarette against the edge of an ashtray on the desk. "Howarya today?"

He ignored the comment and Sam edged forward to stand beside him. Beau eyed the carton and eased into the conversation by saying they'd been sorry to hear that Deirdre was losing her job.

"Yeah, well, I guess that happens." She dropped a

potted plant on top of the collection in the box. "I've found another one already. Another boat captain. His wife isn't crazy about the idea but he needs the help and *she* don't want to answer phones all day. Too menial, I guess, for herself. All I have to do is carry my junk over across the way there and I start the job this morning."

Beau nodded. "Look, I know you've been over this a lot of times but could I ask you a little more about those men who chartered the *Glory Be* that day?"

She gave a weary knock-yourself-out kind of shrug.

"So," he said, "two men came in and said they wanted to go fishing."

She nodded.

"Tell me what you remember about them."

It sounded like a rote recital of facts she'd already repeated too many times. "Two guys, one black, one white— nice tats on that one." Deirdre raised an eyebrow in Beau's direction, until Sam cleared her throat. "Gave their names as Smith and Jones. I wasn't paid to ask questions about that kind of stuff. Then they tell me they want to fish up around the northern shores of the Bay, but I kind of laugh and say they were misinformed, fishing's difficult there— Darragh won't go to places where he's likely to lose all his gear tangled up in rocks. They kind of looked at each other and then decided to leave it up to the captain where to take them. They handed me cash for a full day's trip."

"Euros or dollars?"

"Dollars. I told 'em there would be a fifty-dollar fee for exchanging them. Humph, basically for my trouble to walk down to the bank. Hey, why not? They didn't question it."

"Did you see a third man?"

"Might have." She tilted her head toward a window.

Sam noticed for the first time that the *Glory Be* was in view just down the pier from the office.

"I usually kept an eye open, to see when the boat actually left harbor. Sometimes Darragh would forget to radio his time out, and I was supposed to track it and make sure they were back before their petrol would have run out."

"And when they didn't come back by that night you were the one who reported it and sent the coast guard out looking?" Sam asked.

Deirdre nodded.

"So, this third man. Tell me about him," Beau said.

"Not much to tell. He came walking up to the boat, pulling a bag like those kind you take on the airplane. That looked kind of funny. There was a little conversation amongst them. Darragh must have said it was all right. He had enough gear for everyone to fish. The new guy went aboard and they sailed."

Beau pulled out the photo of Quinton Farrell; Sam hadn't realized that he'd kept it. Deirdre nodded—that was the man.

"Have you seen him again since the *Glory Be* sailed out that day?"

"Nope." Deirdre stubbed out the burned-down cigarette and got busy with her desk supplies again.

Sam and Beau walked back to the hotel's parking garage and retrieved their rental.

"You didn't ask her about these Travellers," Sam said as Beau backed out.

"I had planned to, but did you see her reaction when I asked whether she'd seen Quinton Farrell since the day the boat went out? She was lying through her teeth."

He was certainly observant.

"In case she is in touch with him, I didn't want her knowing where we're going next."

"And where is that, dear husband?"

"I asked a few questions at the hotel desk before you came down this morning. There's a town not far away, T-u-a-m—the clerk pronounced it something like toom—where supposedly there's a big encampment of these Travellers. She showed me on the map," he said, raising the folded sheet. "I also learned that not all of the Travellers move around all the time anymore. The government has even provided them with 'halting places' where they can live semi-permanently. The lady said the effort is to get them to put their kids in school, but they've tried laws like that for decades and it hasn't completely changed their ways."

He handed Sam the map and she studied it to become oriented to their destination. Once they were on the open road she remembered what she wanted to ask him.

"So, do you get the feeling that Deirdre might have actually helped the men? Aided and abetted, or something like that?"

"I don't know, darlin'. I wouldn't think so—but I wouldn't rule it out either. She definitely knew more about Farrell than she was saying."

"Then again, maybe it's only that she found him attractive or something and didn't want to admit that. Sometimes women are funny about those things."

He sent a grin her way before focusing his attention again on the two-way traffic on the N17 highway.

"Hey, at least we're getting to see a bit more of Ireland, all in the name of helping Bridget's family."

The approach to Tuam started out much like any other town in any other place—a scattering of light industrial businesses, some automotive shops and gas stations, as the concentration of traffic grew heavier. The car ahead of them passed a slow-moving tractor and Beau tensed as it became clear he would have to make the same move. Passing on the right, with oncoming traffic, still wasn't coming naturally to him. He finished the maneuver and they began to see residences along the sides of the road, sturdy square two-stories with steeply pitched roofs and chimneys at both ends.

A traffic light, a roundabout, the sight of a tall church spire in the distance—and traffic that was quickly becoming congested. Sam kept checking the map, but since they weren't entirely sure of their destination Beau stayed with the majority of other drivers and headed toward the town center on Ballygaddy Road. It soon narrowed to a squeeze with parked cars along the sides and small shops lining the sidewalks.

"This doesn't exactly look like the area where a bunch of mobile people in caravans would be living, does it?" Beau said.

"We could stop and take in some of the shops and then ask someone where we might find them."

Tuam, it turned out, also had a Shop Street and they lucked into a parking space in front of an antiques store.

"Cute, huh?" Sam said. The stone buildings weren't so different from those in Galway, but maybe the shops were appealing because of the fact that she didn't have to own and operate any of them.

It felt good to stretch their legs and they found themselves keeping up a good pace as they walked by shops and pubs and came to another intersection.

"That direction looks like it becomes residential again,"

Beau said, pointing toward a block of row houses in subdued grays and tans that sat against the sidewalk.

"I saw a spot down one side street that might have possibilities for lunch."

"And directions."

"I'm glad you didn't make me be the wife who has to suggest stopping to ask."

His hand on the back of her neck gave a soft, loving squeeze and she led him toward the open door of a cozy little pub. Inside, the barman took their orders for sandwiches. They were early, they realized, when they discovered they were alone in the place. By the time they'd finished their sandwiches, the few tables had filled and most of the stools at the bar were occupied.

"The guy behind the bar is hopping," Beau said. "I feel guilty asking him to look at the map right now."

Sam scanned the room. "There's a woman at the bar who doesn't have her food yet. Maybe I can ask her."

She picked up the map and opened it. The young dark-haired woman looked up as she approached.

"Excuse me? Could I ask a favor?" She spread the map and explained what they needed.

"Why'd you want to visit them?" the local woman asked. "Just curious. Not many Americans even know the Travellers exist."

"Some friends in Galway suggested we look them up."

"Yeah, well they do make some pretty things. If you go to this area here," she said, indicating with her finger, "you'll see their caravans. They keep pretty much to themselves, but sometimes the old men have stands set up and the women sell crafts and such."

"What's the shortest route?"

The woman took Sam's pen and drew in the turns they should make. Beau watched over Sam's shoulder and nodded as if he knew exactly where to go.

A man's voice intruded. "Goddam knacks. They'll steal you blind, and then they want government services while they pay no taxes toward their keep. Oughtta boot 'em off the dole and send 'em right back wherever they come from, you ask me."

"Watch your mouth," said the barkeep. "We don't need no cursin' and no commentary, Maguire. Everybody knows your opinion already."

"Sorry," the young woman said quietly. "Not everyone around here likes the Travellers much."

"Much?" said old Maguire. "Worthless gypsies, they are."

Chapter 18

S ounds like a sore spot," Beau said as they walked back
to their car.

As he negotiated the series of turns that took them
away from the city center, Sam wondered what they
might be getting themselves into. But when they located
the place, it looked like an ordinary trailer park—perhaps
more crowded than some in America, a mixture of mobile
homes, travel trailers and small motorhomes packed into
close quarters. Interspersed in the sea of metal were a half-
dozen or so of the colorfully painted wagons like they'd
seen near Ballyvaghan. An old man worked under shelter
of a three-sided metal shed, pounding on something with a
wooden mallet.

"Hi, can I help you?" he said, his dark eyes twinkling
under the brim of a flat cap. He continued to knock away

at the narrow band of metal while he spoke, shaping it into a smooth curve.

"We're looking for a family called Farrell," Beau said, doing his best to look unofficial. "Do you know of them?"

The man took the curved metal strip and fitted it against the side of a cylindrical container. Sam could see that it would soon be a teapot.

When he spoke again, all he said was, "Maybe." He gave Beau the eye and tapped the metal strip a few more times to adjust the fit.

"I like your work," Sam said. "Do you sell them?"

"Some. Some's for home. The missus uses an entire set of my pans." He waved his mallet toward one side wall of the shack where two shelves were full of finished pieces.

"Would you sell me one of the teapots?" she asked, belatedly wondering how she would fit it into her suitcase. Well, she would think of a way.

The price he quoted was no bargain, but she was paying more for information than for a teapot. She fished out some money and chose the pot she wanted. He gave her a wide smile, and Sam noticed that he had no upper front teeth. His lively eyes and ready smile caused Sam to smile back, and it was almost as if they'd both heard the same joke. He laughed as he put the finishing touches on the handle for the newest teapot.

"Now about them Farrells you're wantin' to find . . ." Tap-tap-tap. "Half the community is over't the church this afternoon, there bein' a big weddin'. You might find 'em there."

She started to ask directions but Beau gave a little stab at the air with his index finger and she spotted a cathedral spire rising a block or two away, behind a thick stand of trees. She thanked the old man and hugged the new teapot close to her chest. He lit up once more when he saw how much she appreciated his work. She chuckled as they walked back to the car.

"Are we up for a wedding?" Beau asked. "We're not exactly dressed for it."

"Beau! We can't just go crashing it. Plus, I have a sneakier idea."

She pulled her camera out of her pack, along with a small travel journal where she'd been jotting notes about their travels. Sadly, she discovered, she hadn't made a new entry in four days.

"I'm an American travel writer," she told Beau. "You are my camera-dude."

"Sam . . . what kind of trouble—"

"Just find that church."

Doing so wasn't exactly rocket science. He kept the spire in view until it got blocked by a row of buildings, but as soon as they came to an intersection they spotted a hugely long white limo pulling to the curb in front of the gray stone edifice. Sam raised an eyebrow toward Beau but his concentration was on finding a parking spot. She glanced back toward the limo, where a coterie of young women in brilliant turquoise dresses began to emerge onto the sidewalk. This, surely, wasn't a welfare family.

"Let me out here if you need to," Sam said. "I think I've got my story angle."

She slung her pack over one shoulder and clutched her notebook and a pen as she got out of the car and nearly got run down by a vehicle coming unexpectedly from the right.

A pause, it passed, and she dashed across to the front of the church. By the time she got there four bridesmaids were gathered around and the star of the show was stepping from the long car. A patient mother stood to one side, her own dress a palette of vivid blues and greens.

"I love the dresses," Sam said to the older woman. "Do you suppose we might get a few pictures, maybe ask a couple of questions for our magazine in the U.S.?"

The woman regarded her for a long moment, apparently decided she wasn't spoofing them, and nodded.

"Are you the mother of the bride? You actually look much too young to have a grown daughter."

Okay, it was hokey flattery at best, but when Sam saw how young the bride was she pretty much understood. The young woman in white couldn't have been more than seventeen. She glanced toward her mother as the other girls worked at arranging the billows of white satin. A much younger girl, probably a sister, of about ten was dressed in a downsized version of the bride's dress.

"Who is the little one?" Sam asked.

"Oh, she's the mini-bride," said the mother with pride. "All the girls want them nowadays. She gets to dress the same as the bride and carry her flowers and help her until she's ready to walk the aisle."

Sam watched as the ten-year-old mimicked her older sister's moves.

"My photographer should be along any second," Sam said, searching above the heads for sight of Beau. "Would it be all right if I asked a question or two first?"

The young bride noticed Sam's notebook. She drew her shoulders back a little, clearly enjoying her moment in the limelight. Sam gave a one-sentence rundown about how Americans knew so little about the Irish Travellers and how fascinated they would be to know more about the lifestyle, especially the weddings.

The bride preened a little as she explained that the crown holding her veil was made of real diamonds—Swarovski—and that she'd dreamed of this gown and this day since she was a very young girl. Sam supposed it was one of those things that transcended all cultures—girls and their wedding dreams.

Beau showed up just then and Sam had him snap pictures of the bride alone and then the entire procession as all the young women lined up to enter the church. As they walked away, Sam noticed another female standing at the edge of the gathering.

"I'm sorry," Sam said. "I meant to ask the bride's name. For my article on Travellers."

The woman gave a friendly smile. She wore a red skirt and low-cut black top that showed off her ample endowments, went heavy on the eye makeup and the professional sun-streaks in her hair. "Gilmore," she said.

It would have been way too lucky to find the Farrells this easily. "Are you—?" Sam tilted her head toward the wide church doors, where the bride's skirt was being squeezed by her attendants to fit through.

"Oh, no. I'm not a guest. Not all Travellers are automatically invited to every event for the others. I'm Saoirse, by the way."

It sounded like sare-sha and Sam had to ask her how to spell it.

"Sorry," Sam said. "I'm really new to Ireland and the Travellers."

"And you'll not be hearing an accurate story if you ask about us among the settled people. There's so many wild stories—we're stupid and lazy and thieves. The men have nothin' better to do but fight and the women stay preggers all the time. It's total rubbish. So what— our women don't generally have careers. La-di-da. We think it's more important to be good wives and good mothers. And, yeah, a lot of our kids don't do much schoolin'. What do they need it for? The teachers treat 'em rude because we don't stay in one place forever like the settled people do."

Sam realized that the woman thought she was being interviewed for a magazine article so she hastily scribbled a few notes. For good measure, she asked Beau to take Saoirse's picture.

"And so what if we take advantage of the dole if we need it? That's what it's there for." A chime sounded and the woman pulled a cell phone out of her bag. "A message from me daughter," she said as she put it away. "She's havin' her second baby in a month or so."

Sam consulted her notes. "Someone in Galway suggested that we contact a family here named Farrell—do you know them?"

"We've just recently arrived in Tuam, ourselves," Saoirse said. "Come along with me, if you'd like. I can introduce you to someone."

A picture of being abducted by gypsies flashed through Sam's mind.

"It's all right," Saoirse said with a pleasant laugh. "We none of us bite."

She hitched her large red bag up to her shoulder and, with an eye on the traffic, started back toward the trailer encampment. Sam and Beau exchanged a look then headed after her. She passed through the opening in the walled area and wound her way among the haphazardly parked vehicles. Finally, she halted beside a relatively modern small motor home, a little battered and rusty at the edges.

"This is mine," she said. "My husband is off for the day, checkin' out a car that a man wants to sell. My son's all eager to learn to drive and we're not startin' him with the caravan, for certain."

Sam remembered her notes for the supposed magazine piece she was to be writing. "I'm curious about something," she said. "The huge wedding—the fancy dresses, the limousine and all that. How do people who seem to come from modest means . . . well, how do they manage it?"

"A girl's weddin' is the biggest day of her life," Saoirse said. "Every woman remembers how special it is, bein' treated like a princess. *Bein'* a princess, for that one day. Those of us with daughters, we save every penny we can put by to give our girls the kind of day they'll remember."

If the rest of a young woman's life would be spent in one of these small conveyances, moving from town to town, it did seem pretty important to start married life with the one little speck of glamour she would likely ever enjoy. Sam made a few more notes. Maybe she really would write some kind of story about all this.

"Oh, here's Cian now," said Saoirse, nudging Sam.

He walked with the duck-like gait of a barrel-chested man who was no stranger to his Guinness. Forty-ish, black hair trimmed very short, ruddy cheeks and vivid blue eyes— he greeted Saoirse heartily.

"Meet some new American friends," she said. "The lady is writing for a magazine, about Irish Travellers."

"Is she now? Interestin'. How're you finding Ireland?"

"It's beautiful," Sam said. "We've taken a lot of pictures.

Would it be all right if we took yours? And maybe some of the homes too?"

One of the old-style wagons was parked immediately next to Saoirse's place, and Cian told them it was where he lived with his father. Beau caught a few shots of the bright red and yellow wagon and Sam confirmed the spelling of Cian's name—she'd mistakenly thought it was Kane. The Gaelic spellings would confound her forever, she decided.

"They're lookin' for Farrells," Saoirse told Cian. "I told 'em I'm new here but you or your father would know."

"Yeah, Farrell—they've been around for awhile. Why d'you ask?"

"There was an American by that name who recently came to Ireland," Beau said. "We lost touch and thought he might have made contact with family members here."

Cian shrugged. "Could be. Could be."

Saoirse's phone chimed again and she excused herself to go into her coach and take the call.

"Come," Cian said, "meet my father. He knows a lot about the people. Real savvy man."

They followed as he approached the wagon and gave two solid knocks at the door. "Da there's company," he called out.

A small window set in the door opened and a white head poked out. "What's the noise?"

"Da we got guests. From America."

Sam could tell at a glance that the small wagon would be jam-packed with four people inside, especially if Cian's father proved to be as stocky as his son. She wasn't surprised when their host steered them toward a collection of mismatched chairs on the patch of ground that passed for their yard. A large wooden spool, the kind used for rolls of industrial wire, served as a table.

The elderly man stepped outside and worked his way carefully down the wooden steps. He stood about five feet tall, wiry and thin as a whip. The sharp blue eyes were his only feature in common with his son. They took in everything about Sam and Beau at a glance.

They shook hands and Cian gave the story about how Sam was writing an article about Irish Travellers. He introduced his father as James Barlow.

"We were told that an American named Farrell might have family among the Travellers and we wondered if you may have seen him?" Beau asked.

Sam realized that the description of Quinton Farrell might easily fit half the men of the community—the ones they'd spotted so far were all similar.

"What's he done?" James asked, a sharp edge to his voice.

Neither responded right away.

"This Farrell you're lookin' for. What's he done?"

"Well, we're not sure," Beau offered.

"You may be a writer," James said to Sam, "but you, sir, are no photographer. You're a lawman." He raised a palm against any protest. "I can smell 'em a mile away. You're a lawman."

Had they walked into some kind of setup? Sam felt her nerves tighten.

But then James laughed—a good, hearty laugh.

"You've heard the stories, I'm bettin'. Travellers are all crooks and thieves, eh?"

Cian piped up. "It's bull! We're no more thieves than anybody out there."

Protesting too much? Sam glanced toward Beau but his

face was unreadable.

James laid a hand on his son's forearm. "Calm yourself down, boy. We're not, but there's some's are. Don't get yourself all bothered."

Cian clamped his mouth shut.

"Now, then," said James. "The Farrells. Like with any family in any place, there's good ones and bad ones. Happens that a few of the boys in this particular area, they've got their hands in some, shall we say, money-makin' operations."

Cian sent his dad a look, as if to warn him away from saying too much about making money.

"They sell things what ain't rightly theirs, boy. That's all I'm sayin'."

Cian sat back in his chair and folded his arms.

"So, mister lawman," James continued, "again I ask— this Farrell you're lookin' for—what's he done?"

Beau gave a sigh, propped his arms against his thighs, and gave the story. Only the basics, Sam noticed—the man was wanted for theft in the US, he and two cohorts had chartered a boat in Galway and were now wanted in the death of the captain.

James nodded as Beau talked. "Aye, we heard about it."

Sam's face must have registered surprise because he gave her a wry smile.

"We may live simple out here but we're not on the moon. We got television. We watch the news."

She responded with a properly-chastened smile.

"It was that Darragh O'Henry, wasn't it?" Cian asked, leaning forward again. "The one they're sayin' died after he took the Americans out on his boat."

"Right. That's the one."

"And what makes you so sure he wasn't the man workin' with this Farrell from America? Around here the story goes that O'Henry was supposed to help Farrell and get a cut of the money."

James glared at his son. "It's no matter anyway," he grumbled. "Farrells packed up yesterday and left. They're not in Tuam anymore."

Chapter 19

Seriously? Darragh would put his boat and his life at risk and get involved with Quint Farrell?" Sam found herself puffing a little to keep pace with Beau as they walked back to the spot where they'd parked their rental car.

"I didn't say it was true, darlin'. I said I would have to check it out. For sure I would check it out before I said anything to the family."

"Absolutely. At best, it's hearsay. And who knows—maybe the Barlows and the Farrells have some old feud or something. There's no way we could even scratch the surface of the history of that group."

They reached the car and he opened her door.

"Plus, as James Barlow said—the Farrells left the camp and lord only knows where they've gone."

They'd stopped by Saoirse's camper to say goodbye and

thank her, and to casually ask if she'd heard of the Farrell family leaving. She confirmed it, as did the old tinsmith where Sam had bought her teapot earlier. Among the few others they tried to ask, most just closed up. Apparently the stories that the Travellers kept to themselves and didn't open up to outsiders were mostly true. Just in case, Sam had given Saoirse her phone number. Being new to the Tuam community she might be the one who would talk if she learned anything.

"I guess we were lucky to get as much information as we did," Beau said as he maneuvered the car away from the city center. It appeared that they'd badly timed their trip back to Galway, as cars were moving at a crawl.

"I can pass on what little we got about the Farrell family and see what happens," Beau said.

Sam found her thoughts drifting—from the interesting afternoon in Tuam, to the bookshop to her uncle, to the curious tour through his house in which she had the distinct feeling they hadn't seen nearly everything, to the startling discovery of another carved box in Terry's locked bookcase.

By the time they got back to their room both of them were exhausted, it was far too late to call Lambert, and in his present mood Beau didn't feel like dealing with the bureaucracy of finding the right person at the FBI.

While Beau took a shower Sam opened the room safe, thinking she would simply put away the earrings she'd worn to Tuam, but she found herself closing her eyes as she handled her wooden jewelry box and remembering details about the one at her uncle's house. What were the odds of two family members, who didn't even know each other, coming to possess identical artifacts?

A need surged through her, the need to know the truth.

She had to get back into Terry's house, get the other box out of the case and find out its story. A picture of the old Traveller tinsmith popped into her head—could an itinerant craftsman of some type have carved both of the boxes?

Her hands began to warm and she quickly set the box back into the safe. The last thing she wanted at this time of evening was to contract its energy. Experience had taught her to use that energy wisely—and only when she was prepared to work at full speed for several hours.

Beau emerged from the steamy bathroom looking relaxed.

"Your turn. That hot water felt *so* good."

By the time she finished a leisurely shower and shampoo and had dried her hair so it wouldn't kink up in the night, she found her husband fast asleep. She pulled the drapes and turned out the lamps.

The dream began as one of those strange ones where she knew she was dreaming but felt powerless to wake up and start over. Like walking through the scenery on a massive movie set, Sam was merely there to watch the actors play out their roles. A blur of motion drew her attention to the left.

"Out of the way, girl!" a man shouted as he spurred his horse through a crowded marketplace. He spoke in Gaelic but somehow Sam understood.

She saw a small figure go down in the mud and she rushed to grab the youngster out of the way of the next horse and rider who came charging through.

"Come here," she told the girl, pulling her aside. "Are you all right?"

The dirty-faced child looked at her with large blue eyes and a solemn mouth. She shook her head and ran out of sight between two gray stone buildings. Had the little girl even seen her?

Looking around, Sam saw that no one had paid particular attention to the exchange. Other children were dressed similarly—dark clothing of rough cloth, boys in knee-length pants and two layers of jackets, girls whose skirts dragged the earthen road, cloth caps tied over their heads. Not a clean face in the bunch. The adults wore full-sized versions of the same attire. Sam looked down at her own clothing; she was in her cotton nightgown and terry robe, which was unbelted and flapping in the chill breeze. Another glance at the people passing her—not one of them acknowledged her.

Their voices carried on, conversations with each other, in a language Sam didn't recognize. She pulled at the belt of her robe, closing it against the cold wind that channeled up the narrow street, noticing that her feet were bare and muddy.

She was apparently in a small European town—the thought crossed her mind that it could even be Galway—and by the crowds and level of chatter it must be market day. She gathered her robe and gown away from the muddy ground and dropped in behind a woman with a cloth bag over her shoulder and four children trailing her, following until she spotted an open square where tables and blankets were spread with food and wares.

A butcher displayed cages of chickens, squawking wildly, and sides of meat; someone else showed piles of dirt-crusted potatoes and carrots; one woman's table was laden with lengths of cloth. The women who paused there looked longingly at the pieces dyed in reds and blues but purchased the plainer tans and grays which must have been less expensive. An old man under a wooden shelter hammered at a strip of tin, forming the handle for a teapot. In a moment of odd clarity, Sam remembered buying such a pot from a man who, judging by his age, could have been this one's father. She wandered through the throng, watching the trades that were taking place, mildly wondering how she would get home again.

At the far end of the disorganized row of vendors one man sat alone. His small booth consisted of a scrap of rag suspended over four roughly hewn poles, a covering that would hardly protect the wood carvings he was working on in the event the rain started again. He sat with his back to the wall of a stone building on a stool that was nothing more, really, than a wide tree stump. He honed his knife against a flat stone then picked up another piece of wood. An old woman approached and stooped to pick up one of the items he displayed on the tattered blanket at his feet. Her unkempt gray hair fell like a veil across her face.

"Out of here, witch!" he yelled. "You'll not be touchin' my work."

She looked up and gave him a steady glare, laying the palms of both hands over some items he'd stacked there.

"Out!" he yelled again.

She stood slowly, looked straight into his eyes and said something in a low, nearly musical tone. Sam couldn't understand it, and when the man replied she couldn't understand his words either. The old woman slowly turned and walked away, vanishing around a corner.

Sam felt her eyes drawn to the man's blanket to see what they had been arguing over. The woman had touched a stack of three wooden boxes. They were by far the nicest of the work, although not finely done by any means.

Three boxes with a carved quilted pattern, crudely finished, with a yellowish stain that settled into brown lines in the low places. Sam had seen two of those boxes.

She woke with the sensation that she'd fallen from a great distance, landing on the plush top of the king-sized bed at the Harbour Hotel with a jolt.

"Darlin'? You okay?" Beau mumbled, half asleep, rolling over and reaching his arm around her. He nuzzled against her neck and was soon breathing deeply again.

Sam closed her eyes, searching again for the vision of that final scene but it was gone. She willed herself to go back to sleep but rest would not come. When Beau rolled to his other side, she slipped out of bed.

Rummaging through her back pack in near darkness, she came up with a pen and the small journal she'd been using for notes. She carried them into the bathroom where she opted to work by the tiny nightlight rather than subject herself to the harsh glare of the fluorescents above the sink. She jotted the basics of the dream, as many details as she could remember, but it was fading quickly. She left the journal and went back to bed.

By the time sunlight began to stream through the windows, the whole thing seemed almost silly. Sam chalked it up to her imagination running wild after their day spent among the Travellers and decided she was beginning to incorporate the ambiance of all these Irish towns into her psyche. If the dream really had any meaning, wasn't it crazy that she'd been able to understand some of those conversations and not others? She brushed it off as she told Beau about it over breakfast.

What she didn't tell him was that now, more than ever,

she wanted to get her hands on the second carved box. To see if it was the same as hers. Really, that was all. She flicked toast crumbs off her lap and they went back to the room so Beau could make some phone calls.

His first attempt at reaching Detective Lambert ended with his leaving a short voice message. He remembered the name of the lead investigator in Dublin and spent a few minutes tracking down the right department before he got the man on the line. He gave the recap of their day in Tuam to a man who sounded thoroughly sick of his job.

"It's not that I don't believe you," he said, "it's just, I got no patience with the Travellers anymore. You know? They want taxpayer money to live on, but ask their cooperation on a legal matter—hell, ask 'em any kind of question that might land one of 'em in jail—you get nothin'. I'm sick of it."

"Trust me," said Beau, "I'm a small town sheriff and I've seen similar."

"Yeah, I know. They pull out the 'ethnic discrimination' card and want all the favors. And they can't prove they're any different in their DNA than any of the rest of us. Problem is, you can't believe anything any of 'em says."

Beau could see the conversation going nowhere so he thanked the man and hung up.

"Well, there's a severe case of career burnout," he told Sam when he relayed the conversation. "I can only hope he'll pass the tip along to the FBI and maybe work with them. No one seems to be thinking of poor Jacob Goldman." He drummed his fingers on the glossy surface of the desk. "I guess I could always figure out who's in charge of this at the FBI and get in touch with them myself."

"What will you tell them? There are Farrells in Ireland related to this Quint guy—they know that already."

He gripped her shoulders and gave her a kiss. "You are absolutely right. They have contact with any agency they need here, through Interpol. We're on vacation. Let's drop it."

"I just feel badly for the O'Henrys," Sam said. "The case seems to be stalled, on a bad track from their perspective."

"You never know. Not all Travellers are dishonest—not all hard-working fishermen are honest. The facts of the investigation have to stand and Lambert never said anything to me about Darragh as a suspect."

"Okay. You're right. Now, at least we're down to only two things that need our attention while we're here."

"Two?"

"Well, the bookshop of course. I still don't know what to do about that."

"And . . .?"

"I can't let go of the fact that Uncle Terry had a wooden box like mine. It's just way too coincidental, Beau." She sat on the edge of the bed. "I really wish I'd had the chance to meet him, hon. To talk at least once and get a feel for what he expected of me."

"So you should do whatever you need to. Go back to the shop, call that lawyer again . . . whatever it takes. I know you, darlin' and you won't let go of this until you figure it out."

She chuckled. "You are so right about that. And I think I'll do just what you suggested—go to the shop *and* contact Daniel Ryan."

Although she invited him along, Beau opted to act as travel planner, plotting another road trip while she took care of business. She picked up her umbrella and pack, leaving him to pore over maps and descriptions of castles.

The conversation ran through her head, along with flashes of last night's odd dream, as she walked toward O'Shaughnessy's Books.

Could her uncle have known of the twin box in Sam's possession?

Chapter 20

From the middle of Shop Street, the bookshop had taken on a new life. The newly cleaned front windows contained bright displays, and an enticing sign touted the discount prices. People were taking notice. Sam watched as two who were standing at the window turned to go inside, while a young woman edged in closer to have a look at the display. Whether Sam had to take possession of the store or not, at least it now had the look of success about it.

Inside, Ambrose was ringing up the sale of a large stack of the formerly dusty bargain books for a middle-aged woman who looked thrilled to get them. Two younger women were browsing the shelves on their own. Sam glanced around for the other two employees, until she realized that angry voices were coming from the back room. She hurried to the doorway.

"—is absolutely not true!" Bridget said to Keeva.

The young woman's face sparked with emotion, her face a heightened pink. Keeva stood with her arms tightly folded across her chest.

"I'm only sayin', it was on the television news. It's what people are saying."

"Ladies!" Sam uttered through clenched teeth. She tilted her head toward the sales room. "Voices! We have customers."

"Sam, is it true?" Bridget's voice came out in a strained whisper. "Is my uncle being accused of helping those American men who stole all those diamonds?"

"The police haven't told Beau or me anything like that." Sam kept her voice low and calm. Of course, the police hadn't exactly told Beau anything since yesterday's news hit the wires. "Keeva, it would be best not to talk about this."

"I simply said it was what I heard on the TV today."

Sam hadn't watched enough television news here in Ireland to know how it was done. If news anchors handled it the same as in the States—reporting 'breaking' stories with very little in the way of facts before they went on the air—she could well imagine how upsetting this would be to Bridget's family.

"Okay, okay," she said to both of them. "I'll ask Beau to find out what he can. Meanwhile, Keeva, we have customers. Maybe you can see if they need assistance? Bridget, please collect yourself. You can go home if you need to, but while you're in the store I really need for you to not listen to the gossip and just concentrate on your work. Please?"

Bridget watched Keeva leave the room, then she took a deep breath. "I'm sorry, Sam. We've never had words before, Keeva and me. I don't like doing it."

"I know. I know." Sam pulled her into a hug, then handed her a tissue.

"It's just hard, you know. There were reporters at our house this mornin' hangin' about and shoutin' out questions. Dad's taken time from work and Mum's about to go crazy, with him in the house all the time."

Sam smiled.

"If only there was something I could tell them," Bridget said with a sniff. "Let them know the prosecutor won't be smearing our name in court."

"I don't think that's going to happen. They only told us that they plan to prosecute the two men they have in custody—Greenlee and Furns. No one ever said anything to Beau about your uncle being involved in their crime." No one but the Travellers. Maybe they had started the rumors, using the media to shift blame from a Farrell to someone else.

Bridget blew her nose and tossed the tissue into the trash. "I hope they won't speak ill of the dead is all. There'd be no point to it, and our family just wants to put paid to this whole thing."

Sam agreed, but she was about out of comforting things to say when she realized Ambrose was standing in the doorway.

"Someone to see you," he said. "That lawyer fellow."

Daniel Ryan stood near the biography section at the back of the store, seeming to browse but not actually touching any of the books.

"Might we talk?" he said as soon as Sam greeted him.

"Certainly." She hadn't yet shed her jacket so she led the way outside.

A light mist had begun to drift downward but she

ignored it. Ryan led the way to the sheltering awning of a neighboring shop where souvenir hunters were digging through a bin of key rings and magnets. Sam edged away from the crowd around the open door and turned to him.

"You see," he began, "Mick and I have discussed your concerns about the estate. The financial records and all that . . . well, I came by to ask if you would like to visit your uncle's home again."

Sam felt her eyebrows rise. Why this, all of a sudden? He obviously didn't know that Anna Blake had already showed them around.

He sensed her hesitation. "I, um, Mick left the box of business records that you'd gathered when you went there with him. Of course, if you aren't interested . . . it's fine. Not to push you."

Again, her skepticism reared up but she was not going to miss another opportunity to get a look at that wooden box.

"Oh, no. It's a very kind offer. I would love to go." After the battle of wills for more than a week now, she felt a tug of emotion at his thoughtfulness. "Let me tell the employees that I'm leaving."

"Invite your husband, if you'd like," Ryan said. "I don't mean to make you think this is some untoward move on my part or something." He blushed red as he said it.

"I'll call him."

They walked back to the bookshop, where she stepped into the back room and called Beau at the hotel. He wasn't interested in another trip to Woodgrove Lane but wished her well and suggested she could invite Daniel Ryan to join them for lunch if she wanted to. He would roam down to the docks and stop in to see Deirdre Athy and ask if she'd come up with any new clues about the whereabouts of Quinton Farrell. A thought flashed through Sam's mind—what if it was Deirdre who was in league with the Americans?

She started to mention the idea to Beau but he'd already said goodbye. And Daniel Ryan was waiting. She picked up her pack and walked out with him, her mind switching gears and thoughts of the matching wooden boxes coming to focus.

The drive to Terrance O'Shaughnessy's house went quickly and Ryan pulled into the long drive, positioning the car as close to the front door as possible since the rain was letting go in buckets now. "If you have the time, I can show you around," he said, shutting off the engine.

"I don't really need the tour of the entire house," Sam admitted as they shook their jackets inside the front door. She made it sound casual, the way she and Beau had driven by and spotted Anna that day. "What I do want to see is something in one of the bookcases in the study."

Ryan didn't seem surprised at her admission. And once she thought about it, that made sense. Anna was keeping the house in order; she had probably told the lawyers about the surprise visit.

The study looked as it had on the previous two visits— the heavy desk and deep leather chairs were dusted and unmoved. The box of file folders sat beside the desk. The fireplace would have been cozy with a fire in it on a damp autumn day like this, but it had the same cold, blackened hearth as before. She pointed toward the glassed bookcases.

"It's in this one," she told the attorney.

He walked over to a large painting on one wall, a hunting scene, very traditional with horses and hounds. The frame swung to one side revealing a wall safe behind it. He twirled the dial from memory, opening the door and pulling out a wire ring with two small keys on it.

"One of these goes to the desk," he said, "and the other is for the bookcases. Now if I can only remember which is which."

Sam waited, trying not to tap her foot or, worse yet, grab the keys away and do it herself.

The small brass lock clicked, he opened the glass door and reached for the box.

"There you go. I've no idea what this is or why Terrance had it. It's not very attractive, is it?"

The assessment was a polite one. The box—like Sam's—was more than unattractive. It was really ugly. It only transformed itself when she handled it. She reached to take it but remembered what had happened with the first one.

"Could you set it on the desk and leave me with it for a moment?"

He gave a puzzled look but did so. "I'll see if there's any tea in the kitchen these days."

Sam watched him walk back into the foyer, leaving the study door open behind him. She almost closed it, but that might make him think she was up to something. She ignored the impulse and instead stood behind the desk and regarded the box. It had stones mounted at each point of the X's in the design, but it was hard to see them or determine their color. Hers glowed blue, red and green when she handled the box but at other times they were dull and quiet like these. The stain and varnish looked the same, too, a dull yellowish brown.

She placed her hands on the box. It was cool to the touch. Nothing special. She opened the lid.

As with the other one, this was plain inside. A few vintage postcards with postage stamps in single-digit denominations lay inside. She lifted them out; a quick glance suggested they might be from her uncle's travels. She would go back to those later.

When she had received the first box from the dying woman at a property she was charged with cleaning and caretaking, the old *bruja* had told Sam that she was meant to own the box. Pressing it into her hands, Bertha Martinez told Sam to use the box wisely.

Now she wondered—was it possible for one owner to have two of these, to perhaps double the power with the possession of two? She pulled her hands away. The power of the first box had frightened her at times and had helped her at others. Did she dare take the chance of unleashing those forces once again?

She touched the lid, flexed the hinge—open and closed—a few times until it moved smoothly. Across the room, the clock chimed the half-hour. Daniel Ryan would return any minute.

She laid the lid open once more. A faint set of carved letters were barely visible along the rim, perhaps the craftsman's name, nothing that made sense to her. As she'd done with the first box, she ran her fingers around the inside of the empty compartment. When she completed the circuit of the four sides . . . nothing. She touched all surfaces of both the lid and the box. She felt no reaction, no increase in heartbeat. The box displayed no reaction either, no golden glow of wood, no sparkle from the stones.

Sam's breath whooshed out. She hadn't realized she was holding it.

Bertha Martinez was right—each box was destined to belong to someone. Perhaps this one had been Terrance's.

Daniel Ryan was standing in the doorway when Sam looked up.

"Sorry. I was about to say that the kettle's on. Sam? Are you all right? You look a little shattered—I mean, you know, tired. Everything okay?"

She took another deep breath. "Fine, yes."

He regarded her closely.

"Really. I, uh, found these old postcards in the box. I wonder if I might take them, just to look them over. My uncle had an interesting life, didn't he?"

"I suppose so. About his life, that is. Very interesting. And, sure, I don't see why anyone would miss a few old postcards."

Sam closed the empty box and stacked the cards.

"Beau suggested that we have lunch when we were finished here. Join us?"

He glanced at his watch, formulating an answer, but he never got the chance to give it. A loud crash sounded above their heads.

"Someone is in the house!" she said. Without a second thought she rushed out of the study and up the stairs.

"Is anyone there?" a woman's voice called out. "I need help please!"

Sam followed the sound of the voice, dimly aware of Daniel Ryan coming up the stairs behind her.

"In here!" came the woman's voice again. "The end of the hall."

Sam opened a door to discover Anna Blake on her knees beside a white-clad prone figure. It was a very elderly man, with twig-like legs sticking out from the knee-length gown.

"He got up." Anna practically grunted the words as she worked to get her arms under the man's head and shoulders. "I tried to tell—"

"Anna, I'm here too," Daniel said. "Do we need to call the EMTs?"

The downed man spoke in a reedy voice. "No—I can get up."

He struggled mightily, but it took the other three to get him up on those shaky legs and to guide him to the hospital bed near the windows. He leaned back into his pillows, breathing heavily, after Anna tucked his legs under the sheet.

"Let me get him settled," she said. She made eye contact with the lawyer. "Then I expect you'll want to talk."

Ryan took Sam's elbow and guided her out of the room.

"What is going on here?" she demanded once the door closed. "Is that—"

"Yes. He's your uncle."

Chapter 21

Sam came back into the bedroom when Anna opened the door. Terrance O'Shaughnessy's color had returned and Sam suspected that the caregiver may have administered some kind of medication. The old man's hair was snow white, obviously thinning, although it still covered his entire bony scalp. Milky blue eyes surrounded by deep creases watched as she walked toward his bed and took one of the deeply veined hands.

"Hello, Samantha," he said. His voice came out stronger than it had ten minutes ago. "I suppose I should introduce myself."

"Uncle Terry, why didn't you tell me? I could have come by to see you every day."

"Have a seat, girl. It's a complicated story."

Anna brought a chair and then left the room. Daniel

Ryan had already disappeared to another part of the house.

"We all believed you were dead," Sam said. "Your will? The trust . . . What was that all about?"

His knotted fingers twitched on top of his blanket. "I'm going to tell you, child."

She had to smile. It had been forty years since anyone had called her a child.

"Who was the man who said that reports of his demise were greatly exaggerated? It doesn't matter—I must say that the same applies to me."

"But you sent us airplane tickets and you're paying for our hotel room?"

"Aye, I must confess to a tremendous ruse, dear. I've conspired to trick you, along with others about whom I care greatly."

"Why?"

"Call it an old man's insecurity . . . or perhaps it's an old man's form of security. No matter. The fact is that I was testing all of you."

Seriously? Sam waited.

"I regret that I didn't stay in touch with my American family in a better way. It was easier when Maggie was alive. She wrote the letters, handled the gifts at the holidays, put my name on them even though I hadn't a clue what she had purchased. I was too busy making money then—scoring a big real estate deal, flying off to the Continent. When my beloved wife died I discovered how pitifully I had wasted my chances. But then, did I change my ways and do a better job of it? No, sadly, I moped around this big old place for a few years and then I went right back out and did it all again. Sad, isn't it, that a man can create a fortune and have no one to share it with."

Sam squeezed his hand. "Your charities will benefit. That's a very good cause."

His eyes closed for a long moment and she wondered if he was too tired for this. About the time she thought of leaving quietly, the eyes opened again.

"The charities. Well, yes, they will get their due. There's money in the bank for them." His mouth pursed and relaxed. "But it was the bookshop and this house that I cared about, the home I shared with Maggie and the shop she always wished we would have, together, when she was alive. Samantha, I'm afraid I've always done things too late. Wanted to do the right things, you understand, but I came around to it a bit after the fact."

Sam nodded. Everyone probably felt that way at some point.

"I've been almost completely stuck in this damned bed for the past year. And partway through I began to wonder . . . what if I died without ever doing the right thing. It was a very real possibility, you see. So I began to think about that and wondered what it would be like to die but to stay around so I could know how everyone reacted to my death."

She began to see where this was going. "So, you took Anna and your lawyers into your confidence and staged it all?"

His thin lips stretched even thinner and he gave a dry chuckle. "Pretty sharp girl, you are. That's exactly what I did."

Ambrose had railed about the fact that Terry's coffin was closed at the funeral home, and the cemetery director had no record of the second half of the double plot being used.

"And you're probably wondering why." He waited for

her nod. "I was curious, as I told you. Wanted to see what people would do."

Sam felt herself beginning to smile at the supreme joke. "And were you surprised?"

"In some ways, yes. In other ways . . . not a bit." He was enjoying this and Sam let him play it out.

"What surprised you, Uncle Terry?"

"Well, I suppose the biggest came even before my so-called *death*, when I informed the directors of my charitable trust that a condition of receiving my fortune would be that they keep the bookshop open. You should have seen their faces. Glances all around the table, smug little looks. Daniel Ryan was in the room with us, and he reported to me how the conversation went after I left. Keep the shop until the day after the funeral, they all agreed. What the old man doesn't know won't kill him. Laugh, laugh, har-har—joke's on Terry. I revoked the trust and fired them all the very next day."

Sam chuckled at his glee, but remembered how close she'd come to having those same thoughts about dumping the dusty little shop herself.

"That's when I decided to change things up a bit and see what happened. Ambrose Piggott has been a trusted employee and the most loyal friend a man could want. I know he thinks of me as a father but the feelings went deeper. His very life is that shop."

"Terry, you should have left it to him. I didn't expect anything at all. And you are so right, the shop means everything to Ambrose. Change it, please, so that he gets to keep it."

He wagged his index finger at her. "Not so fast."

"Were there other tests? Was I being tested? And the

other employees?"

"Well, of course you were. Everyone."

"And?"

"Certain reactions made me happy. As I've told you, some did not."

He coughed and signaled for the cup on his bedside stand. Sam held it, turning the bent straw so that he could sip.

"I was not pleased with the way Ambrose treated you when you arrived. I was not pleased with the condition of the shop, although I have to admit that I began letting it go, as part of the challenge to see how the directors of my charity would greet the news that they would soon own it."

"Ambrose was just—"

"He was rude—no excuses."

She regarded him from the corner of her eye. "How did you know this? A fly on the wall?"

"Ah—nearly that good. Two gossipy women. Anna was charged with getting information on my behalf."

"But I never saw her in the shop."

"She and her sister enjoy a glass of stout together almost every night. Anna would see me to bed after my supper, slip out for an hour or so for a break, come back in time to stay the night in her room here and tell me all about what was going on in my shop the next morning over breakfast."

Sam had another thought. "The pranks. Once we began fixing up the shop, there were two occasions where our work was torn apart. I kept looking for signs that Ambrose was secretly doing it to run me off."

"Anna again, my dear. All part of the test. I was curious how each person would react. Would they fall upon each other, blaming all around? Would the incidents escalate as one of them tried to outdo the other? Would you throw up your hands and flee the country?"

"I suppose it doesn't help my case if I admit now that I nearly did walk away from it."

"You, my dear niece, passed every test. You showed calm in the storm, organization in the face of chaos, unflappability when it seemed the place was infested with leprechauns and faeries. Yes, even that little bit got back to me. Keeva and her superstitions—ha!"

Sam sat back in the chair, shaking her head in amazement. "You are quite the orchestrator, for a man in his nineties."

"Ah—I was quite the orchestrator in my younger years, too."

"So, what happens now? Is it still a condition that I own the shop for two years?"

"Samantha, I know better. I would never ask it of you, to make you leave your new husband behind and stay here to keep a bookstore running."

"He will be most appreciative of the consideration."

Terry chuckled again and set off another small coughing fit. "I'm an old man, Sam," he said after another sip of water. "I wasn't supposed to last this long, and I can promise you, the next time you hear of my death it will be the real thing."

"Don't say that. You're so sharp. You have a wonderful sense of humor."

His eyes rested for another moment. "If one could only live a hundred years on one's humor. Unfortunately, the body gives out and believes otherwise."

"You're tired and I've stayed too long," she said. "I want you to tell me what to do, but we should save the talk for another day. Maybe I can come back tomorrow?"

"Do not wait too long," he said, his eyes coming open again.

She considered that. "Okay, there is one question that I have a feeling only you can answer for me."

"Name it."

"There's a wooden box in your bookcase in the study, carved, with some small inset stones."

A smile crept over his face. "I know the one. It's special in some way, isn't it?"

"Where did you get it?"

"Ah, a rather long story."

She could tell his energy had completely faded. "Tomorrow, then. I want to hear all about it when I come back."

His eyes closed again and he nodded.

Sam stood and kissed his cool forehead. "I'll get Anna, in case you need anything before you go to sleep."

Downstairs, she found Anna and Daniel Ryan at the kitchen table, empty tea cups in front of them. The daylight had faded and Sam was surprised to see that it was nearing mid-afternoon. She'd missed lunch with Beau and hadn't heard from him—he must have stayed busy somehow.

"Anna, my uncle may need you. He was getting very tired and I hope we didn't overdo the visit."

"I'm certain he loved every minute of it," she said. "It was the reason he'd gotten out of bed in the first place. He heard voices and when he learned it was you, he wanted to go down and find you."

Clearly, Terry's trying to negotiate the stairs would have been impossible.

"How did we not know he was here the other times I came to this house?"

"When you were with Mick O'Connor it was arranged that the visit would take place during Terry's nap."

"Mick was very secretive with me. Now I understand his obstinacy about not letting me see the place."

"When you and your husband drove along that other time, it gave me quite a fright. I wasn't certain Terry would still be asleep. I couldn't be sure but I hoped that you didn't figure out that you hadn't seen nearly all of the upstairs rooms." She stood and went to the door. "I'll be seeing to Terry now."

Sam gave Daniel Ryan a steady stare. "It's a good thing I got this chance to hear all this from my uncle. I wouldn't have appreciated the humor, once I learned the truth, if I'd gotten it from you or Mick."

He started to say something but when Sam's phone rang he got busy clearing the tea things. She didn't recognize the number on the readout.

"Is it Sam?" the female voice said over the phone. "It's Saoirse here. In Tuam."

Sam walked out to the front hall, hoping to keep the call private.

"Yes. Have you got new information for us?"

"I believe so. It's about that American man, the Farrell."

Daniel Ryan had come into the hall, jacket over his arm.

"I'd like to call you back later, if that's all right," Sam said. Saoirse agreed.

The lawyer stayed quiet during the drive back to the center of town, and she was too busy mulling over everything Uncle Terrance had told her to initiate conversation. As they came to the dock area, she informed Ryan of her intention to visit Woodgrove Lane again the next day. He delivered

Sam to the curb in front of the Harbour, offering to drive her in the morning if she wanted him to.

Over-helpful after stonewalling all this time? She gave a noncommittal response and went up to the room, which was dim and empty. Beau must have found an errand to keep him busy. She filled the kettle with water and flipped its switch, setting up a mug and teabag, looking forward to a few minutes' quiet. She was eager to tell Beau about her afternoon but still had a lot of information to process.

While the water heated, she dumped the contents of her pack on the bed, determined to lighten the inevitable clutter that seems to grow inside every purse or bag that a woman carries. Spotting her cell phone she remembered that she'd promised to call Saoirse back. She looked at the number but dialed it on the room's landline rather than incur the high international rates on the cell.

"You asked me to let you know if I heard word of the Farrells," Saoirse said as soon as Sam identified herself. "My son tells me he heard they've taken up with another camp on the north side of Galway. Or maybe it was the northeast . . . we come from the Limerick area, ourselves, and I'm not so familiar with the popular places here. I don't know if the one you're lookin' for is with them, but maybe this helps."

Sam thanked her for the information, a little surprised that a Traveller would talk so openly.

Chapter 22

The kettle let out a ribbon of steam and shut itself off. Sam poured the boiling water over her teabag and dunked it up and down with the string. Maybe Saoirse was so willing to talk to them because she wasn't a native part of the Tuam group? Or maybe she was just hoping to be included in the article Sam was supposedly writing. Either way, it was potentially good information that Beau could pass along to Detective Lambert, especially if they had a way of establishing for sure that Quinton Farrell was with the Travellers, before they gave the lead to the police.

She looked up to see the door opening.

"Hey, darlin'. Glad you're back. I've got a lead on Quint Farrell—want to come along?" He rushed into the room and picked up his jacket, his face alight with the excitement that she recognized whenever he felt that a case was breaking.

She scooped everything back into her pack, abandoned the freshly brewed tea and trotted to keep up with him on the way to the parking garage.

"I never did like the story Deirdre Athy gave us when we talked to her the first time," he said as he unlocked the car. Twice, she opened her mouth to tell him about discovering her uncle alive, but Beau had already started the engine by the time she opened her door. Her news would keep awhile longer, she decided.

He went on, almost breathlessly. "So I went poking around the docks and found where she's working now. Got the chance to talk a little more."

"So she knew more about Quint Farrell this time? Did she tell you where he is?" If so, why wasn't he handing this to Detective Lambert, rather than checking it himself?

He circled the block around the parking garage and pulled to the curb across from the marina, where masts of sailboats bobbed gently on the early evening swells.

"The little white building up there," Beau said, pointing. "Seaward Charters. It's where Deirdre works now. They close in fifteen minutes and I'm betting she's going to lead us to something interesting."

Sam passed along the information she'd just gotten from Saoirse, about the Farrell family relocating somewhere around the north side of town. "Unfortunately, she didn't seem to have any solid information as to whether Quint would be with them. It does seem funny, though, that they decide to pack up camp right when he shows up in the country, don't you think?"

He nodded, keeping his eyes on the front door of Seaward Charters' small office. "Yeah, but to come to Galway? Scene of the crime . . . local police on alert.

Wouldn't they likely go much farther away?"

That made sense. Saoirse's information might be worthless. Or, another thought, it could have been given with the intent of throwing them off the trail. Sam realized her thoughts were going circular—she was hungry and tired. She wanted to slide down in the seat and close her eyes, but she forced herself to snap awake and concentrate. Somewhere along the way, surely she could talk Beau into feeding her.

"What makes you think Deirdre will contact Quint tonight?"

"It was more in her manner than what she actually said. She got real edgy when she saw me again. Remember when we talked to her that day, when she was clearing out her stuff, how she seemed very cooperative about all the little details of the charter, up until we started getting specific about Quint? Then she stalled and I could tell she was lying."

Sam nodded.

"Well, this afternoon she really got jittery when I walked in. I could see it in her face that she regretted letting me know that she would be working nearby. And regretted saying as much as she did about the three Americans. I would bet that she's been in touch with Quint since that day. He's promised her something . . . I don't know. But my gut tells me that he'll try to see her again. He didn't think twice about putting Jacob Goldman into a coma. Deirdre's life could be in danger if she knows too much about Quint."

Sam considered that. Only a handful of people had direct contact with Quint Farrell since he'd arrived in Ireland—Darragh O'Henry and Sean Bareth were dead. Hank Greenlee and Trucker Furns were in jail, awaiting trial. Only Deirdre was walking around free, with information about Quint in her head. Unless she gave testimony to the police and then went into hiding—soon—her life wasn't worth much.

"There she is," Beau said, starting the engine.

Deirdre headed up the street, away from their car, crossed at the next light and walked out of sight behind an apartment building. Beau cruised slowly to the corner, turned and spotted her nearly a half block ahead. An impatient motorist tooted his horn at their slow pace, dodging around them when Beau gave him a little leeway.

"Not easy," he said, "trailing someone on foot this way. I had assumed she would get into her own car and I could match her speed."

In Taos, where people rarely lived within walking distance from of work and where they drove their cars to go two blocks, his idea would have no flaws. Here, Sam realized, Deirdre could do nearly anything: hop a bus or train, stop for food, do some shopping, or simply go into any of the apartments or small row houses that lined the streets. They got their answer when she walked into a pub called O'Leary's.

"Now what?" she asked Beau. "Wait for her to eat, drink and be merry? This could take some time."

He drove past and pulled to the curb, eyeing O'Leary's in his mirror.

"How about this—I'll go in and get us something to eat," Sam said, "see if it looks like she's staying awhile."

"Most pub food doesn't exactly come in takeout boxes," he reminded her.

Her hand was already on the door handle. "I'll think of something."

"Sam—don't let her spot you."

True, Deirdre would know her face; they had met on more than one occasion. Sam remembered a scarf among the jumble in her pack. She fished around until she felt it, and draped it over her hair. Carrying only a few euro bills, she hoped the look was different enough that Deirdre wouldn't immediately pick up on who she was. And even if the woman should spot her, Sam could always make light of it, claim she'd just been out for a walk in the neighborhood.

The small pub was packed for happy hour or teatime or early diners, or whatever they called it here. A quick scan assured Sam that Deirdre wasn't seated at the bar, where she would almost certainly be forced into a conversation with the woman. She spotted a display of packets of potato chips, pretzels and such which would provide an excellent excuse for her visit. She walked up to the barkeep and asked for two bags. While he plucked them off the rack and made change, Sam turned to give the room a gander.

Deirdre Athy was seated at a corner table, her chair facing the room. She looked up, a smile lighting her face and Sam noticed a tall man with dark hair. He approached with a heavy limp and spoke to Deirdre. She laughed at whatever he said and he pulled out the chair across from hers. It was Quint Farrell.

Sam felt her heart rate pick up. Beau could nab him, right here.

Her hand shook as she snatched up the two bags of pretzels and took the change the barkeep offered. She concentrated on not running out the door. At the street, she rushed to the car and yanked open her door.

"He's in there!" she told Beau. "With Deirdre at a table in the corner—at the right side of the room. She didn't see me."

Beau, to her disappointment, didn't leap out of the car. "What should we do?" she demanded.

"Hold on. What we *should* do is call Lambert and tell him Farrell's location. Get in the car, Sam, so we don't call attention to ourselves."

"But Lambert isn't even after Farrell any more," she said as she closed her door. "He said so himself. He's concentrating on gathering the evidence against the other two."

"Yes, but Farrell is still an FBI-wanted felon. They'll be depending on local authorities to apprehend him on sight."

"So, call!"

He held out his hand for her phone, dialed Lambert's number, came up with voice mail. "That's not going to work. The man is just too busy." He punched 999, the local emergency number.

"I'm an American law enforcement officer," he began. After a couple more identifying codes that Sam didn't really understand, he informed the dispatcher of the suspect's name and location and told them he intended to keep Farrell in sight until their officers could arrive.

"It's the best I can do," he said, handing Sam the phone. "Was this the only door to the pub?"

She pictured the interior, trying to remember the layout. "I think so. It's not a very big place."

He chewed at his lip, staring into the rearview mirror. Sam listened for sirens, watched for flashing lights—nothing yet.

"I don't like this," Beau said. "I'm going to stand by the door so I can grab him if he tries to leave." He leveled his eyes to hers. "You stay here. Do not move."

She felt a pout coming on.

"I don't want you hurt. He could very well be armed."

"Okay. But I don't want you hurt either. Be careful, Beau."

She turned to watch him walk toward the lights of the pub. Still not a siren in earshot. She fidgeted and ripped into one of the pretzel bags, stuffing two of the crunchy sticks into her mouth as she kept her eyes on her husband.

Beau strolled slowly past the lighted windows, trying to look nonchalant, paused outside the door. A couple walked up and blocked Sam's view for a minute. When they moved, Beau was gone.

She jammed the pretzel bag into a cup holder on the console, ready to yank her door open, but when she looked up again, Beau was in the doorway of the pub, staring back and forth at the sidewalk.

"They got away," he said when she rolled down her window. "I took a quick peek—the table you described was empty. They weren't anywhere in the place."

Sam's earlier adrenaline rush drained away. "What now?"

"I'll talk with the police when they get here, tell them what happened."

That part of it took far too long, and Sam had consumed both bags of pretzels and paced the short stretch of sidewalk four times before Detective Lambert arrived.

"So Quinton Farrell's back in Galway," he said. Stating the obvious. And showing up way too late.

Sam tamped down her impatience.

"My wife went in to buy a snack and spotted Farrell inside sitting with Deirdre Athy," Beau said.

Lambert seemed surprised. Sam wasn't sure whether he'd worked so many new cases in the last few days that he'd forgotten details of this one, or if he'd never actually considered that Deirdre might be involved with the criminals and therefore partially to blame for Darragh and Sean's deaths.

"I'd like to help work on this," Beau said. "We've met a few of the Travellers and might be able to offer some assistance."

"I can't let you take it on your own. The press would have a field day and the courts might disallow some of the evidence." He made a 'halt' motion with one palm. "And I can only spare one man. Aiden can work with you. And we appreciate your help."

Lambert called over his sergeant and explained what was expected of him—accompany Beau who would be the liaison to the American authorities and report everything back to the detective squad. Surprisingly, both men seemed entirely agreeable to working that way.

By the time Beau broke away from the cluster of cops, Sam was decidedly grumpy—no lunch, no dinner, and pretzels weren't cutting it. Plus, she was tired of getting the suspicious gazes of every passerby who saw her as the only obvious civilian in the sidewalk gathering.

"Okay, my little princess," Beau said, making up for forty-five minutes of ignoring her. "Let's get some dinner and relax."

They ended up staying at O'Leary's for dinner; the car was already parked and the choice didn't involve making any mind-straining decisions. Taking a table in a hidden alcove, Beau pointed at another exit, obviously the way Deirdre and Quint had gotten past them.

"Don't fret over it, darlin'. They may not have seen you.

Likely, Quint knew about this other door and it's how he came into the pub in the first place."

"Yeah, you're probably right," she mumbled with her mouth full. She'd spooned into the bowl of Irish stew nearly the moment the waiter set it on the table. "Now I'm worried about her safety, after what you said. Do you think Quint still has the gun with him?"

"No telling. It's a strong piece of forensic evidence. He would have been smart to dump it in the ocean after he killed Darragh and Sean. But criminals don't always do the smart thing." He cut into the lamb chop on his plate. "Anyway, let's relax tonight. There's an APB out on Quint so every uniform in town will be watching. Tomorrow I'll get together with Aiden Martin and we'll start asking questions."

"Oh! Tomorrow! I completely forgot to tell you my big news."

When she dropped the bombshell that Terrance O'Shaughnessy was still alive, Beau went completely still.

"What the hell was he thinking?" he demanded.

"I know. Not exactly fair play, if you look at it that way. But I do get what he was trying to do."

She went on to explain, as much in Terry's words as she could, why the charitable trust had fallen apart and how her uncle wanted to test people's reactions before finalizing his will. Beau didn't look too happy about the deception—honesty might well have been his middle name—but he let her tell the whole story.

"And," Sam said, "do you remember the carved wooden box he had in the bookcase in his study? When I asked Anna to open the door so I could examine it closer?"

He'd gone back to his mashed potatoes. "Not really."

"Well, I got the chance to see and touch it. It's nearly identical to mine, a little larger. When I asked Uncle Terry about it he said there was quite a story behind it. He promised to tell me about it tomorrow when I go back."

Beau smiled at her. "Sounds like you won't mind, then, if I spend a little time in the morning with Aiden Martin, asking around about Quint Farrell."

Sam felt a momentary tug. As much as she enjoyed helping Beau whenever he let her, learning more from her uncle and solving the mystery of those odd wooden boxes was more appealing to her right now. She felt a lightness of spirit as they finished their meal. Finally, she would have answers.

Back in their room, Beau turned to her. "I missed you today."

"I'll miss you tomorrow, too," Sam said. "My plan is to wrap up the details of Terry's estate in the morning, make sure someone else's ownership of the bookshop is finalized and airtight, and be done with that worry."

"My plan is to get enough information on Quint Farrell that the Irish authorities can nab him and extradite his ass back to New York."

"And then both of us will have the last few days of our honeymoon to spend doing nothing that isn't completely enjoyable."

To emphasize the thought, he took her in his arms and planted tiny kisses across her forehead, along her right temple, to her mouth, and down her neck. Somehow they fell onto the bed and all those clothes managed to come off.

"I like this honeymoon stuff," she murmured as he ran

his hands over her body.

Sometime later, she drifted into a dreamless sleep and didn't remember even rolling over until she awoke to bright sunlight the next morning. They lingered over a room service breakfast until the phone rang, Aiden Martin informing Beau that he'd arrived to pick him up.

He gave Sam another lingering kiss and left her with the keys to the rental car. She showered and dressed then gathered her pack and the map of the town. After a few minutes in the driver's seat, studying the unfamiliar layout of the controls, she headed toward Woodgrove Lane.

The moment she approached Terry's house her plans shattered, her mood plummeted. In the driveway sat a gleaming black hearse.

Chapter 23

A man in black came out the front door, directing two assistants who wheeled a gurney with its cargo, which made only a small lump under the white sheet. They guided it toward the dark vehicle while Sam parked and got out of her car. Her eyes began to blur. He'd been so frail, but so sharp in the way he made plans.

On the doorstep, Anna Blake watched Terry's body leave his home for the last time. Sam looked up at her with a thousand questions.

"He was at peace with goin'," Anna said as the hearse drove away.

The two women walked into the house together.

"Last night before he fell asleep, he told me he was happy to have met you, Sam."

The tears wouldn't hold back. Sam felt her shoulders shake.

"Let it out. It's all right." Anna handed her a box of tissues. Her own face was still a little red and puffy. "I found him when I woke up before daylight. Cold already, he was."

The door to the study stood open and they drifted that direction, settling into the two leather chairs in front of Terry's massive desk. A hundred thoughts went through Sam's mind, not the least of which was to wonder about the bookshop and its employees.

"I've called Daniel Ryan," Anna said. "Terry had a big envelope, his instructions. He told me where to find it last night."

Sam noticed a thick mailer bag lying on the desk. Beyond, the carved box was back in its spot in the bookcase. The painting covering the wall safe was back in place. Ryan or Anna had probably put everything back after her visit yesterday. She thought of the conversation she and Terry were to have this morning, how he was going to tell her the history of the box and how much she'd hoped it would give clues to the origins of the one she owned, as well. Regret flooded her and the tears flowed again.

Anna quietly rose, saying something about tea, and left the room.

Sam stared at the box in the bookcase, collecting herself. What was it about old people and these boxes? Did all of them have to die when they passed the boxes along?

What am I thinking? This box isn't automatically mine.

But she knew. Unless he'd specified some other disposition for it, she knew Terry wouldn't mind if she took this one. That line of thinking led her to the bigger question. What *were* Terry's final wishes? Yesterday he'd only told her that the charitable trust didn't exist anymore and that she didn't have to keep the bookshop. But what *had* he done with all of his assets?

The thick envelope stared at her, but she didn't think it was her place to open it.

Anna appeared in the doorway again with a tea tray in her hands and the news that Daniel Ryan had arrived. She set the tray on the desk and began to pour. The lawyer came in, offering condolences to both women. He picked up the envelope, bent the metal clasp upward and opened the flap. A glance inside, then he started to place it in his briefcase.

"I'd like to know what it says," Sam said. "My uncle and I talked yesterday. I would like to know if his wishes were put in writing."

Ryan reopened the envelope and pulled out a sheaf of papers. "I'm sure they were. He signed this only a week ago."

"Terry used to think of things at the oddest moments," Anna said, handing Sam a teacup. "He would call me in and say 'write this down.' I would make notes and he would initial them. I suppose he thought, you know, in case he went in the night or something."

"After you arrived in Galway," Ryan said, "your uncle seemed satisfied that he was ready to finalize his plans. We gathered all those little bits and put it together into this document. It was signed and all made duly legal."

"May I see it?" Sam asked.

"No harm, I suppose. This was his copy. We've another at our offices." He handed the pages to Sam. "I would suggest a reading of the will after the funeral. One of those documents includes his wishes for that, as well."

Sam reached for the envelope and placed the pages inside. She would read it all later. Privately.

"If you have any questions, don't hesitate to call me," the lawyer said. "Mick will be back in Galway tomorrow.

He'll certainly be available to you as well."

"I'm afraid I don't know what to do and I can't even formulate a question at the moment," Sam said. "But thank you for being available."

"Hardiman's can handle everything. Or you may become involved if you wish."

Sam remembered the undertaker's professionalism at Darragh's services. "Thank you."

She set her empty cup on the tray and stood up. "I suppose I better go by the bookshop and make sure everything is all right there."

Leaving the Tudor house, Sam felt the scenery passing in a blur. A hollow feeling settled in her core, so different than when she'd arrived an hour ago filled with anticipation at the stories her uncle would tell. When a horn blared at her because she inadvertently crossed into the wrong lane, she realized that she better be paying attention to driving on the left. She decided to park the car at the hotel and walk to the shop, rather than figure out the complex maze of one-way streets and limited parking in the shopping district.

She walked in to find Keeva and Bridget in a somber mood.

"You've heard about Terry."

They both nodded. "Anna called me," Keeva said. "I'm afraid I had a few choice words for my sister over the idea that she'd known of the deception all along."

"I know. I was stunned by it too," Sam said.

"Ambrose nearly went into shock. Certainly wasn't fit for working with customers after gettin' the news. I took him home. He's likely taken to his bed over this."

Sam thought of the older worker and his attachment to her uncle. Poor Ambrose.

"I suppose we should talk about holding a proper funeral this time," Sam said. "I'd like Ambrose to be in on the planning, if you think that would be wise."

"The poor dear never did find closure over Terry's bein' gone. It's generous of you, Sam, to include him now."

Sam didn't know about generous—mainly she wanted someone to guide the way so all the correct traditions would be observed.

"Would it be all right to go by his house? I could talk to him about this."

Keeva nodded agreement.

"Can you tell me how to get there?" Secretly hoping it was close so she wouldn't have to get out in the car and traffic again.

Bridget spoke up. "It's a mite tricky to describe. I'd be happy to watch the shop if you want to take Sam over," she said to Keeva.

"That's best," Keeva agreed. She retrieved a jacket from the stockroom and joined Sam at the front door.

"It's not far," she said to Sam as they walked along Shop Street.

The day had turned surprisingly warm with a touch of Indian summer and a clear blue sky. The street made a dogleg turn and Keeva turned into a tiny alley, not wide enough for two to walk side-by-side. Sam followed into the gloom created by the three-story walls that rose above them. Fifty yards in, a set of stone steps rose to a green door. Keeva turned to Sam.

"It's not much, I'll warn you. Ambrose can certainly afford better, but he's a complete cheapskate. Keeps this bone-chiller little *box* and then puts his money by in the bank. For what? Some rainy day? As if we don't have those all the time."

He answered their knock and stood back silently to admit them. After Keeva's warning, Sam found herself surprised to enter the neat little square room, an efficiency apartment with a Murphy bed built into the wall. A closed door probably led to a bathroom. There were two upholstered chairs that had seen better days but were clean and neatly slipcovered. A short worktop with a small sink held a miniature microwave oven, and an under-counter dorm-sized fridge completed the cooking facilities. Mainly the room was jam-packed with shelves and books. Clearly, Ambrose's love of reading extended into his entire life.

His face seemed blotchy with color, his eyes puffy. Sam could only imagine his shock at having to face his mentor's death for a second time. She leaned in to hug him and he actually allowed it and accepted her words of condolence. Keeva excused herself to go back to the shop, leaving Sam and Ambrose alone. They took the two chairs.

"I met my uncle yesterday," Sam said, relating how it happened that she'd been at his house when he fell and how their introduction came about.

"I felt very lucky to talk with him awhile. I could see that his feelings for you and for the shop ran very deep."

The old man's eyes became moist again. He cleared his throat a little too gruffly.

"Ambrose, I would like your help," she said, going into the explanation that Terry had left certain instructions but that Sam wanted input from his closest friend. "Would you mind being the family liaison with Hardiman's Funeral Home and getting the arrangements put in place?"

"If I could make a request," Ambrose said, his voice coming out clearer now. "A proper wake—at Terry's home?"

"Of course! We should absolutely plan that. Perhaps you and Anna can decide on the food and get the word out to Terry's closest friends? Naturally, I wouldn't expect you back at work for a few days. Take your time, and don't worry about the expense. I'm sure there is plenty to cover as nice a party as you want to do."

Ambrose sat straighter in his chair, leaning forward a bit as he spoke. "Oh, I won't spend a grand amount," he assured her. "But it should be done correctly."

"Thank you, Ambrose."

As she left the tiny apartment and retraced her steps, Sam felt the energy drain out of her. What a morning. She turned toward the docks a block sooner than normal, deciding not to stop in at the bookshop. Keeva and Bridget would handle it just fine. At the moment all Sam could think of was finding a quiet hour to process everything that happened this morning and to read through the documents in the envelope from her uncle's desk.

She rode the silent elevator and let herself into the room, glad for the first time ever that Beau wasn't in. She dropped her pack on the bed and shed her jacket, thinking of tea. Maybe she was more Irish than she'd ever imagined, she thought with a tiny smile as she switched on the kettle.

She'd just settled into a chair, freshly brewed cup of tea on the nightstand beside her, the copy of her uncle's written funeral instructions in hand, when the door suddenly opened. Beau strode in, full of motion and smelling of fresh air.

"Oh, hey," he said. "I didn't expect you back yet."

She gave him the nutshell version of what had happened and he immediately knelt beside her.

"I'm so sorry, hon. You were so excited yesterday after you met him."

She nodded, not quite trusting herself to talk about her emotions.

Beau held her a minute. "I told Aiden that I would be right back. I needed to grab something and the hotel was on the way . . . But I can tell him to go ahead without me. I'll stay here with you."

"Don't be silly, Beau. I'll be fine."

He began rummaging through a dresser drawer.

"So, tell me about your morning. Where are you guys going now?"

"We found a small Traveller camp on the north side of town, just like Saoirse said. And there were some Farrells staying there. But no Quinton Farrell. At least that's what they *said*. But I could tell that seeing an American lawman on their doorstep was a little unnerving. They were prepared to bluff their way through a conversation with the local police, but they kept giving me the eye, like they weren't sure what my connections were." He pulled his cell phone out of the drawer and pressed a button.

"Uh-oh, this thing's dead."

Sam set her papers aside and pulled her own phone out of her pack. "You can use mine. So, what happened?"

"We got another lead. An old man, nearby, not one of the Travellers. Looked like an old retired guy with nothing else to do. He was strolling the neighborhood and stopped to gawk a little when he saw us pull up. When we walked away from the caravan where we'd been talking to one of the Farrells, this man motioned us over and said he'd seen the guy we were asking about."

Sam had set her papers aside and watched Beau buzzing around the room, filled with nervous energy.

"So, you're heading out to check this lead?"

He paused long enough to give her a close look. "Are you okay, being here alone?"

"I'll be fine." Another wave of sadness washed over her and she felt her eyes well up. "I guess I'm not completely fine. Could I come with you? It would take my mind off all this other."

He debated for a second, torn between agreeing and staying in the room with her. "Darlin', I'm not sure—"

Her disappointment must have been evident.

"You'd have to stay in the car."

"Okay. Deal." She grabbed up her jacket and pack and caught up with him at the door.

Aiden Martin seemed surprised and not entirely happy to see Sam but he kept his thoughts to himself as she slid into the back seat of his unmarked government car.

Beau gave a short explanation that included an explanation of the ways Sam had helped him in the past with his own cases. It sounded better than 'she was feeling a little blue so I let her come along.' Sam decided he was just being kind because, after all, it was their honeymoon and they'd ended up going off in different directions much of the time.

Aiden drove and Beau turned around in his seat to give Sam a short briefing.

"The old man I told you about, he said that Quint had come around with a blond woman, and that the two of them had left together. Doesn't sound like Quint was quite as tight with the Travellers as we'd thought, or that they are harboring him."

"We believe that Quint and the woman are still together, that he's using her to help him get around," Aiden said.

"If Deirdre has gone home, it's possible that Quint may be there too. Or neither of them may be there. Until we know his location, it's not worth calling out all the forces. We don't plan to apprehend Quint ourselves, unless he should give up easily. Our job is to locate him, then we'll call in extra men, maybe even an armed Emergency Response Unit depending on the situation, to actually bring him in."

"Interesting, why would Quint come back to Galway at all?" Sam said. "You'd think he would want to put some distance between this town and himself."

"There has to be something," Beau agreed. "What's Quint's strongest motivation?"

"The money, the diamonds?" she said.

"Are you sayin' that Quint might have hid the loot somewhere nearby after he escaped the *Glory Be*, and now he has to come back for it?" Aiden kept his eyes on the road as he joined the conversation.

Beau spoke up: "It makes sense. Quint gets off the boat but it's the dead of night and he's washed up on a shoreline, God knows where. Maybe he's hurt—Sam, you said he was limping when he came in the pub to meet Deirdre last night."

"He was. So, maybe when he washed up on the shoreline he lost track of the bags containing the money and diamonds and he's come back to look for them. Or he stashed it all somewhere. Maybe the Travellers took him in and he thinks they took the gems."

"He went to the Traveller camp in Tuam, according to Cian and his father, but no one else we talked to actually admitted seeing him there."

"There's a fairly well-known fencing operation within the Travellers," Aiden said. "It's quite likely that Quint heard of it and wanted them to buy the diamonds."

He cruised slowly down a narrow lane of dingy gray row houses with small windows. Most looked small and dim, uninviting in the shadows cast by gathering clouds.

"Number twelve, just there," he said to Beau, pointing ahead. He guided the car to the curb, staying about three houses away.

Sam felt the energy level in the car escalate.

"Stay in here," Beau instructed her. "We don't know what we'll find."

Aiden glanced over his left shoulder, verifying that she wouldn't give them trouble over the order.

Sam nodded, only slightly impatiently.

The two men got out and closed their doors quietly. They crossed to Deirdre's side of the street and edged toward her door, Aiden taking the lead. They stood on either side of it before Aiden reached out and knocked. Thirty seconds went by. He knocked again; this time Sam could hear it.

Nothing.

Beau edged past Aiden and approached the unit's small window, cupped a hand around his eyes and looked in. He said something to Aiden, who twisted the center-mounted doorknob. It opened.

Both men edged in, staying sideways to the opening. Sam caught herself holding her breath.

After one of the longest minutes of her life she saw Beau come back out, jogging toward the car.

"Deirdre's been beaten—can you come help?"

Chapter 24

The front door opened into a hallway so narrow that Sam had to follow Beau. A small living room was on the right and she could hear voices.

". . . back soon." Deirdre's voice sounded thick.

When Sam stepped into the room, she saw why. The woman's lower lip looked like a balloon and one eye had swelled nearly shut. She sat in an old armchair, clutching a washcloth to the puffy side of her face.

"She says Quint went out for food. He'll be coming back," Aiden said to Beau. "We need to get her out of here."

"Can't leave," Deirdre mumbled. It sounded more like *cad leeb*. "Quint comin' back for me."

He did this to you and you want him back? Sam stared.

"Bringin' me diamond—"

"Don't try to talk," Sam said gently, kneeling beside the

chair. "We'll see about the diamond later. Right now, let's think about getting you to a safe place."

Not the car. Quint, returning, would easily spot her there and Deirdre wasn't doing much to protect herself. She would probably leap out and go with him.

Aiden left the room, saying he would check on something.

"Did you see the diamonds, Deirdre?" Beau asked. "Did Quint leave them here?"

She shook her head but the motion made her flinch.

"Do you know where they are?"

Another shake, smaller this time.

"Deirdre, Quint is a very dangerous man. He beat an old man badly enough to put him in a coma. He probably killed two others. We need to get you out of here." Beau spoke gently and Deirdre paid attention.

Aiden came in, and Sam heard someone else out in the hall.

"Your neighbor says you can come to her house, dear. Let's get you going," Aiden said, stepping over to take her arm.

Sam could tell that both lawmen were edgy, expecting Quint to come walking in. She stood and took Deirdre's other elbow, helping her to stand. She was a little wobbly on her feet for the first few steps.

"Shouldn't we be calling an ambulance for her?" Sam whispered to Beau.

"Don't want to alert Quint. We'll get her to a hospital soon."

A young woman was standing in the hall. "Deirdre, what's happened?" She looked at Aiden. "I'd drive her to hospital myself but I'm late to pick up my kids at school and take 'em to their football practice."

"It's all right," he said. "If we can only let her rest at your house until the danger's passed?"

The woman blanched a little at the policeman's warning of danger. She dropped a key into his hand and scurried out.

"Sam, if you don't mind . . . I'll ask you to sit with her?" Keep her from rushing back over here into the arms of Quint Farrell, he meant.

Sam accepted the house key and tried to get Deirdre to pick up the pace. She kept clutching at her side, and since she could only see out of one eye, taking the steps became a little tricky. It only took two minutes to get safely behind the neighbor's door, but the time in full view on the street felt like an hour.

Sam closed and locked the door immediately. The floor plan looked the same as the one next door, although the furnishings were a degree or two nicer. Sam left Deirdre standing in the hall while she checked the place. The hall led to a kitchen at the rear of the house, where a back door gave way to an alley full of trash cans. Sam checked that the kitchen door was securely locked. Stairs led to a second story, presumably where there were bedrooms. Back in the living room, Deirdre had seated herself on a sofa, but Sam noticed that the drapes were fully open to the view of the street. She pulled them closed.

"Can I get you some water?" Without waiting for an answer she went back to the kitchen, pulling the shade over the one window before filling a glass.

Deirdre's copper-blond hair hung in strings around her

face, and she brushed them back without making much difference before accepting the glass. While the woman sipped clumsily at the water, Sam stepped to the side of the window and moved the curtain a tad. Not a soul was moving on the street.

Her imagination threatened to take over. Quint was armed. Beau was not. She'd noticed that uniformed police officers here didn't carry guns, only a strong truncheon. But both Aiden and Lambert, as detectives, did have guns. She could only pray that they could surprise and subdue Quint before gunfire became inevitable.

Deirdre perked up a little after draining the glass. She got up and walked over to a mirror on the wall, groaning when she saw her face. She'd brought her washcloth and Sam offered to wet it again.

When she returned from the kitchen, Deirdre was gingerly touching the sore spots that, by morning, would be horrific bruises.

"Did Quint Farrell abduct you?" Sam asked. "Force you to drive him?"

She knew better, even before Deirdre spoke. She'd seen the woman greet Quint with a smile in the pub last night.

"He promised me a diamond the size of me thumb," she said, dabbing at dried blood on her chin. "Said he'd be selling a bunch of 'em but he'd save me the best one. Do you know what that would be worth? I could have meself a grand ring made, or I could get the money and pay off all me bills and buy a new car as well."

Sam waited.

"All I had to do was take him out to see the Travellers. But then the man he wanted wasn't at Tuam and he found out they was moved back here to Galway. So then I had to bring him back. He got real nervous about that, with the cops looking for him here. Said if I'd let him stay at my house he'd make it two diamonds. Two diamonds! I never had such."

Sam didn't point out that she didn't exactly have them now, only a collection of bruises.

"Why did he hit you?"

Deirdre gave a few more dabs with the cloth. "Ah, you know men. Least little thing sets 'em off. I had no food in the house and he got upset over it. What was I thinkin'? Course I should've stocked up some things a man would want."

Sam would have bet money that the thing Quint wanted from Deirdre wasn't limited to food. Or a safe place to stay. She didn't say anything.

"How long was he here?"

"Couple of days. He's eager to get this business deal finished."

The *Glory Be* had been towed in more than a week ago. Where had Quint Farrell been all that time? Sam remembered his limp.

"Was Quint injured when you picked him up?"

Deirdre turned too quickly and flinched. She adjusted to smaller steps and made her way back to the couch.

"He'd a nasty gash on one leg. Some stitches in it that looked homemade. Bruises on his shoulders and ribs."

"How did he get those injuries?"

"He didn't say. I didn't ask." Deirdre sat down with a groan. "Could I get some ice for my lip?"

Since it was difficult trying to understand the woman's

speech through the fat lip, Sam chided herself for not thinking of the ice sooner. She headed back to the kitchen and tried to piece together the sequence of Quint Farrell's movements as she searched drawers for a plastic bag and the small freezer compartment for cubes.

The trawler had gone out with three passengers and two crew. Somewhere out at sea, the three Americans had killed and dumped the crew. Who did the shooting was still a matter for the police to figure out, but it seemed clear that it was at a later point in the trip when Greenlee and Furns ended up in the lifeboat. And Quint? At some point he abandoned the trawler and came ashore. How? And where?

The coast guard had reported the trawler coming very close to the rocky shore, saying it probably would have been dashed on the rocks a few hours later. Maybe Farrell had thought he could judge the tides correctly and slip over the edge, swimming to shore when the tide was low enough to be safe. If he'd planned incorrectly, he might have been bashed against the rocks himself. Lucky for him, he didn't die in the effort.

She carried the ice pack to Deirdre and paced to the window again. It was still very quiet next door. She remembered something.

"Deirdre, someone hinted at the idea that Darragh might have been in league with the Americans, might have been trying to help them get away, and they turned on him."

The woman had to move the ice pack aside to speak, but the look on her face affirmed Sam's earlier feeling that Darragh had known nothing of the robbers' intentions when he took them out to sea.

She peeked out from behind the curtain again, still nothing. She felt antsy.

Apparently, Deirdre was feeling the same way.

"This is crazy," she said. "I told him the nearest market is only a few blocks away. He should have been back by now."

"Maybe he went to a pub."

"And not come back with food for me, too?" She sounded incredulous, but settled into the realization that it could be true. Quint was proving to be not quite the gentleman Deirdre had imagined.

Sam watched the emotions cross her face, not wanting to bring up the possibility that Quint had simply stolen her car and was miles from the city by now.

"What's your phone number?" Sam asked. "I'll call over there and ask the men if anything has happened."

"I only have me cell," Deirdre said, pulling it from her pocket.

Sam sighed, wishing Beau would tap on the back door or something. She thought of doing that—going out the back door of this house and tapping on the window at Deirdre's—but it didn't seem like a good idea to take the chance of messing up their capture. He would let her know when they considered it clear.

Meanwhile, although she'd been able to learn a lot from Deirdre, she half wished she'd stayed at the hotel to finish going through her uncle's papers.

The light outdoors began to dim. Deirdre woke from a little doze on the couch, giving a mighty groan when she tried to get up. She got to her feet and hobbled down the hall in search of something for the pain. They really needed to get out of here before the neighbor and her kids came home. About the time Sam was ready to break her word and find Beau, she heard a tap at the door. Beau stepped inside when she answered.

"We're calling it off," he said. "Quint has either figured out we're there or he's skipped. He may never come back."

"Never?" cried Deirdre. *Neber*, with the puffy mouth. "My car! He's stolen my car?"

Chapter 25

Ineed to get out and *do* something," Sam said when Aiden Martin dropped them off at their hotel. "Too much sitting around."

They'd gotten Deirdre settled back in her home, cautioned her to double-lock everything and not to let Quint Farrell back inside, no matter what he promised. Beau had very little hope she would comply, but there was only so much they could do.

"We could take a walk," Beau suggested.

It was getting dark but the streets were crowded with people on their way home from work or going out for the evening. It wasn't nearly as late as it felt to Sam. After the emotion of the morning and the boredom of the afternoon, she couldn't be sure what she wanted. They circled the dock area and found themselves meandering along the water's edge, following the park-like berm, crossing the bridge, walking out to Nimmo's Pier.

A breeze came onshore, bringing fresh air and an assortment of detritus that collected along the shoreline. Although she'd wanted to put everything out of her mind, Sam found herself relating Deirdre's conversation to Beau.

"She said he had a gash on his leg and someone had stitched it up. Homemade, I think was the way she put it. I wondered who would have done that, and then I got to thinking about Quint's actions. He was with the Travellers in Tuam at some point and then he got Deirdre to drive him to the newer encampment here. Do you suppose he came ashore, injured, and the Travellers found him and patched him up?"

He pondered that. "Except that Tuam isn't on the coast."

"True." She looked out across the water. "But one of them might have been driving along, saw an injured man by the road . . ."

"I suppose it's possible."

She felt on a roll. "He wakes up in somebody's camper, sees or hears something that leads him to believe they could fence the stolen jewels."

"Except that would be pretty iffy. He steals all these diamonds in New York and comes to Ireland, on the off chance he would accidentally run into a reliable fence?"

Hmm. She chewed at her lower lip.

Beau spoke up. "But let's say he came to Ireland because he arranged with someone to meet him here. For some reason, this is a place the police wouldn't immediately think of looking."

"He's going to meet them in Shannon, where the plane arrived, and then hop another flight right away. But how would he plan to end up in Galway, chartering a boat?" she asked.

"The FBI agent in New York told Lambert that Quinton Farrell had posed as a jewelry wholesaler when he boarded the plane, giving him a reason for all the diamonds and to carry a weapon. The gun had to be checked but he had a legitimate-sounding reason for it and apparently created the right documents."

"Okay, so posing as a jewelry dealer he flies into Shannon, gets to Galway and charters the boat. He was meeting someone. It had to be that."

"Makes sense to me," he said, as they started the long walk back toward the bridge. "But who? And where would this meeting be taking place?"

Sam shrugged. "No idea."

"I have to give it some thought. For now, though, what would you like for dinner?"

"Room service and our big comfy bed?"

He took her hand as they walked. "You got it."

Beau placed the food order while Sam took a quick shower. Snuggled into her silky gown and robe, she decided to get some details out of the way before completely calling it a night. Ambrose answered his phone right away and assured Sam that he and the funeral director were managing arrangements for the services. There would be a viewing the following evening, with Mass and burial the day after. And there would be the wake at Terry's house afterward, as they had already discussed.

Considering her involvement in Beau's search for Quint

Farrell, Sam couldn't imagine having the time to get the house ready and make the requisite sandwiches and desserts. She called Keeva.

"I'd love to do it," Keeva said. "I'll enlist the help of Anna and Bridget. Don't you worry about a thing."

A random thought touched the edges of Sam's brain— something she meant to ask Keeva— but she forgot it the moment a knock came at the door. She told Keeva to call if she needed anything for the wake, as a waiter wheeled their dinner table inside.

Over dinner she remembered the large envelope Daniel Ryan had given her, so the minute they finished eating she pulled out her uncle's legal papers and leaned against the headboard to read.

There were listings of Terry's possessions, with a few special bequests to local people who'd apparently helped him at one time or another. A hunting rifle for his gardener, a collection of Waterford crystal for Anna along with a cash bequest, small keepsakes for several people whose names Sam didn't know. The will itself named the larger items: Bank and brokerage accounts were to be divided by percentages to a variety of individual charities (no mention of the charitable trust); Ambrose was to get the bookshop (Sam felt a shot of joy at this); Keeva and Bridget would receive decent yearly bonuses as long as they remained employed at the shop; Sam would inherit Terry's house and its contents, except as otherwise bequeathed.

Wow. She set the page on the duvet beside her and took a deep breath. It was far more than she'd expected—both as a gift and as a responsibility. She read on. Another clause, farther into the document, granted her the right to dispose of the property in any manner she saw fit. It was too much to think about now, at the end of a very long day.

Beau had edged under the covers beside her and she shoved all the papers onto the nightstand and snuggled into his warmth. Secure and comfortable, she began to dream.

She was in her uncle's house, facing the task of sorting his possessions and deciding who should get which of them. Continually drawn to the carved box in the bookcase, she told herself that she'd already ruled out any magical effects with it, but each time she set it back in the cabinet she would turn around and find it back on the desk. She picked it up and held it close, the same way she sometimes did with her smaller one. The wood warmed slightly but there was no other reaction. Someone called to her from another room and she set the box on the desk.

She walked from Terry's study out a door, where she found herself standing on the rocky coastline, completely alone. Above, she could see grassy fields stretching into the distance. Terry's house was nowhere to be seen. She watched the tide lapping at the rocks, idly wondering if it was going out or coming in at the moment. It was a peaceful setting but Sam found it unsettling to be there—how had she come to this place and where were Beau and the others who'd been at Terry's house?

She scanned the coastline in both directions, catching a glint of light off some object. As she looked, there were more of them. She thought of Taos and the way an entire field would sparkle with light after a snow—sunshine hitting ice. She bent to touch the spark, expecting cold. It was a stone, a diamond. She picked it up and stared at it in the palm of her hand.

Another flash caught her attention—green. An emerald, then a yellow diamond, then a sapphire. The beach, for meters in each direction was littered with gemstones. She gathered a dozen of them, all sizes and colors, gripping them tightly as she walked among the rocks. She thought of her wooden jewelry box; she could fill it with these gems and have enough to replace the box's dull ones with these beautifully cut, vivid ones. But she didn't have the box with her. What could she use to carry them?

A few yards ahead she spotted something, a dark pouch of sturdy fabric. With its straps and buckles, it would be easy to fasten it around her waist and fill it with the treasure. She headed toward it, caught her toe on a rock and started to fall . . . gripping the diamonds tightly in her fist, she went down.

Beau was gazing down at her when her eyes came open. Sam felt herself panting. She stared at her tightly curled fingers, opened them slowly. Of course there was nothing there.

"You okay?" he asked. "You must have had a doozy of a dream. You were thrashing around and breathing hard."

She sat up. "Whoa. Such a vivid scene."

He brushed her hair back from her face.

"I'm okay," she said with a little smile at his outline in the dark room. "Just a very weird dream."

"Do you need a glass of water or anything?"

"No, I'll be fine. I'll just go back to sleep . . ." She eased back down into the curve of his arm and fell asleep again almost instantly. The dream didn't return.

Chapter 26

Beau was in the shower when Sam snapped awake. She sat up and shook her limbs. Snapshots from the dream stayed with her, along with the strange sensation that she'd just been unconscious for several hours. She turned on the electric kettle and dumped double-strength instant coffee and three sugars into a mug.

"Hey, you," he said with a smile when he emerged, shirtless, in jeans as she was pouring boiling water. "First you were restless, then you slept like a dead person."

"What's with this anyway?" she said, blowing on the steam from her cup. "Second really weird dream this week. Maybe there's something they put in this Irish food."

"Or the fact that you are on sensory overload? Between an uncle who came back from the dead and then went there again, a bookshop to clean up and operate, and chasing a jewel thief all over the countryside . . ."

She laughed. "It's not exactly been an uneventful trip, has it?"

"I suppose we should check on Deirdre this morning, be sure she's doing okay," he said as he buttoned his shirt.

"She was pretty banged up. Emotionally, too." Sam flipped through the hangers in the closet, trying to decide what to wear. "I could call her."

She dressed in jeans and chose the last shirt that hadn't been worn at least once, then dialed the phone. Deirdre said she was on her way out the door.

"Have to go to work or there's no money for the rent, much less comin' up with a car." She sounded bitter.

"Surely the police will find yours. It's not like an American can do a whole lot with a stolen car here. He'll abandon it somewhere and then try to leave the country," Sam said. "Beau can ask the police to watch the airports and ferry parking lots."

She realized the local authorities would have already thought of that, but it felt like she was somehow reassuring the distraught woman.

Deirdre cut the call short, asking Sam to phone her if they got any word on her car.

"I take it Quint never came back," Beau said as Sam replaced the receiver.

"Nope."

"Let's get some breakfast in you. This time I'll tell them to leave out the vivid-dream ingredient." He handed Sam her jacket and held the door open.

They stopped in at a little dockside restaurant they'd noticed earlier in the week, sitting down to another of those hearty full Irish breakfasts.

"You know, Deirdre's new office is just up the block," Beau said, stabbing a section of sausage with his fork. "We could pop in and ask again if she can think of where Quint might have gone. She may have had some ideas during the night."

"I get the feeling she had plenty of ideas, mainly of ways to render a slow and painful death to the man."

"Good. You know what they say about a woman scorned—she's likely to talk."

Deirdre's face looked only marginally better this morning. The swelling was down considerably, but she'd depended on heavy coats of makeup to hide the bruises. It was only partially successful. She lowered her sunglasses when Sam asked about her black eye, but immediately put them in place again.

"He'll not leave this area until he's found the diamonds," she said to Beau's question about whether she could guess where Quint might have gone. "It was the thing he talked about all the time, losing those stones. He truly thought the Travellers had taken them while he was out of it."

"So that's why he went back to Tuam?"

"And again why he followed that group of 'em down here. He said they swore they never took anything from him." She touched the side of her face gingerly. "I never asked how he asked the questions. You could likely follow a trail of bloodied faces."

She reached for a cigarette pack, lit one and took a shallow draw on it.

"Your ribs are killing you, aren't they?" Sam asked.

Deirdre nodded, blowing out a ragged stream of smoke.

"You should see a doctor."

"Can't afford it. And what's he gonna do? Tell me to

put ice on the bruises and not strain the ribs. Everything will heal in time, he'll say. I can save the money and tell it to myself."

She pressed the glowing tip of her cigarette against an ashtray, putting out the fire and preserving half of the little pleasure stick for later.

"I'll tell you one thing. Quint's a bit rattled that an American lawman is after him. He doesn't know who you're with, what agency, but it's unnerved him that you got here so fast."

Sam looked at Beau, whose expression was unreadable.

"He's desperate," Deirdre said. "Be careful of him."

"Thanks. We'll watch our backs."

The telephone rang and they used the interruption as a reason to go.

"How, exactly, are we going to watch our backs?" Sam said as they walked toward the hotel.

The plan was to get their rental and take one of the drives Beau had planned a few days ago, get away a few hours before they had to appear at Terrance's viewing this evening. But Sam caught herself glancing nervously over her shoulder.

"The same way we always do, darlin'. Just be alert."

Fine. She could only see about a thousand places where Quint could be waiting to jump them or a million vantage points where he could pull off a shot. Taking the car and getting away from town seemed like a good idea. They decided to stop by their room first, collect the maps and pick up umbrellas just in case.

I know one little layer of alertness I can add, Sam thought as Beau slid his card key into the lock. She used the excuse that she wanted different earrings and pulled her wooden box from the room safe, carrying it with her into the bathroom and closing the door. Setting it on the countertop, she placed her hands along its sides. The wood began to warm.

What the heck. She picked it up and cradled it close to her body. Within a minute or two the warmth had spread up her arms and into her chest. When her hands began to tingle she set the box down. Her palms were deep pink. Immediately, the glowing wood began to dim and the stones lost their vivid color.

She flushed the toilet to explain why she hadn't immediately come back, then carried the box back to the safe.

"I thought those were the earrings you were already wearing," Beau said.

Oops.

"Changed my mind." She regretted not telling him the whole truth, but there were still some things it was better not to share.

She locked the safe and joined him for the walk down to the parking garage.

"I thought we might drive the north shore of Galway Bay today," he said, handing her the map and starting the engine.

She studied the route in case he wanted help figuring out which turns to take. All at once, the print on the map blurred. When Sam squeezed her eyes shut she saw the coastline. A black parcel floated in on a wave and as it hit the beach it hung up on a large rock. The wave receded. She blinked away the vision and the map became perfectly clear.

Okay, what was that?

Beau's eyes were on the road and she didn't mention the weird feeling. They chatted as they drove through the area known as Salthill and past several golf courses, the road veering closer and farther from the shoreline in different places. They came to a spot with an overlook and Beau pulled over without asking.

"Good place for some pictures?" he suggested, reaching for the camera bag in the back seat.

Sam set the map aside and they walked across the springy grass to a low wall where a few lovers had scratched their initials in the rock.

"Sit there," Beau said. "I'll get you with that winding coastline in the background."

She smiled when he told her to, and he snapped two before walking over to sit beside her and hold the camera at arm's length for a shot of the two of them. Then a shot of the two of them kissing.

"Oh, yeah, that's going in the family album," he said as he looked at it.

When he showed it to Sam she felt her vision blur again. She spun around, half expecting someone to be coming up behind them. Aside from two people crouching at the water's edge, a hundred yards away, there wasn't another person in sight. She tracked the water line and it happened again. A quick vision of a dark package lying almost invisibly against the dark rocks.

Quint Farrell's face flashed before her. This was it!

"Beau! There's something here—near here. Do you know anything about tides?"

"I grew up on a ranch, darlin'. Tides are beyond me."

"I need to know when the next high tide is. There's

something . . . I don't know how to explain it, but it's going to get washed away when the next high tide comes."

"What are you saying? What thing?"

"I'm pretty sure it's Farrell's missing diamonds."

He gave her a sideways look.

"Beau, it's like the other times—when I saw those fingerprints, when that guy's aura glowed so brightly—you know I can't really explain what happens . . ."

"But you've proven it works. I believe you. Where's your phone?"

She pulled it from the pocket of her coat. He dialed a number.

"Aiden? We've come across a clue in the Farrell case. What time is the next high tide?"

He nodded a few times, repeated some numbers.

"Today will be the highest tide of the month, he says. At 2:14 this afternoon. He wants to know what it has to do with the Farrell case."

Sam wiggled her fingers and took the phone from Beau. "Aiden, I can't really explain how I know this, but the missing diamonds have washed up in a black pouch, somewhere along the shore on the R336."

"Sam, that's miles long. Do you have anything more specific?"

She looked out over the water. "It's close to where we are now." She grabbed the map from the car and gave him the name of the last little town they'd passed through. "The bag washed up on the tide last night. If today's tide is higher, it will get washed back out to sea unless we can find it. Can you round up enough officers to search several miles of coastline?"

"Round them up and conduct a search—on less than three hours notice?"

When he phrased it that way, she realized how impossible it would be.

"And what do I have to go on?" Aiden was saying. "It'll be my head if I muster all these men and it turns out to be nothin'."

Beau sensed how the conversation was going. He took back the phone. "Aiden, I don't know how to explain it either . . . Are you superstitious?"

"All Irish are superstitious."

"Then let's just say that my wife has the gift of sight. She's helped me solve several cases, based on these . . . hunches, visions . . . whatever they are. We need to believe her."

A huge sigh came over the line. "I'll do my best to gather enough help. Please don't get me demoted over this."

Beau assured the man that he would stand behind him. He clicked off the call.

"My cell phone bill will be astronomical," Sam said, "but thanks for trusting me."

"We could start looking before they get here," Beau said. "I can't imagine sitting around for the next hour or more until the rest of them arrive."

Sam nodded. "Bring the camera, in case we have to photograph evidence or something."

"You're already thinking like a cop." He ruffled her hair. "Half cop, half psychic. Do you know how flaky most law enforcement think those people are?"

She rolled her eyes, not at all wanting to be lumped in with either camp—those with true insights or the charlatans who put up plywood signs with a big palm print by the side of the road.

"Let's start walking," she said.

They rounded the end of the low wall where they'd been sitting minutes earlier and decided they could cover more ground if they went opposite directions.

"I'll head east, you go west," Beau said. "If we end up far apart, I'll come back for the car and catch up with you so we can work a different section."

Sam hoped the police would get there before they had to hike too many miles on the rocky shore. Her sneakers weren't exactly ideal for this.

She described the bag she'd seen in the dream. "It will be between the high tide line and where the water is now. If you find it, do this." She stuck two fingers in her mouth and gave an eardrum-piercing blow.

"Where'd you learn to whistle like that?" He smiled at her.

"Doesn't matter." She felt her mouth form a grin. "Okay, an old boyfriend. In high school. Go. Get busy."

She covered ten yards slowly, realizing what a challenge it would be to spot a black bag among the wet gray-black stones on the shoreline. Patches of sand were few and far between, and she remembered someone saying that it was a frustrating place for fishermen because they spent more time retrieving tackle than catching anything. She glanced back at Beau. He'd covered only a little more ground than she.

Work smarter, not harder, her father used to say. She closed her eyes and tried to bring up a picture. Between last night's dream and the sudden vision she'd had at the overlook, surely she could call up an image of the rock where it lay snagged.

She concentrated.

She saw it again.

She opened her eyes but all the rocks looked so much alike. A big sigh and she walked on, eyes to the details on the ground.

Twenty or thirty minutes passed. She and Beau were now more than shouting distance from one another. He seemed equally intent on the goal. She stretched her neck and shoulders, which felt permanently frozen at the awkward angle she'd been working. While her shoulders rolled she tried to call up the vision again but with the passage of time it was getting dimmer. The lapping waves were also coming closer to her feet.

Get the big picture, she told herself. She looked out at the flat horizon. *I can do this all day. My father gave me a zillion of these little pep talks.* She focused westward, down the shoreline that seemed to go forever, around one curve and then another. She sighed and took yet another step forward.

And there, not another ten feet away, she spotted it. A black bag, with straps. Not quite the same as the dream, but she registered a moment of shock that she'd actually gotten it fairly accurately. She scrambled over the rocks and picked it up, dodging the incoming wavelet that splashed over the bag.

Her heart raced as she stood up and turned to face toward Beau. His familiar form moved in the distance, now a small stick figure.

I better be sure before I call him away, she thought. She held the bag close to her body and tugged at the zipper closure that ran the length of it. It was caked with sand and wouldn't move. She thought of dunking the zipper in seawater, hesitated because, after all, there were probably diamonds inside. Then she chided herself. The thing had been in sea water for days. She couldn't possibly do it any more harm.

She held it in a firm grip and swished it in a small tide pool that had formed with the last outgoing wave. Most of the sand came off. She stepped a little higher, away from the waves, tried again to open it. This time the zipper slid, just a little.

With small tugs she finally got it open enough to poke her fingers inside. She felt plastic bags, pulled one out. It did, indeed, contain diamonds. She stuffed it back inside, pulled the zipper shut and raised her fingers to whistle for Beau.

"Don't even try it," said a voice from her left.

Quinton Farrell stood there and he had a gun aimed at her.

Chapter 27

Screw this! The thought formed in the same instant that she blew the longest whistle she could muster. Beau turned. He was probably a half mile away. Over the rocky ground he would never make it to her in time.

Farrell came at her, slowly, limping but keeping the gun aimed at her heart.

Sam watched his eyes. The man was cold and dead-set on getting the bag of gems. For a split second she considered simply handing it over, letting him get away. Bridget's face flashed before her—Quint Farrell had shattered that family's peace. Not to mention the potential of young Sean Bareth or the loss to the Goldman family in New York. She couldn't do it.

Farrell's eyes never left her face as he covered the twenty-yard gap. She weighed the possibilities but no matter what she came up with, she would never outrun a bullet. A wave lapped at her heel, the chill soaking into her sneaker.

She could stall, but only until the sea took her feet out from under her.

"Hand over the bag," he said.

Sam gripped one of the bag's straps and held it at arm's length, letting the pouch dangle over the foamy wavelets.

"I'll throw it into the sea," she said. "Put the gun down or I'll do it."

He was calculating the distance, wondering if he could make it to the bag before it would be carried away.

"You do that and you're dead," he promised.

Sam glanced toward the dangling pouch but she really wanted to catch sight of Beau. So far Farrell hadn't acknowledged the sheriff, but Sam had no illusions that Quint wouldn't shoot her and then take aim at Beau once he had the pouch. Another murder or two wouldn't make much difference at this point. But Beau was out of sight. Where had he gone?

"How did you figure out the pouch would be here?" she asked. "This country has a lot of coastline."

"You led me to it," he said with a smirk. "I knew it had to be along this particular coast. Those gypsies told me where they found me—some old guy and his wife took me to their motor home. Once I chased around and figured out that they didn't have my bag, it made sense that I'd lost it in the water or on this shore."

"So you bailed out of the trawler and just started to swim for it?" She had a hard time picturing the scene. The *Glory Be* had been found adrift miles south of here.

"There was a dinghy tied to a private pier on some little island. I grabbed that, towed it along until I had the bigger boat well out to sea. Got in the dinghy along with my stuff and started her up. It was a good way to put myself miles from where the old guy's fishing boat would have been bashed against those cliffs."

She waited, wanting to edge her gaze to the side to see where Beau was.

"Stupid little thing ran out of gas. Like a mile offshore. But I've always been a good swimmer. Figured I could make it. I thought the suitcase with the cash would float, but it sank right away."

He stared out to sea for a moment and Sam briefly thought of running. But his attention was back on her in a few seconds.

"I strapped the pouch around me, headed in. Damn rocks—by the time I got to shore I was so weak. Next thing I know I'm waking up in this couple's camper and I got this huge cut on my leg."

Quint had regained his strength and stolen Deirdre's car and now here they were.

"You didn't say how you knew to follow us." Her eyes went to the right—where was Beau?

"Your FBI guy—I've seen him go in and out of the police station. I saw you both show up at Deirdre's yesterday."

He thought Beau was FBI. And they'd missed him by minutes.

"An hour ago I started down from the road up there, saw you both prowling around . . . figured, what the heck, let you two do the work. Not strain this stupid leg of mine. I get my stuff back and I'm outta here. Won't bother you a bit more once you give me what's mi—"

The fierce blast of an auto horn sounded, long and

hard. Then a series of short blasts in a pattern. It might have been Morse code, for all Sam knew. She only knew that Beau had reached the car and was signaling someone.

By the time Farrell turned around to see what was going on behind him, a dozen Garda officers were racing over the berm. Quint began to hobble toward Sam, his eyes on the bag. She snatched it close to her body and dodged his lunge. His toe caught on a rock and he went facedown into the shallow water. Without a thought she kicked his right wrist and jammed her knee into the small of his back.

"Sam! Sam, let him up. You'll drown him." Joe Lambert was there, huffing.

It wasn't exactly true. The wave had receded enough for Quint to catch a breath, but it wouldn't be long before the next ones came and the tide rose to cover the whole area. She let the detective take over. He directed two uniformed officers to handcuff Farrell and drag him up the bank.

Sam followed. Once she reached the flat area on top, she saw that a dozen police cars had congregated. Beau's eyes were scanning, looking for her and she ran toward him.

"Oh, I guess you'll need this," she said, handing the black pouch to Lambert when he walked over to join them. "He thought you were with the FBI, Beau. That's why he was both dodging us and keeping an eye on our movements."

Lambert opened the pouch and let out a whistle when he saw what was in it. "Begorra! This'll make our evidence safe a richer place, at least until someone comes to take custody of it." He pulled the zipper shut again.

Across the grassy way, Farrell glared at them from the back seat of a cruiser. Its lights came to life and it roared off to deliver the master jewel thief and killer to his just reward.

Chapter 28

The debriefing, in which Sam had to relate everything Farrell had told her during the standoff, took far longer than she liked so it was with a quick step and a bit of fluster that Sam rushed into Hardiman's Funeral Home for the viewing. She and Beau had raced through showers and quickly donned their only sets of mourning wear in order to be there.

As Terrance O'Shaughnessy's only relative, it fell to Sam to greet the visitors and observe the proprieties that had been missing the first time Terry died.

Bookshop customers, employees, and a large contingent of those who had done business with Terrance O'Shaughnessy over the years crowded the funeral home. Blatantly missing were the former directors of the charitable trust Terry had formed and subsequently dissolved. Having their endowment snatched away had evidently caused some hurt feelings.

Ambrose got his wish for the chance to say a proper farewell to his longtime friend and mentor. Sam left him alone with Terrance in the viewing room and he stayed quite awhile. Keeva, Anna and Bridget acted as hostesses, offering tea to those who'd already said their goodbyes.

Sam caught up with Mr. Hardiman in a quiet alcove.

"So, how did my uncle pull this off the first time, a fake funeral, I mean?"

Hardiman shifted from one foot to the other, stalling. When he finally answered it made perfect sense.

"He paid. I visited his sickbed at the house and he called in his caregiver and lawyer. He told me what he wanted to do and the witnesses confirmed it. I was aghast at first. Simply shocked. But—what can I say?—he pulled out a check and paid for two funeral services. I told him what we absolutely could not do—that was to file a false death certificate or to bury an empty coffin. His friend, Mr. Piggott, was very unhappy about it all, and I thought we might have a spot of trouble over it." He cleared his throat a little uneasily. "I don't want to say that I'm happy to see Terrance dead at last . . ."

"But it's made an honest man of you."

"Something like that."

"I wish I'd had more chances to spend time with him," Sam said. "He seemed a very caring person."

Ambrose emerged from the viewing room and approached Sam. Hardiman vanished into the woodwork somewhere.

"Thank you, Sam. I'm so grateful for your thoughtful treatment of the situation. I'll be happy to stay on at the shop and offer whatever help I can."

She thought of the will but didn't reveal anything,

thanking Ambrose for his part in making the funeral arrangements.

The next day crawled—the funeral Mass at the church, burial beside his dear Maggie which touched everyone's emotions, and finally gathering at Terry's home for the remembrances and reading of the will. Sam had asked Daniel Ryan to wait until everyone but those actually named in the will had left.

Now, gathered in Terry's study with a collection of chairs from other parts of the house and the lawyer seated at the desk, Sam watched the reactions as each bequest was read. Ambrose nearly wept when he learned that he would own the bookshop, and Keeva and Bridget were thrilled with their financial bonuses. Those who received Terry's collections and small items seemed pleased with the elderly man's choices.

When Ryan got to the part about Sam receiving Terry's home and the remaining contents a hush settled over the room.

Ever since she'd read the will, Sam had thought about this. As lovely as the place was, she knew she would never be able to give it proper care. Nor was it likely that she would get to Ireland often enough to spend time enjoying it. Home and family were simply too far removed from the island republic. She stepped forward.

"I am so grateful for the chance to meet all of you, for having you as part of my life these two weeks. It means a lot to me, and to my family, that all of you were here for Terry during the years we had lost touch."

A sniffle from Bridget, but the others merely looked at Sam expectantly.

"I've made a decision about the house. Since my uncle gave me sole discretion over the house and its contents, I would like to make my wishes known, here and now."

Bottoms shifted in chairs, fingers fidgeted on laps.

"I will be unable to give this home the care and attention it deserves. That much is clear and will be even more clear once I leave for the States again. I would like to claim some small item as a remembrance for myself and something for my sister and a few American relatives who knew Terry in his lifetime. Beyond that, please let me pass along the house, the property and Terry's vehicle to Ambrose Piggott."

The man's face went white and Sam was momentarily afraid he would swoon right there in his chair. Tears began to run down his face and his shoulders shook. Sam walked to his side and embraced him.

"You meant so much to my uncle," she whispered.

The others gathered around and soon Ambrose was on his feet, receiving hugs from everyone. Sam and Beau stepped aside, and in a few minutes Daniel Ryan announced that he'd brought a bottle of good whiskey if anybody was interested in retiring to the parlor.

Stories began to flow as glasses were drained. Sam noticed that Beau limited himself to a few sips, since they had to drive back to their hotel tonight. In the morning they would pack and ride back to Shannon for the long flight home.

While the others remembered Terry in story and song, Sam thought about her choices. The carved wooden box called out to her. As the bigger brother to her own, she felt a pull to take it as her own keepsake. She removed it from the bookcase and set it on the desk.

Flipping through the postcards she saw that they were correspondence between Terrance and Maggie in their younger years, well before email and even in a time before telephone usage was common. The cards came from a variety of European cities, showing that both of them had been well-traveled people. Her mother, Nina Rae, collected family history and would enjoy those.

For her sister Rayleen, Sam spotted a shamrock pin. By its size it must be green glass—surely there was no emerald that size. Certainly not one left in a bookcase rather than locked in a bank vault. But it was the kind of bling her sister would love.

She remembered a beautiful English riding saddle among the items in the garage. It would be perfect for her cousin Wilhelmina—Willie—who worked with, lived with, and loved horses more than nearly anything else.

Among some boxes in a cabinet in the dining room, while they were recruiting serving dishes for the wake, Sam had found two exquisite Waterford Christmas ornaments. They would be perfect for her aunt Lily, the other niece Terry used to remember at Christmas when Lily and Nina Rae were children. She walked into the dining room to collect them.

Daniel Ryan was putting his coat on when she came back into the hall. She told him about the items she wanted and he offered to see that they were packaged and shipped. She left the little collection on the desk, except for the wooden box.

"I think I'll carry this one on the airplane with me," she said. "I'll put it in the car and get the addresses for the others."

She walked out into the misty evening and set the wooden box on the back seat of their rental. Her pack was in there and she retrieved her cell phone with all the family addresses in it. When she stood up, Saoirse the Traveller woman was standing at the end of the driveway.

"I wanted to come to the funeral," the woman told her. "To pay respects."

"I didn't realize you knew my uncle," Sam said.

"I didn't." Saoirse gripped the strap of her big red purse. "It's just that . . . I've only learned what a good man he was. He's done something incredible to help us."

Sam felt her brows flex. What was the woman talking about?

"A lawyer came to our camp today, and he told us that a teacher's bein' paid to come to us and start giving classes for the adults. I'm finally going to learn readin' and writin'."

"You don't know how to read and write?" Sam knew her amazement was showing. "But your daughter sent text messages."

"Ah, well. I know my numbers and some letters. She makes up little codes to give me a message sometimes. I've learned to fake my way through a lot of things. It's just that proper schoolin' wasn't considered necessary when I was a girl. The government made laws to require it but a lot of us ignored them. At least the young ones today are gettin' some basics."

"And my uncle is paying this teacher?"

Saoirse nodded, giving Sam a big smile.

"Come in then," Sam said. "Join us."

But Saoirse was already walking away. "I only wanted to thank you, Sam." In a few seconds she was out of sight in the mist.

Sam walked back inside where Daniel Ryan was organizing his papers in the study.

"My car and driver can take you to the airport tomorrow," he said. "If you'd like I'll arrange the return of your rental car and drive you back to your hotel now."

"Thanks, but I want to make a little stop along the way."

"Fine, then. Shall I take these items for shipping?"

She gave him the instructions and thanked him again. Beau walked in as they were winding up the details.

"About ready?" he asked.

The long day was taking its toll on their energy and Sam nearly dozed as they drove back toward the city's center. She came awake in time to tell him what she had in mind. He parked as close as he could get to the pedestrian-only Shop Street and they got out.

They walked through the evening mist, toward the streets of shops that were closed now. Within five minutes rain began to come down earnestly and they dashed back to the car to avoid becoming completely soaked. Sam opened the back door, knowing she'd left an umbrella there. Terry's wooden box was gone.

"Oh no!"

Beau pulled out the umbrella and opened it over their heads.

"The box. It was the one gift I had asked my uncle for." Her spirits sank. "He never got the chance to tell me the story about it. And now it's gone."

Beau brought her close and she rested her forehead on his chest.

"I'm sorry, darlin'. I don't know what to say."

When had it disappeared? Sam thought of Saoirse walking away into the night. Then again, they had just now left the car, accidentally unlocked, for ten minutes. They'd seen no one on the street, but anyone could have spotted the box and taken it. She stared toward the nearest row of shops and the scene blurred before her teary eyes.

Gone were the modern offerings of jewelry and sweaters and tourist trinkets. Primitive vendor stands rimmed a dirt pathway; figures in rough, dark clothing milled about. A young girl with blue eyes in a muddy face turned away from Sam and walked toward a man who was selling wood carvings. At his stand, she picked up a small box . . .

Sam felt her breath catch, a small cry escaping her. The medieval scene vanished.

"Sam? You okay?"

She let out a ragged breath, nodding to Beau. She couldn't explain the fleeting scene or the fact that she somehow felt better about losing the box.

He kept one arm around her shoulders, the other hand holding the umbrella, as they started back on their walk. Rain sparkled on the cobblestones, rendering everything shiny and new.

The bookshop came up on their right. O'Shaughnessy's front window was softly lit now by tiny lights that gave a magical quality to the colorful books on display. Sam noticed that Bridget was changing the selection each day now. A lamp on one of the big display tables inside cast a warm glow through the store, giving it the cozy feel of a home library where you would want to spend all your days. Her mood lightened.

"It's changed so much, hasn't it?" she said to Beau.

He nodded and gave a smile. "It was your doing. You turned it around."

She sighed. "It's so charming now . . . I wouldn't mind

working here again."

He turned and stared at her, a dimple forming as he grinned at her. "Mrs. Cardwell . . . be careful what you wish for . . ."

What *would* she wish for? The history behind those mysterious wooden boxes—Sam knew in her heart she wouldn't rest until she knew it. But their time in Galway was at an end, sadly. She smiled up at Beau and they kissed as the Irish rain became merely a light patter above their heads.

Author's Note

A very special thanks to Stephanie Dewey and Ashley Quigley for the pleasure of your company in Galway, and to Elizabeth Grimm for sharing your Irish travels with me as well. I must also give credit to my friend Margaret Norrie who first told me of the Irish Travellers and led me on a quest to learn more about their unique culture. Thank you.

My thanks go out to Susan Slater; the books are always better with your editorial touches. Shirley Shaw has been a remarkable help to me in catching the gremlins that inevitably sneak into any manuscript, and to Kim Clark thanks for giving it that final read-through. And of course to all my readers—
I keep writing them for you!

Connie Shelton is the *USA Today* bestselling author of two Amazon.com bestselling mystery series and of several award-winning short stories and essays. She formerly taught both fiction and non-fiction writing courses, and was a contributor to *Chicken Soup for the Writer's Soul*.
She and her husband live in New Mexico.

Sign up for Connie's free email mystery newsletter at
www.connieshelton.com
and be eligible for monthly prizes, notices about free books, and all the latest mystery news.

Contact by email: connie@connieshelton.com

Follow Connie on Facebook, Twitter and Pinterest

Discover all these books by Connie Shelton